T0552576

DEEP GRAVES

THE THORNHILL VAMPIRE CHRONICLES BOOK 2

LUCIUS VALIANT

THORNHILL PUBLISHING

He ne'er is crowned with immortality Who fears to follow where airy voices lead.

- John Keats

DEEP GRAVES

THE THORNHILL VAMPIRE CHRONICLES BOOK II

LUCIUS VALIANT

ONE

F ull moon nights are my favorite; they're the closest
thing to daylight, and I'm pretty sure I treasure
them more than I ever did the light of day when I
had it.

Stepping out onto the curb outside Deep Graves, I was
bathed in the welcome ghostly glow of the low-hanging full
moon above Highgate Cemetery.

The cemetery is just across the street from my undertaker premises, and tonight everything in it looked as if it
had been dipped in liquid silver. The graves looked neater
and better kept now than they had been decades ago. Still,
weeds were, as ever, in the process of reclaiming the tombs
and stone angels.

Let me cut to the chase. My name is Gabriel Graves, and
I'm an immortal.

Ironically, perhaps, I've made quite a name for myself in
the death business. My family was in the death business,
fulfilling the various tasks of undertakers, long before the
undertaker profession existed in its current form. You
might call it a family tradition, laying the dead to rest. And

it is a tradition that I've personally carried forward since 1665. There's a special pride that comes with having been in your profession for that long; it has become a part of you, and you have become a part of it.

I've long since made my fortune and could have retired, if I wanted to, but why would I? I may be 391 years old, but in my immortal state I will never age or grow tired. I carry the weight of centuries only in my spirit. Besides, I love what I do. Over the centuries, I've honed every aspect of what it takes to be the perfect undertaker to near perfection. Being an undertaker has become so much more than a profession for me - it's an avocation, a vital creative outlet.

I turned and locked the heavy door behind me, then lowered the iron bars in front of it. There were only two sets of keys for each door; no other copies had been made. I trusted only my long-term mortal assistant, Hyacinth, with a key and left it to him to let Rita in whenever she was needed. Good help, I mused, is so difficult to find these days, but Hyacinth and Rita made the cut.

I could run Deep Graves on my own. But the truth is that I enjoy having my two mortal assistants around. Of course their presence forces me to slow my pace to match theirs, lest I frighten them, but it is a sacrifice worth making.

I don't mean to make Hyacinth and Rita sound useless or like they're not pulling their weight at Deep Graves, even though they're both millennials. They're in fact invaluable to me. For example, without them, Deep Graves wouldn't have a beautifully maintained web presence across multiple platforms; no one would be responding to potential clients' endless questions over Facebook Messenger or in Instagram DMs, whatever those are.

And of course, the majority of the funerals we conduct

take place during the day, and for those, I unfortunately can't be present due to my "rare skin condition."

This is how I refer to my vampirism in conversation with the uninitiated. My mysterious condition also explains my insistence on low lighting at all times; there are no bright lights at Deep Graves, or in any of my cars. "Andy Warhol had a similar condition," I've told my mortal assistants and they've never questioned it.

Oh, they suspect something; they believe me to be a top shelf eccentric, but of the truth, they're blissfully ignorant. I pay them too well for them not to respect my secrecy, and so they never prod. Any mortal who's ever worked for me and was nosy by nature, I'm afraid I've had to... let go.

All in all, after all these years, I know exactly how to pass for a mere mortal. I know the exact conditions required for maintaining the illusion, and everything in my life and in my business is perfectly and meticulously orchestrated to continuously weave it. My mannerisms and speech I can easily modulate to mimic those of a mortal man. The unusual hours I keep aren't unheard of in a place like London; measured against some of the city's well-known free spirits, I don't even believe myself to be in the game. No, all that is easy.

It's my appearance that is my most obvious giveaway, and it's one I can't do much to control. My skin is as pale, smooth, and poreless as marble. If you were to touch it, you'd flinch at the discovery that it is also just as cold. My hair and nails have a hollow, glass-like luster, no longer filled with the ruddy vitality of human life but with the unnatural glow of the dark flame that keeps me inexplicably animated. The result? I look inhuman, flawless, ageless, hyperreal. If you get too close, or see me in bright light, or touch me, or catch me in a moment where I believe myself to be unobserved, you'd know immediately that I'm not like you. You'd know that I'm not one of your tribe, that I'm a threat.

In day-to-day terms, it's the not aging part that poses the greatest challenge to remaining at the helm of Deep Graves. And of course I've thought about it, but closing my business is really not an option; it's my life's work.

Is there a limit to how many times I can retire my mortal staff then disappear for a few years, only to return in the guise of yet another young successor in the line of Graves? I haven't reached that critical line yet, but when and if I do, I'll have to think of some solution. I'm sure it'll come to me.

With the doors firmly locked, I crossed the street to the cemetery. Highgate Hill slopes dramatically, and Deep Graves is, as it has been since 1839 when the cemetery was also built, located at the very bottom of the cemetery and across the street, looking up at it. It is the perfect place for an undertaker's business to be.

My marketing strategy wouldn't work for businesses that depend on quick sales, but in the death business, it's one big waiting game. And when you've got all the time in the world, like I do, you can take your sweet time. Whenever someone visits the cemetery, they drive or walk past Deep Graves, which sits there like a spider's intricately spun net, subtly reminding them that when the time comes, they will know where to find me. I've acquired whole family trees of customers thanks to my location alone.

Reaching the foot of the west side of the cemetery - by far the most beautiful and lush of the two sides, if you ever visit - I swung myself easily over the tall fence.

Landing soundlessly among the vines and dirt on the inside, I began to walk.

A thick, coiling mist had started creeping along the ground, seeping down from further up the hill and rolling over the tombstones almost like a blanket. The earth smelled damp, dark, and deep - the best smell in the world. Well, it comes second after the coppery smell of blood gushing from a freshly torn artery.

I loved this place, loved it as much now as I had when it was built. What a remarkable time that had been in my personal history. I'd been the only non-human member on the board of directors for the London Funeral Company, though of course the others hadn't known. We'd been on a mission to solve the city's problems of overcrowded inner-city cemeteries, and I dare say we succeeded.

I lifted my gaze until the towering ruin of Thornhill Mansion filled my vision, looming as always above the cemetery with its many floors, spindly turrets, and the stained glass domes above the library and above the great hall, both newly restored after years of neglect.

Of course it is true that houses of this magnitude never truly fall to ruin, but Lyrica - for a time the only member of the Thornhill clan to reside in the mansion - had let it get pretty close.

According to my observations, Thornhill Mansion had stood empty between 1861 and 1969, close enough to a hundred years. But from 1969 onwards I'd occasionally see Lyrica in the garden, or in the cemetery itself, a delicate and willowy figure; she might as well be a ghost. We'd even exchange a few words, but only when the occasion demanded it. Too much history. Too much bad blood between her family and mine.

Recently, an even bigger drop of poison had been added to the mix.

Just a few weeks ago, Lyrica brought her last remaining mortal descendants to Thornhill Mansion to be reunited with the accursed clan. And I can only conclude that it must have been one of these descendants who let Venedict Thornhill - Lyrica's cousin, lord of the mansion, and the closest thing I have to an arch nemesis - out of the chain-wrapped casket in which he had been confined since 1861.

I'd long since gathered from eavesdropping on Lyrica's thoughts that she was the one who put him there, hoping to prevent him from creating any more vampires. A wise move, if you ask me.

I would have preferred it if Venedict had stayed locked away forever, not least because I have to raise my hand right now and admit that I am the one responsible for turning him. I infused him with my blood, naively believing that we shared a deep and affectionate bond.

Of course the brat was only ever interested in himself, and in the dark and formidable powers that the vampiric blood gave him. I rarely make errors of judgment, but when I do, they're of a certain magnitude.

But as I was saying, someone let Venedict out.

And once he was out, he, Lyrica and one of their mortal descendants, a hunter of our kind, came looking for me.

Under sneaky pretenses the three of them gained access to my home; my beautiful, peaceful villa deep in Queen's Wood. There they accosted me on the eve of my sister Elizabeth's resurrection.

How unfair of them to interrupt my plans, merely because I had chosen as the host for my darling incorporeal Elizabeth the body of Venedict's sister, Octavia.

Now, let me make one thing perfectly clear, before you

rush to label me the villain. I did not evict Octavia's spirit from her body so that I could offer it to Elizabeth. No, I would not have done such a thing. Octavia's consciousness was long gone by the time I retrieved her beautiful, immortal shell from the Thornhill family mausoleum. And you'll have to agree that it would be a crying shame to leave a perfectly good vessel like Octavia's to gather dust in the tomb when my sister's spirit could do with a body just like hers.

Yes, yes, I know this is all rather convoluted, but try to follow along.

Elizabeth lost her own body to the plague of 1665. This remains my greatest source of regret. Despite swearing to our parents that I would always protect my little sister, I failed to intercept between her and the specter of the Black Death. I only succeeded in saving myself. By the time I was given the immortal blood and went to share it with her, that it might shield her forever from harm, it had already been too late.

The memory of Venedict and Lyrica interrupting the process that would have drawn Elizabeth's spirit into Octavia's body and anchored it there was still fresh in my mind - it still stung. Because of them, my poor darling sister was still out there, roaming the ether, every bit as disembodied as before.

Blocking Elizabeth's entry into the physical realm had been their greatest sin that night, but not their only one.

As part of their vicious attack, they had also critically injured both my brother and my nephew, my only remaining family. Thomas had lost one of his eight tentacles but was now recovering well. Yes, my brother is his own kind of monster, what of it?

With Dwight, his son, it was a different story. His brain

must have sustained some damage when Lyrica drove a bayonet up through his chin and out through his crown. He had survived, but his inability to speak or to even recognize me didn't bode well.

The Thornhills had been avoiding me since that night. It was no small feat considering their home's proximity to Deep Graves. I hadn't as much as glimpsed any of them since they fled my villa with Octavia, Venedict and Lyrica carrying their wounded mortal scion between them.

A question lingered: Why on earth had I decided to let Harlan Thornhill in when he rang me on the intercom that night, claiming to be a client? I'd never laid eyes on him before, but I knew perfectly well who he was. I knew that he was a vampire hunter.

It was an uncharacteristically careless move on my part, but I suppose I must have felt intrigued, unable to resist the game of cat and mouse that I sensed would ensure. There is that, plus I really am a sucker for a pretty face.

Either way, he had lost a lot of blood to Elizabeth's failed resurrection and must have perished soon after. Served the Thornhills right.

No doubt they thought that they had thwarted my plans, that they had banished Elizabeth to wander the astral plane forever, desolate and alone.

How wrong they were. There was still one way I might be able to finally right the historical wrong of her death.

The three vials of ectoplasm I had left jangled hushedly in my pocket.

I'd wasted one, pouring it into Octavia's mouth to help Elizabeth manifest there. I would not make the same mistake again. I had one vial that would transport me, two more to ensure mine and Elizabeth's safe return - there was no spare for luck.

As I walked on, Thornhill Mansion grew larger and larger in my view - an obnoxious and monstrous building, a perfect reflection of the Thornhill family itself. But tonight it was of no significance to me. I would deal with the Thornhills, once I'd rendered my own family complete again.

Turning left, I walked up the worn stone steps and then the gravel path which leads to the Circle of Lebanon. Grand and mysterious, the Circle had always been the cemetery's crowning achievement, the jewel in my design.

The Circle is built into the steep hill directly below Thornhill Mansion's garden. The entrance is flanked by tall Egyptian-inspired columns, behind which an alley of tombs rises on either side before you get to the Circle itself.

Tonight, silvery September mist was pouring from the Egyptian Avenue and pooling at its entrance. I stepped through it and walked between the familiar tombs until I reached the great circle of tombs within.

Until recently, an ancient cedar tree had loomed on top of it, its crown the only part of the circle you could see from the gravel path outside. It had saddened me when the tree, struck one too many times by lightning and branded a danger to visiting mourners and tourists by the Highgate Cemetery Trust, that wizened band of bookkeepers, had been cut down and removed.

Adrenaline fuelled my next steps. This was the moment when my journey to bring back Elizabeth would not only begin but also succeed. Or not, but I was determined not to dwell on the possibility of failure.

Like a great spider having spun my web, I'd watched generations of mourners come and go in the cemetery. I'd heard and seen them water the earth with their tears, and slowly, over the course of centuries, they had charged up the Circle with their potent human emotions. These strong emotions and the charge of the ancient ley lines that converge in this place would ease my journey.

Tonight, I would unleash the powerful, tragic magic that had gathered in the Circle of Lebanon, like a giant battery finally being put in a device and switched on.

I could only hope that it would all click into place, that it would work. I wasn't asking for much. I needed just a small crack in the fabric of time and space, big enough for me to slip through.

To onlookers, it might have seemed that I levitated, but really I just took off from the ground and leapt up onto the roof of the circle of tombs. Jumping six feet or more is no obstacle for me.

Landing in the grass next to the charred remains of the grand old cedar, I reached for the shovel, which I had left here the night before.

After digging a suitable grave, I gently laid down in the soft, damp earth. My view was of the distant stars and orb of the moon, all of it framed by swaying grass.

Soon, I would be walking through the crooked and narrow streets and lanes of 1665 London once more. But only for as long as it took to track down and retrieve Elizabeth. I would turn her into a vampire swiftly, and then transport her back here. No matter how tempting it might be to have a little stroll around in 1665, for old time's sake, I wasn't going to linger. This trip had one purpose and one purpose only.

I reached into my breast pocket, retrieving one of my vials of ectoplasm in its tiny, skull-capped crystal vial. It glowed bright silver in the darkness, nearly the same color as the moonlight.

"Here's to 1665," I said out loud, as if I was making a toast.

Removing the small crystal skull topper with one hand, I let a few drops fall on my tongue. The rest I downed in one gulp.

I shuddered at the indescribable taste, and the intense heat gliding down my throat, heating up my chest like a slow, liquid fire. I hadn't felt this warm in years - indeed, I did not remember ever feeling this warm before. Burning.

Realizing that they were unnecessary, I removed my lambskin gloves and put them in my pocket, before removing my jacket. I am usually unaffected by temperature changes, but this was something else.

Already, the landscape around me had begun to blur and spin and change. Slowly at first, and then faster and faster until it was as though I was on a large, cataclysmic merry-go-round.

The circle of tombs under me seemed to ripple as the larger circle of tombs around it spun and spun; I couldn't even have told you in which direction. The mist filling the space between the tombs was now glowing phosphorescent green, or perhaps I was imagining it. I certainly was feeling rather dizzy.

I strained to look over my shoulder, to glance in the direction of Thornhill Mansion, which should be behind me. I could only see the blurry outlines of its imposing structure. When was it built? Before the cemetery. Early Victorian Era. I looked again and now it was gone. The very ground under me was spinning faster. The cedar tree was there, but young and vital. I longed to cling to its trunk to steady myself, but as I reached for it its trunk turned into a sapling and disappeared into the ground.

This had better work.

Pressure was building inside my skull, building its momentum toward the unbearable. I could feel myself dissolve. My body simply ceased being solid, fading into the surrounding darkness. I couldn't see anything, and I could barely hear. I reached helplessly for something to steady myself with, anything, but suddenly I was falling. Falling down and down through the darkness. I was Orpheus descending into the misty, dangerous realm of the underworld.

Someone cried out, but I couldn't tell if it was me. I was thrashing and flailing wildly, trying to grab hold of something. But there was nothing but falling. Then I felt myself dissolve and disappear.

For a while there was only blackness, and then I sensed ground under me again. The ground was spinning, or was it my head?

Slowly, very slowly, I opened my eyes and looked up into the night sky and its distant stars. The stars were still the same, and yet, something about the atmosphere was markedly different.

I was lying on my back in a muddy field. It was 1665, surely, and the cemetery would not be built under my careful supervision and subtle influence, for nearly another 200 years.

I lifted a hand to rub my eyes with the back of my sleeve when I found that it was covered in dirt.

And wait, what was this?

Mesmerized by the sight of my own hand, I momentarily failed to grasp the perfectly obvious. My hand was still my hand, no doubt about that; my long, slim-boned fingers wiggled and moved as I commanded them to. But it was warm, with clearly visible veins and pores. It was pale, but not marble white. There was no luster to my skin whatsoever.

A half-choked sound of terror escaped my throat as the realization settled over me.

"No. No, no, no, no, no!"

I was looking at the hand of a mortal. Two of them, in fact - this became clear when I thrust my other hand out in front of me. I clasped both of these warm and unfamiliar hands against my face and let out an indignant howl.

A cold feeling of dread nestled in my stomach, which now seemed to be churning and growling, in the throes of half-remembered mortal digestive processes.

My mind was struggling to comprehend it, to take it all in. I'd clearly succeeded in traveling back in time, yes, but I must have gone too far. The sluggish and alarmingly weak form in which I now rose from the field and started walking towards the road was my own familiar body, but from before the vampiric blood had transformed it. The proportions were right but the material was all wrong.

After nearly four hundred years I was a mortal man again.

Had I missed it?

Oh, don't be ridiculous - of course not!

Being mortal again was a dreadful feeling after nearly four centuries of sweet, sweet immortality. And I knew better than anyone that London in 1665 was a particularly bad time to be mortal.

TWO

Once I recovered from the shock of realizing that I was mortal again - assuming one can truly recover from such a disheartening setback - I pulled myself together and started making my way uphill towards Highgate Village.

Down one vial of ectoplasm, I still had two left and could have turned around right then and there. Being mortal again meant being at significant risk, but having come this far I wasn't about to turn around without Elizabeth. I might never be able to return here again.

At first, locomoting by means of my mortal legs felt like attempting to walk underwater. Step by step, though, I was becoming more sure-footed until I was walking at a brisk mortal clip.

Then, as if to mock me, the heavens opened and it began to rain as it can only rain in England. I had to use my beautifully tailored Italian jacket to shield myself from the onslaught. The rain was mild, but even so I was quite damp and annoyed by the time I reached Highgate Village. My Italian dress shoes squelched with each step and my pale blond hair cleaved to my neck and forehead like ghostly seaweed.

Highgate Village had been and was now again an actual village, separate from the ever growing, ever sprawling London city. Small, thatched-roof cottages and pubs lined the narrow streets, their windows glowing warmly through the curtain of downpour.

Resisting the temptation to enter one of the pubs in search of a warm fireplace and other forms of sustenance, I coaxed myself to continue around the corner and to keep walking until I found myself standing in front of a stable. There, I put some of the coins I'd brought with me from the present to good use purchasing a horse; a fine, glistening black steed that I immediately named Comet. This was an admittedly twisted reference to the comet that had been seen in the sky above London on New Year's Eve 1665, and which was later said by many to have been an early omen of the plague.

Comet carried me easily downhill from Highgate, through fields and lanes, and then through the narrow streets of the city until we reached my old parish, St Brides. The smells of the Thames flowing nearby hit me with a powerful wave of nostalgia. But just underneath the brown smell of water was a darker, decidedly putrid scent. I recognized it and shivered.

Fleet Street looked somber in the gray drizzle, but my heart still leapt at the sight of all the narrow timber-framed buildings, the crude hand-painted signs and shingles in wood and hammered metal hanging above most of their doors, all signaling that I was close to my old home.

Turning down Bride Lane I finally dismounted in the courtyard behind my father's coffin builder's shop. I tied Comet to a rusty metal ring in the ground. My family had never owned a horse so I made a mental note to myself to come up with some explanation for how I had been able to afford one.

Ah, but my original plan had been so simple! Travel back to 1665, turn Elizabeth, bring her back with me to the present and be done. But that wasn't to be. My plan now would have to involve several extra steps, and one of them was going to be a reunion with my father.

There was an utterly surreal quality to standing here in the drizzling rain, facing Graves & Sons, a place that had ceased to exist for nearly four centuries.

Well, the narrow and crooked timber-framed building on the corner of Bride Lane and Fleet Street still stood. It was one of the few structures in the area that hadn't been reduced to ashes during the Great Fire of London in 1666. But the humble coffin shop that my father started from nothing had come to an end with his death in the summer of 1667. I closed my eyes, half expecting Graves & Sons to evaporate like a mirage. When I opened them again, it was still there.

The windows glowed from within, their thick panes misted. Through them I could make out the familiar silhouette of my father. I was bursting to enter the shop and to envelop him in a hug, but I hesitated, pacing nervously on the cobblestones. I suppose I was afraid that the illusion would shatter.

Drawing in a deep breath, I steeled myself and grabbed the door handle.

The little brass bell above the door jangled as I stepped into Graves & Sons with its low beams and warm scents of wood polish and fresh pine. I also picked up on the scents of herbs in little bundles, meant to ward off the plague's grim miasma. So I'd arrived too early in 1665, but at least I was in the right year. That was something.

And there was my father. His slim, slightly crooked frame was leaning over a worktable at the back of the room, pale eyes and dexterous fingers working his tools. He barely glanced up at the sound of the bell.

I took a few steps further into the narrow shop. He kept on working by the light of the petroleum lamps, I cleared my throat and raised my voice. "Father."

Michael Graves looked up and his face crinkled in a smile. "Ah, there you are. You go get some rest now, I'll be fine here on my own. This is the last one, nearly ready for tomorrow." He greeted me as if I'd only just left and come back in.

When I made no move towards the narrow wooden stairs that would take me to the living quarters above the shop, my father looked at me again, a questioning look forming in his eyes.

"But what is it you're wearing?" My expensive, tailored suit had caught his attention. "Certainly not a suitable ensemble for grave-digging, son. And now you can't wear these fine clothes for the Bakers' funeral tomorrow."

"You still scold me as you would a child," I said with a wry little smile. How this tendency of his had annoyed me in life! And how I'd come to miss it since. He was right, too. Looking down at myself, I could see how I must look to him in my smartly tailored woollen suit and expensive hand stitched shoes, all soaked and caked with mud.

Grimacing, my father straightened his back. No doubt he was aching from being hunched over and working for unbroken hours on end. "Well," he said, "when all of this is over, you ought to start thinking about finding yourself a wife who can worry about you. Your mother and I may not be around forever."

I frowned slightly, recalling how, throughout my mortal life, my parents had never entirely stopped nudging me - at first with growing desperation, then with weary resignation - about the possibility that I might one day want to find a wife.

My disinterest in women had never seemed to wound them too deeply, though. Thanks to my siblings, Thomas and Elizabeth, the continuation of the Graves bloodline had never hinged on me. I had made my own contribution to the family legacy, transforming my father's modest enterprise into one of London's leading funeral businesses.

If only my father could have witnessed the evolution of Deep Graves over the years. He would have loved what I'd made of it.

"No, thanks. And if the fancy takes me to dig graves in my Sunday best, then that is what I'll do."

"Very well," my father shook his head, but it was a gentle gesture, not really a disapproving one, "I suppose you know best. Regardless, I'm too tired now to argue."

I stepped closer to him, anxious to reach out and touch his arm or shoulder, to reassure myself that he was really there.

Hesitantly, I did, finding his arm warm and solid. He was no ghost. I looked into his eyes; green like mine, but a little darker and with flecks of hazel.

"Please go upstairs Father, I can see how tired you are. What more needs doing here? Leave me to finish it."

Michael Graves took a seat on a high-backed wooden chair next to the workbench and wiped his hands on a linen cloth. "No need, son. I'll wait for Westminster to collect, and then I will rest," he said, patting the small coffin on the workbench with his hand. Then he took a sip of water from a cup and looked over at me again, his expression still slightly quizzical. "Gabriel, you look a little pale."

"Don't worry about me. How are Elizabeth and Thomas? How is mother?" I hoped these questions didn't sound completely inane. He had no clue that I'd been gone for centuries, but was under the impression that I had only been out for a few hours to dig graves commissioned by the parish church. In his timeline, who knew where we were at? I needed to know.

"Ah, you know," My father's face grew sad and infinitely tired, "Thomas is threatening to head back out to sea. He doesn't mean it, of course, but his mere toying with the idea is enough to give me palpitations!" He chuckled slightly, before a dark cloud drifted over his features. "As for Elizabeth, I must admit I worry about her more than I do about you boys. Don't get me wrong, the three of you are my angels. But she's my youngest, my little girl. And of course I worry about your mother too, and about Dwight. How I hope that these grim times," at this he made a helpless gesture to indicate the streets outside, "will soon be behind us."

"They will."

"Who knows if those preachers we've heard in the streets could be right, after all. Perhaps this really is God's way of punishing this city."

"No, never. If there is a god, as I know you and I both have our doubts, he wouldn't punish the whole city. London is full of good people, well, and a few rotten apples. Anyway, it isn't like you to speak like this, to take such a dim view."

My father had never been a religious man, despite

working closely with the parish church, instrumental as he was in every Christian burial in St Bride's Parish.

He rubbed his closed eyes with two fingers. "I know, I know. I'm just a tired old fool."

"Nonsense. Now, please listen to me and let me take over. Let me wait up for Westminster." I stepped a little closer to the glow of the oil lamp. "And I promise I'll speak to Thomas in the morning and turn his thoughts from heading out to sea. I'll make him see that he can't simply shrug off the responsibilities he has here."

"Thomas has always looked up to you," My father patted my hand and gave me a weary smile so full of trust that it made my heart ache. "Your words will probably carry more weight than mine. Just try not to bring it up before the funeral - it'll put him in a glum mood. Speaking of glum. Westminster will be here any moment with the bodies."

As IF ON CUE, the door swung open with abrupt force. The brass bell above it rang out in alarm as Malm Westminster, the plague doctor of St Bride's Parish, strode into the shop.

He wore the instantly recognizable black cloak and grotesque beaked mask of his profession, but he slipped off his beaked hood and tucked it under his arm as soon as he was inside.

Westminster was a large man, both tall and thickset. His wrists had to be as thick as my neck, and what was visible of them between his shirt and the heavy leather gloves he had on was covered in dark hair that reminded me of a wild boar's bristles. A mirthless smirk crept across Westminster's pronounced, stubbly chin and his small, hard eyes gleamed as they scanned the room. Still standing near the door, he greeted us in a bombastic voice, "The *esteemed* coffin builders! I hope you have the coffins prepared?"

Past the outline of Westminster's heavyset shoulder, I was able to make out the silhouettes of a cart flanked by two men. On top of it lay a bulky, formless cargo covered by a sheet. From one corner, a child's graying hand dangled limply. Icy fingers ran down my spine at the sight of it.

Now, I'm very accustomed to seeing the dead. After centuries both as a vampire and as an undertaker, countless dead have passed through my hands and into the expertly crafted, silk-lined caskets for which I have become known. But there was simply something about seeing this dead child's grayish skin, merged with the unpleasant awareness of my own currently mortal state that made me feel both queasy and weak at the knees.

"Of course, yes. I've just put the finishing touches on the last one. Come right this way," my father, ever the professional, gestured towards the back room where all of the completed coffins were kept. Westminster followed him, and after him followed his two companions, grunting as they carried the lifeless, cloth-wrapped forms of the four members of the Baker family.

We all stepped through the low-beamed door that led to the back room. Here, simple but well-built coffins in all sizes lined the walls, stacked up against each other. Some had been polished or painted, but most were made of raw and simple pinewood, our bread and butter.

I still had one of these specimens on display in the Deep Graves casket showroom which is adjacent to my villa. Surrounded by the many more opulent and artistically expressive caskets I've delved into creating since, it is there to remind me of where I come from.

My father indicated the three coffins laid out in a row on the floor with their lids next to them, ready to be secured in place with hammer and nails. Two were adult sized, one slightly smaller for the family's teenager. My father then turned around to pick up the fourth and smallest coffin from his workbench after quickly securing the bottom panel with a few more nails.

Westminster's companions unceremoniously placed the corpses into their requisite coffins. Despite the layers of cloth they were wrapped in, the odors rising from the skin of the dead was unbearable. It was clear that they had been left in their home for quite some time before being collected. That was the way of things; plague victims would often be left in their houses for weeks on end before they were finally carted away.

Westminster instructed his assistants to take the filled coffins outside and to wait for him in the courtyard. He then turned around to face my father and I. "It's been a long time, Graves."

My father nodded curtly. "So it has. I hear that you've made quite a name for yourself as a witch finder. And now that the plague is back, so is your beaked mask." The disapproval in my father's tone was palpable.

Westminster's chuckle, dark and resonant, was not too dissimilar to an old tomcat purring. "Precisely. One must go where opportunity abounds, Michael. Don't tell me you're blind to the golden opportunity that is presenting itself right underneath our noses?" His beady eyes gleamed like pieces of jet. "For the next month, perhaps only for the next few weeks, you will be golden, building your boxes. But then, people will be dying by such numbers that coffins and funeral rites become wholly unnecessary. Believe me, I visit our neighboring boroughs frequently enough to know the truth. The official death toll, the one you see posted on the bills of mortality, well, those numbers are vastly underplayed. The reality is that the Black Death has gotten much more of a stranglehold on this city than those in power care to admit."

My jaw clenched reflexively. I remembered Westminster all too well.

When I'd first been introduced to him as a child, he'd already been a full-grown vulture. I knew from my father that the guy had been a plague doctor during the outbreak in 1645, and that he had garnered quite the reputation as a witchfinder general since. Here was a man who laid claim to whatever position of power would bring him the most wealth and reverence at any given time, a man who thought nothing of ascribing the deadly label of witch to anyone who might glance at him sideways. And now he was calling himself a doctor once more. It had been half a millennia since I'd last had the displeasure of being in his presence, and after five minutes of it, I'd already had enough.

"And what then, Michael?" Wesmintster leaned close to my father. "How will you feed your family when chaos reigns? You could don the beaked mask, but I suspect you'll let the opportunity pass you by, just as you did twenty years ago."

Westminster grinned broadly at my father and I, and I got the sense that he was testing us.

"Opportunity?" Anger and disgust deepened the lines on my father's face. "I see devastation around us, Malm."

The plague doctor's chuckle filled the shop, setting my teeth on edge. "I am telling you, as an old friend, that when the Black Death is truly upon us, no one will give a damn if a few fistfuls of gold coins go missing from someone's drawers or if a few pieces of jewelry are lifted from the fingers or throats of the dead. You talk of devastation, but devastation is merely the unforgiving truth of mother nature. The plague merely hastens the natural order of things. The weak fall while the strong rise. And why shouldn't I rise? The last outbreak lined my pockets well. But that was a long time ago. You remember it well, don't you? We were young men then, and while I made the most of what fate presented me with, you kept building coffins and digging graves, a loyal lapdog to the parish."

"I made my choices and you made yours, Malm."

"Admittedly," Westminster said, ignoring my father's input, "you've done well enough for yourself and your family, all things considered. But as a friend, I'm urging you not to sleep on the opportunity. This wave, if my intuition is right, promises to be even greater than that last. And I mean greater in every sense of the word! What we're seeing now is only the early days. Get your head screwed on straight, make much of the circumstances. They're here whether we like them or not."

I could feel my father's restrained fury radiating through his skin as I stood next to him. "So the suffering of our friends and neighbors is our opportunity to fill our coffers, Malm? I beg to differ."

"All I am saying is that the Black Death reaps its harvest, and I am simply the reaper collecting my due. There's no sin in that. With the help of your sons, you could make a fortune. They're strapping lads. Well," Here Westminster paused to eye me up and down with palpable suspicion, "Gabriel is tall, at least."

Indeed. Next to my small-framed father, I stood at six

feet tall. I put it down to my mother's Dutch heritage and decent nutrition.

My father had grown up under very different circumstances than the humble but comfortable ones in which he'd been able to bring up his own children. Hailing from a long line of gravediggers, a young Michael Graves had somehow landed an apprenticeship with a carpenter who had taught him how to work with wood. To imagine that such a simple thing had forever changed the destiny of the branch of the Graves family tree from which I'd sprouted.

I looked over at my father and met his gaze. It was clear that we shared a mutual loathing for the man with the beaked mask under his arm.

Westminster, of course, was either oblivious or indifferent to this. "Who knows," he mused, "if perhaps Gabriel here sees things more like I do. Ah, but there we have the lovely, radiant Elizabeth Graves! How she has blossomed."

Westminster's remark tore me from my thoughts. I followed his gaze as his brutally chiseled face turned towards the staircase.

There she was! My long-lost sister, radiant and alive. She was in her white nightgown, only a few shades paler than her long blonde hair and pale skin, as yet untouched by the plague. For a moment, I couldn't remember how to breathe. "Elizabeth!"

I moved swiftly around Westminster and closed the distance between us. I had forgotten how petite she was. At sixteen, she had likely reached her full height of 5'5", the same as both of our parents. I wrapped my arms around her in a tight embrace, partially lifting her off the ground while simultaneously obstructing Westminster's predatory view.

She looked up at me, surprise and a smile on her face. "You just saw me a few hours ago!"

"Well, it feels like it's been much longer," I struggled to hold back the tears that suddenly welled up in my eyes. It was all becoming overwhelming – seeing my father and now Elizabeth, my reason for embarking on this wild journey.

Westminster was still talking behind us, directing his words to our father. "I see why you've kept her hidden away. She has grown into quite the magnificent creature, I can see that. How old is she now?"

"Sixteen," Elizabeth replied curtly, her tone clipped as I ushered her towards the staircase. I didn't want her anywhere near Westminster, and I was completely positive that my father didn't want that either.

Westminster smirked, craning his neck, all the better to wolf her down with his eyes. "Ah, I see. Yes, I would have guessed at least that. You are surprisingly well-proportioned and developed." The plague doctor's eyes roamed over Elizabeth's slight form. "I suppose you haven't yet started looking for a suitable husband? Perhaps, young Elizabeth Graves, you should come work for me at Clayfield, the new pest house being built not far from here. That way, you and I can get to know each other a little more intimately."

"Who exactly are you?" Elizabeth demanded in a stern tone, folding her arms across her narrow chest.

"Malm Westminster, at your service." He bowed slightly, in a way that came across as ironic.

"Isn't it about time you leave?" I turned around to face Westminster. I knew, logically, that he was a powerful man, and that he was well known for abusing it. It wasn't wise to provoke his wrath or to create any trouble, but I wanted him gone. And I suppose centuries as a powerful immortal had distorted my perception of who I was and what I was up against in this mortal man. In other words, Westminster didn't intimidate me. Though he appeared alive and imposing, in another sense, he was dead, his bones long since turned to dust.

I fixed him with a challenging glare. "Goodnight, Westminster. You can see yourself out."

"Well," Westminster said, brushing himself off as if I had just thrown a handful of dust at him, "I expect a busy evening, so yes, I'll be on my way. But you can be certain that I will be back. Perhaps when I return we will be able to have a real conversation, Gabriel. You're too young to remember much of the plague's previous onslaught, but believe me, our true selves are revealed when we are put under pressure. Some will sink, others will soar. It'll be interesting to see what you're made of."

I moved towards the door, opening it and holding it for him, making it clear that it was time for him to depart. And so he left, marching out without a backward glance.

THREE

"Do you think Westminster might be right, about this wave of the Black Death being worse than any other?" Elizabeth asked in a whisper. Her pale green eyes were clouded with concern that had little to do with the four coffins containing the members of the Baker family that Thomas and I had just lowered into the ground. Having played our initial part in the funeral proceedings, we stood back now while the parish priest, Father Dalmane, was saying the traditional prayers.

I stood between my two siblings, all three of us looking down into the hole that was dug much deeper than the usual six feet, and wider as well. Wider in order to accommodate the four Baker coffins, deeper because it was believed that the deadly miasma was able to rise through several layers of dirt to claim new victims.

The Bakers' was the first family grave to be prepared at St Bride Churchyard in Fleet Street, a tranquil and sacred space that I knew would soon be filled with similar graves. Hindsight really is 20/20. I knew for a fact that we stood on the precipice of a great tragedy, that our parish was about to witness a rapid descent into darkness.

But there was no point in burdening either of my siblings with what I knew.

"No," I replied, shaking my head with conviction, "Westminster exaggerates. And of course he would; he's made a profession out of exploiting misfortune, first as a plague doctor, then as a witch finder, and now again as a beaked harbinger of death. He follows the trail of tragedy and opportunity wherever it leads him. He sees others not as real people, but as resources for him to feed on." All right, I admit it, I might have been projecting a little here, but it was still true. "We mustn't fall prey to such a bleak outlook, Elizabeth. I remember the previous plague twenty years ago - you weren't yet born. It was a horrific ordeal, and then, as suddenly as it had begun, it ebbed away. Life resumed its rhythm. Well, not for everyone, of course, but for most. The Black Death will never get its claws into you, I promise."

The million-pound question was how I was going to deliver on this promise.

Last night, before retiring to my living quarters in the attic of the Graves building, I'd asked my father to remind me of the day's date. He'd answered promptly that it was July 27, 1665. I'd had the poor man repeat it to me several times until it finally sank in. The horror of it was that July 1665 was four long months *before* I'd become a vampire. In other words, the vampiric gifts I had come here to bestow upon Elizabeth were only a glimmer on the horizon. Standing here in the churchyard, bereft of my immortality and glancing down at the pinewood coffins in the ground, nothing set me apart from the rest of the assembled mourners. Ick.

"But no one," Thomas interrupted my thoughts, "can control or predict how bad this wave is going to be, despite the best efforts of all the fortune tellers, doctors, and politicians. The truth is, no one knows what the next few weeks or months have in store. Not even you, Gabriel. Which is precisely," he continued, "why I'm considering heading back out to sea. I've already told Father, and I've been meaning to tell you. The last thing I want is to be stuck here building coffins and digging graves with the Black Death stalking the streets."

I shot my brother a sharp glance. There was only eleven months between us, yet I'd always felt like a much older sibling. Centuries older.

The two of us looked rather alike with our clean angular features, green eyes and blond hair. Thomas was a little shorter than I, but built all the more solidly. He was muscly; I was wiry. If we ever had to arm wrestle I had no doubt who would win. But only I had the power to subdue my brother with a single, devastating glance.

"Out of the question, Thomas. The family and the business both need you. Must I remind you that you have responsibilities that you cannot simply shrug off into my lap? Must I remind you that you have a son?"

"But the sea, Gabriel, her siren song-"

"Enough," I said curtly, lifting my hand.

"Hear me out. The sea is calling out to me, louder than ever, now that this is happening to the city."

"That I can believe."

Had I really allowed myself to forget how exasperating I'd sometimes found my brother back when the two of us were both mortal? I suppose immortality and wealth had insulated us from ever having to argue about our deepest values. But back when we were both alive and human and down in the dirt, we'd often clashed. Now I remembered it clearly.

In 1665, Thomas really had left the family behind as the plague raged to pursue his own destiny at sea. When our paths finally crossed again in 1989, we'd both found immortality, though in very different ways. I had wandered the world as a vampire since November 1st 1665, and he had been transformed by a sea witch who fell in love with him during one of his many seafaring voyages. But whereas my brand of immortality allowed me to pass through the centuries among humans, his was a little more... noticeable.

The tentacled lower body that was part of his condition had made him first a formidable and legendary pirate, and later on, a captured animal in a wealthy man's private collection.

"Your life and your destiny, Thomas, belong to the family," I reminded him. "You're a Graves. If we were nobles with no obligations and the means to stay out of the plague's reach, then yes, by all means, your destiny would be yours entirely. But that's not the reality we're living in."

Thomas looked down, his cheeks burning with hurt and anger. His fists clenched as he kicked up a bit of dirt. It fell into the still-open grave while Father Dalmane intoned prayers and words of comfort. As I regarded my brother, I wondered how I might (and indeed whether I should) prevent him from boarding the ship that would take him away from me for centuries. If I were to share the vampiric blood with him before the sea witch could get to him, I could spare him the stress and trouble of a form that would never be able to move unnoticed among mortals.

Father Dalmane's voice wove through the air, like a comforting golden thread. And yet, I couldn't help but pick up on an underlying panic that caused a slight tremor, like the sounds of a Theremin.

"Let us share a moment of silence," he entreated the gathered mourner, "for the souls of the Baker family. They were taken from the world and from our parish too soon. Much too soon, in little Becky's case."

As heads bowed, my mind wandered, conjuring the haunting whine of my own theremins back home at Villa Graves. I had amassed a whole little collection of these strange instruments ever since I had first come across one in the early 1920s. If you want my opinion, their ethereal tones are the perfect accompaniment to solitary nights under a silvery moon.

I missed my theremins. I missed my piano. I missed my records. Not to mention my walk-in wardrobe and my over-sized marble bathtub.

Right now, in the murky, gathering twilight, with the cold damp air rising off the river and seeping into my clothes, my collection of theremins, my lush villa and everything I had left behind in the present seemed worlds away. It had been scarcely a day since I'd embarked on my mad journey back in time, and I was already desperately homesick. And I wasn't any closer to completing my errand now than I had been yesterday.

I was startled as Thomas put a hand on my arm. The funeral was over, the crowd beginning to disperse. Their torches and lanterns formed a procession of fireflies against the encroaching night as they filed out of the cemetery, our parents and Elizabeth among them.

Thomas and I lingered as the others drifted toward the warmth of the nearby pub. We had graves to fill. Yes, we were coffin-builders, not mere gravediggers as our father had been when he was young, and as his father had been before him. Still, St Bride's currently had more funerals than sextons, so our help was needed.

"You carry duty like it's simply a part of you," Thomas said quietly, breaking the silence as he picked up a shovel. "You've always shouldered it effortlessly while I..." His voice trailed off, and he handed me the other shovel. "I appear to be made of a different material, let's just put it like that."

Soon Thomas and I were both shoveling dirt like two perfectly timed pieces in a clockwork.

I had always been the serious one, the responsible one. I'd always carried myself with a solemn gravitas and the funeral business had suited me right from the start. I had no formal education, but our mother had taught me all I needed to know about reading and counting, and by the age of six, I had become an indispensable assistant to my father. I'd actually been interested in learning everything I could about building coffins and running the business. I'd spent countless hours meticulously copying the letters from the signatures our wealthier and most educated patrons left on order notes until, eventually, my hand-writing became indistinguishable from theirs.

But Thomas was, as he had just pointed out himself, cut from a different cloth. He was the dreamer, the free spirit, always chasing some adventure. One of those adventures had led to us having an extra family member - Dwight, his illegitimate son. There were other children around St Brides and Fleet Street that carried varying degrees of resemblance to Thomas, but none of them were confirmed fruits of my brothers' loins.

"You've always been our parents' favorite," Thomas continued, glancing sideways at me, as if he was hoping I'd dispute it.

"Nonsense," I assured him, my muscles tensing as my

unfamiliar mortal arms continued to shovel dirt. "We both have our flaws."

The Baker grave was soon completely filled up and my arms were aching. I put down the shovel.

"Come on," I said, wiping my hands on a piece of cloth which I produced from my coat pocket. Thomas also wiped his hands, but on the back of his breeches. "The others are already at The Seven Stars, drinking themselves into a stupor. We should join them."

We both set in motion towards the cemetery gate. I stood back to let Thomas walk out first, and as he did, something compelled me to cast a backward glance over my shoulder. What I saw made my blood run cold.

There, standing on or rather hovering just above the freshly dug Baker grave, was the instantly recognizable figure of Octavia Thornhill.

"Thomas, you go ahead. I'll join you in no time. There's something I forgot, and that I must attend to."

"I'll see you at the Stars," Thomas gave me a wave over his shoulder without even looking back as he continued walking. His footsteps were soon disappearing up the cobbled lane towards Fleet Street.

I walked back over to the Baker grave, approaching it somewhat hesitantly. Octavia was still there, but was it really Octavia? She didn't appear to be fully solid. Although she was nearly opaque, I was able to make out the outlines of headstones and hedges behind her, through her.

"Octavia," I addressed her in the most steady voice I could muster - as if seeing her here didn't shock me at all. "Have you died - are you a ghost?" Why beat around the bush?

"No, ducky." Her voice was surprisingly resonant, as if she were really here. And yet, it seemed to come from nowhere in particular - certainly not from the semi-transparent figure standing before me. "At least not in the usual sense."

She was glowing softly in the gathering gloom that had accrued in the cemetery. Everything about her was luminous and pearlescent white, from her skin to the gently billowing dress she was wearing. Everything except her hair, which fell in bright, cherry red ringlets around her small frame.

"You're not physical," I pointed out. I didn't have to reach out and touch her to know, and I vaguely wondered whether doing so might be rude. I had a feeling that if I did attempt to touch her, her form would both feel and spread like thickly condensed mist.

"You're very perceptive, Gabriel, I'll give you that."

"How are you here? Also, why?" Perhaps that latter part was more important.

I was standing near enough to her that I could easily see her facial expressions, and there was no doubt at all that she was fully aware of my presence. Her head was tilted, turned slightly towards me, and she was watching me with alert, non-physical eyes.

"I've been roaming far from my body for quite some time - you should know, you considered it an empty shell, a shell that you could offer as a gift to your sister's spirit." Her voice, which had been soft and lilting, turned into a sneer at the end of the sentence.

"Well," I said, slightly embarrassed. This was completely true, but I'd never expected to be confronted about it. "Yes. Yes, I did. I really didn't think you were particularly attached to it; in fact I didn't think you were attached to it at all."

"And so my body was up for the taking?" she frowned,

and I was amazed that I could see the slight wrinkling of her small button nose.

"Admittedly, yes."

"Eco-conscious, are you? You thought you could recycle my immortal body?"

"We've already established that fact. Now, why don't you answer my questions; how and why have you come here?"

"Very well. During all that time that I spent roaming beyond the confines of this immortal flesh prison, I became rather adept at what you might call astral projection, or spirit travel. That's how I've come here. I was roaming the cemetery last night when I saw you crossing the road. I sensed that you were up to something and I followed you."

"You followed me back in time without ectoplasm?" I stood in stunned amazement. This was outright phenomenal.

"Indeed. But as you can see, I'm only here in spirit, not in the flesh."

"So where is your body now, while your spirit is here?"

"I'm not telling you. You've stolen my body once before."

Touche.

"Fair enough," I bowed my head slightly.

"Actually, this brings me to why I've come. I've gathered that you're here on a specific errand. I've come to help you, if I can."

I was stunned. Octavia Thornhill, here to help me? No, that couldn't be.

"Oh, don't look so shocked, Gabriel!" Octavia laughed rather uproariously. Her demeanor had an interesting way of veering from demure Victorian to something really quite forthright and brash, and back again within the same sentence. "I'm not precisely offering my help out of some altruistic sentiment. Rather, it's a preventative measure. If you succeed in turning Elizabeth, as I've gathered that you intend to do, you'll have no reason to make another attempt at stealing my body. See? In this case, Gabriel, I want your plan to succeed."

I did see, and I liked what I saw.

"Well, thank you. Whatever your motivation is, I'm certainly not above accepting your help. In fact, I could really do with a bit of assistance."

"Truer words were never spoken. You've landed yourself in quite the pickle, Gabriel. You went back too far - I saw your disappointment and I heard your muttered curses last night in that muddy field in Highgate. Tell me, how does it feel to be mortal again?" Her amber eyes sparked with curiosity that she made no attempt at hiding.

"Dreadful," I replied. I saw no point in lying. And just then, a thought occurred to me. "Given my predicament, Octavia, how do I know that you're here to help and not to impede my plans?"

"You don't know. I suppose you'll simply have to trust me. But ask yourself, do you really think I want to jeopardize you not becoming a vampire and thus undoing your entire bloodline, to which I happen to belong? If you never become a vampire, Venedict never becomes a vampire, and neither do I. "

"Well, that's convenient. How do I-"

But she was gone, poof, instantly evaporated. Whether she was still listening or watching me I had no idea, but our conversation was clearly at an end.

∼

WHEN I ARRIVED at The Seven Stars public house, where the rest of the funeral party was already gathered to commemorate the Bakers, I walked in on a tense scene.

Ethel Nesbit, a local seamstress, already drunk on the wine, had risen from her table and was gesturing with her gnarled, arthritic hands. Her bonnet had fallen back from her head and was dangling precariously by ribbons tied underneath her warbly chin. Thin strings of steel gray hair flew about her head as she turned it this way and that to make sure that she was commanding everyone's attention.

"I'm telling you all," she proclaimed in a slightly slurred but no less attention-grabbing voice, "there's witchcraft in our midst! Simply because the plague is here doesn't mean we can afford to overlook the signs of the dark arts being practiced. The saying goes, 'no rest for the wicked,' and indeed, the Devil's foot soldiers never sleep, no, never, and their numbers creep through the land and the streets more or less unseen and uncontested."

One of the parish sextons, James Pennyfield, raised his voice from the bar where he leaned, clutching a pint of the pub's famous potent brew. "What do you mean, Widow Nesbit?" From his tone it was impossible to tell whether he was challenging her or was merely curious to hear what she had to say about the Devil's foot soldiers since she was apparently the expert.

Ethel Nesbit, barely needing the encouragement, continued, "I know the signs of dark workings when I see them. At seventy-two, I've lived longer than most of you here, and I've witnessed the presence of witches in various forms and disguises within our community over many decades. I grew up in St Bride's! So mark my words and don't tell me later that I hadn't warned you."

"What signs of witchcraft have you seen, if you don't

mind me asking?" my father inquired from the corner table where he sat with the rest of the Graves family. His tone and demeanor were as infallibly polite as ever, and yet the aging widow frowned, as if she hadn't expected to have to actually justify her veiled accusations.

"Well," she blustered, "the signs are of course perfectly clear and easy to see for anyone who cares to look. Why, I have seen dark, beaked shadows moving across the walls of my home." She paused, perhaps to come up with more signs of witchcraft, perhaps for dramatic effect. "Also, I've found items of clothing missing from my washing lines. And worst of all, since yesterday evening I have sensed a dark aura in our midst, something unnatural that has entered this community. It could be the Devil himself, disguised as a regular man, with the sole intention of preying upon us."

I suppressed a shiver as the widow's pale, watery eyes wandered around the room. The devil in disguise, was I? Oh, I wish; alas, until I was able to find and convince my vampiric patrons to share their cursed blood with me once more, I would remain a mere mortal, and a rather harmless one at that.

"Now, now, Ethel, let us not jump to any conclusions." Father Dalmane suggested. Despite being the religious pillar and custodian of the community, he was slow to reach for superstitions and reluctant to make accusations. I'd always liked that about him. I knew he'd grown up in a small village in Oxfordshire, and he still had much of the farm boy's salt-of-the-earth earnestness about him.

"I'm telling you," Widow Nesbit reached for her cup of wine, and as she picked it up some of its contents sloshed out onto the wooden table in front of her, "The Black Death is God asserting his wrath upon this city, this much I know for certain. And no doubt the actual witches and necromancers among us function like magnets for the disease. Why else, pray tell, would the Black Death have come to the doors and into the homes of our community? Why is this happening to those in our midst, like the good Baker family, while my family members in other parts of the city report no pestilence, no deaths?"

"The plague never unfurls equally everywhere all at once," Father Dalmane reminded her in his resonant, soothing tone, but the widow, on a roll now, refused to let go of her audience so easily.

"Let us ask ourselves," she insisted, "Who prospers when death is rife? We all know the answer to this one. It's the undertakers, the gravediggers, and all that feast on the misery of God's purest souls."

"If that's the case," Thomas said, rising from the table where our family sat, "then shouldn't the professions you mention also include tailors and seamstresses, like you and your kin, Ethel Nesbit? Isn't it true many commission mourning clothing and armbands when loved ones perish from the plague? Haven't you received a surge in orders recently?"

The widow's cheeks burned scarlet with anger, her red-rimmed eyes flashing at Thomas. She cut a tiny figure, and yet I have to admit, her demeanor made her small crooked frame seem at least ten feet tall.

Moving over to our family's table, I placed a hand on Thomas's arm, trying to silently urge him to be cautious. Widow Nesbit had a sharp tongue and a flair for the dramatic, and I would rather we stayed off her radar. To provoke or anger her was no different to poking a sleeping, famished bear. I already had enough concerns without adding potential witchcraft accusations.

Glancing sideways at Thomas, I noted his flushed cheeks and the fiery spark in his eyes. I shared his frustration, but perhaps time had granted me a perspective that allowed me to step back from the heat of the moment. I knew that engaging in word-to-word combat with the widow would only bring us trouble, so I refrained.

Before Thomas could retort again, Father Dalmane, still in his clerical attire and carrying himself with the aura of authority it demanded, stepped into the middle of the room, lifting his hands, determined now to silence Widow Nesbit's wagging tongue.

"To extend on Thomas's point," he began, "it could be said that priests, such as myself, have seen a growing number of congregants in church. Indeed, St Bride's has received more donations recently than in many previous years. People seek Christ's comfort in these dark times. Would you count that as witchcraft?"

Ethel Nesbit seemed at a loss for words. Her strong faith made it difficult for her to counter the priest. Her anger was palpable, but her eyes now held a touch of fear, perhaps realizing she might have overstepped. Her mouth opened, then closed, as her gentle daughter, Justine, tenderly encouraged her to sit.

All eyes remained on Father Dalmane, awaiting his next words.

"Let us not let fear overcome us. In challenging times, it's tempting to look for someone to blame - for someone to crucify, even. But let us not reach for harsh judgments. Undoubtedly, some professions thrive more in dire circumstances than others. But our community needs its grave diggers and coffin builders, just as it needs its seamstresses, tailors, wagon builders, innkeepers, bookkeepers, and bakers. And there's no dishonor in striving to support one's family through a reputable craft. After all, wasn't Jesus Christ a carpenter?"

Several heads nodded in agreement, while others absorbed the priest's words in silence. A few were even gazing deeply into their cups, as if embarrassed that they had been ready to sharpen their pitchforks. As the tension in the room ebbed away, conversations resumed their usual cadence.

Widow Nesbit sat quietly at her table, but I noticed her occasionally sending sharp glances in the direction of the Graves family throughout the evening.

"Pay her no mind," my mother, Marie Graves, said in a hushed voice, "Ethel is not truly mean-spirited. I don't believe we have much to be concerned about."

FALLING asleep after the Baker funeral proved impossible. With the rest of the Graves family asleep, I paced the creaking floorboards of the attic restlessly. Thomas was already snoring soundly behind the floor length curtain that served as a wall, dividing our humble bachelor pad in two.

My half was furnished with a simple wooden bed, a table and a chair placed against the garble wall, and a chest I'd made myself. This was filled with clothes and linens, and it was where I'd tucked away the little stash of gold I'd brought from the future. The vials of ectoplasm I'd decided to keep on my person at all times - and to facilitate this, I'd spent my first evening here sewing hidden pockets into every article of clothing I'd found in the chest.

The crammed, enclosed quarters with their sloping

walls made clear thinking difficult, and yet clear thinking was what I needed to do.

Since my arrival in 1665 some thirty hours ago I'd found myself immediately plunged back into my old life, with all of its demands and distractions. I was overjoyed to be reunited with my parents and would have loved to share with them everything that had happened to me after the end of their mortal lifespans.

But I needed to focus on my only reason for coming here. The first thing I needed to do, surely, was to regain my immortality. Everything else would follow on from there. Without the dark blood flowing through my veins, there was no point to any of this. I might as well lay down and die.

The question was, how would I approach the twins, Isadore and Isadora? This was July 1665. In July 1665 I hadn't known what the Elysion twins were. I'd known that they were different from me and from anyone else I'd ever met, but I had not even suspected the truth. If I were to turn up on their doorstep now, in the middle of the night, demanding their vampiric blood, how would they react? Probably not favorably.

I didn't like to admit it, but there was a very real chance that either my knowledge of what they were, or my desperation to become like them, would make them turn away and deny me the blood. Why, they might even decide to kill me. Imagine that! Gabriel Graves, the vampire, returning to his mortal form only to wind up a victim of his former makers. Now, wouldn't that be a hoot!

I shook my head forcefully, willing this particularly dreadful possibility to go away. I couldn't allow this to happen, couldn't risk putting all of my cards on the table for them to see.

But what then? Would I have to simply wait it out between now and November 1st all over again? Four months - four long months during which anything could happen.

I needed to not only convince the twins that I was worthy of the immortal flame all over again, and I needed to do it as soon as possible. Without tipping my hand to them, without letting them know that I knew what they were. It was going to be a difficult line to tread, no doubt, but I would do it. After all, there was no other way.

I'd already risked everything by coming here, hadn't I? I'd put my own immortality on the line.

Maybe Octavia could help me.

It's a sign of a dire situation, I suppose, when you are accepting help from the sister of your most bitter enemy. Particularly when you aren't certain you can trust her.

FOUR

T he hallway I was navigating had a distinctly Victorian quality to it. It was clear that it had once been grand but had now fallen into a dreadful state of neglect. The ceiling above me was vaulted, the walls clad in faded ornate wallpaper. Along them on both sides hung an assortment of portraits and landscape paintings, but each time I attempted to focus my attention on any one of them, it faded from view, as if it was being enveloped in a blurry mist and hidden from my sight.

The floor underneath my feet was covered in a threadbare carpet with a dark swirling pattern, and on top of this a thick, soft layer of dust. I noticed with some surprise that my feet were bare, and going by their marble-white luster they were vampiric in nature, just as they should be. Looking down at myself, it appeared that I was wearing the same white breeches and voluminous nightshirt that I had gone to sleep in.

But what was this place? It seemed so familiar, and yet I couldn't quite put my finger on it. Just like the paintings on the walls, the name of this place kept eluding me.

It seemed like I had no other - or certainly no better - option than to continue along the hallway. Sooner or later, I was bound to either reach the front door, or to encounter an inhabitant.

Now this end of the long, slightly curved corridor was something else. Here, there was no dust, and the bare walls appeared to have been freshly painted in a deep peacock shade of turquoise.

I noticed now that there were doors on either side of me. One of them, a set of double-wide doors, stood ajar. I lifted my hands and pushed them open, stepping into the library beyond. In a rush of clarity I knew precisely where I was. This was the library at Thornhill Mansion - the home of Octavia, Lyrica, and Venedict, my most wayward fledgling. There were the tall, tapered windows overlooking the garden and Highgate Cemetery beyond it. It was nighttime and only moonlight filtered through the branches of the tall trees outside, falling at my feet in rustling, rippling squares. Bookshelves, thrice my height, covered the walls from floor to ceiling. Far above, a stained glass dome kept the soft drizzle of autumn rain at bay.

The question was, what on earth was I doing here?

Footsteps. Footsteps coming nearer. Someone was making their way up the dark mahogany staircase from the ground floor.

I waited, hesitated, my breath caught in my throat. Who was approaching, and how would I explain my presence here?

The double-wide library door swung open and in stepped Octavia. She saw me immediately, outlined as I was in white against the dark windows. She let out a sharp exhale of air, her hand fluttering up to her chest. She was wearing a Victorianesque dress with plenty of plum colored lace - but it was much too short to be an authentic Victorian piece. So where were we, in 2024?

"Gabriel, what the blazes?" She stepped into the room, closing the door swiftly behind her.

I shrugged and lifted my open palms in an open gesture.

"What are you doing here?"

"I wish I could tell you. All I can say for certain is that I went to sleep, in my own bed in Bride Street in 1665 - and now I appear to be here. But I think appear to be might be the operative phrase here. Unless I am mistaken, I'm only here in spirit."

"You do look semi-transparent, at least to me." Octavia acknowledged. Her eyes widened as she looked up at me. "It seems you, too, are able to travel. In spirit."

"The thing is," I admitted, "I have no idea how I've accomplished it."

"Spontaneous out of body experiences, I've read about them." Octavia gestured towards the shelves behind her. "They're nothing special."

"Traveling out of body like this certainly doesn't solve my problem, either," I mumbled, as much to myself as to her.

The moment I'd said it, everything around me began to fade, including Octavia.

It was like awakening from any dream - try as you might to sustain it, to will the dream to continue, you ultimately are not able to.

I JOLTED AWAKE, propelled myself into a seated position in bed and collided with my forehead against the slanted wooden ceiling. Dizzily I rolled out of bed and stood swaying in the middle of the room. It was so narrow that I could have easily reached out and touched both walls with the palms of my hands. For a moment, it seemed to me that the walls themselves were billowing - as though they weren't quite solid. As I stood there, the dream came flooding back to me, more real than than this moment.

And yet this was what was real; this was where I was. The creaking wooden floorboards beneath my bare feet were solid enough, as were the walls when I reached out and placed my palms against them. And the sunlight, falling in a dusty beam from the small round window in the garble wall.

I inched forward until I stood in that beam of light, as if I could bathe myself in it. When I said that I didn't really miss the light of the sun, it was only because I'd forgotten how wonderful it is. With closed eyes and upturned hands, I relished it now.

I didn't really want the moment to end, but below and all around me, the city was waking up. Thomas had awakened before me - or at least, his profuse snoring had stopped.

"Thomas?"

No answer. So he was already awake, probably already downstairs working.

I washed, shaved and dressed, annoyed at how long it took. There truly is a lot of dreary maintenance work involved in having a mortal body.

Ready to face the day, I pulled the curtain aside to get to the wooden ladder leading downstairs. Thomas' half of the attic looked surprisingly neat, the bed made and the chair tucked in under the desk. And there, on the desk, leaning against a fresh bouquet of wildflowers, was an envelope.

My attention snagged on it and I immediately crossed the room to grab and tear it open. I held the heavy parchment in front of me. My eyes quickly scanned the words, absorbing the enthused sentences written in my brother's unmistakable, blocky handwriting.

GABRIEL,

I hate putting it like this, but by the time you read this letter it will be too late for you to stop me. I urge you not to try.

I know that you will NOT approve of my decision to leave, but please try to feel a little joy for me as I stand on the precipice of the adventure of a lifetime!

I have taken work onboard a ship bound for China. No, I am not telling you which one, because I know you too well. If given the chance, you will attempt to stop my departure, you will drag me from the ship!

I'm sorry for leaving all of you behind, but trust that I will return with formidable tales to tell. I trust in your capable hands to uphold our family's legacy in my absence.

Please convey my deepest affection and apologies to our dear parents and Elizabeth. And to Dwight. You have always been a better role model for him than I.

May the coming days be filled with prosperity and happiness for our family, even in my absence. Know that my thoughts will always be with you.

Until we meet again,

Thomas

I CRUMBLED the letter in my hand. Once again, it was too late. Too late to stop Thomas from venturing out, too late to keep sight of my brother for centuries.

Or was it?

A glimmer of possibility hit me like a lightning bolt. Back in the original turn of events, I'd found this letter, or one much like it, and had raced through the cobbled streets of London, desperate to halt Thomas and convince him to turn back before the ship set sail. Our family's home was not far from the River Thames, but once I'd reached the harbor I had struggled to locate the ship amidst the chaos. By the time I had the right one, Thomas had stood on the deck, waving to me as he spotted my exhausted figure on the pier. Panting and out of breath, I'd had no choice but to turn around, defeated. It had been an impossible race against time. I had been too late.

But not by much. And this was where the glimmer of hope came into it; if I rode Comet, the steed I'd purchased in Highgate, I'd be able to reach the harbor much faster. Besides, I knew which ship Thomas was on, anchored at the very end of the harbor.

Breathlessly, I shoved the crumbled letter into my pocket and raced down the ladder, taking the stairs four or five at a time. The echoes of my footsteps filled the air. Elizabeth emerged from her bedroom when I thundered past, still groggy from sleep, her mouth slightly agape in surprise at my hurried departure.

"No time to explain!" I shouted over my shoulder as I left the house and made my way to the shed we had cleared out and thus turned into a stable. I didn't bother with a saddle or harness, but swiftly mounted Comet, urging him forward towards the harbor through the narrow and winding streets.

The early morning hour meant the streets were not yet crowded and I had relatively unhindered passage to the harbor. An elderly gentleman with a cloud of white hair called out from a doorway, imploring me to slow down, but I paid him no mind.

Within minutes I'd reached the bustling harbor. The Docklands seemed to be the only part of London that still teemed with energy and movement. Everywhere, men hauled boxes, crates, woven baskets, and bags filled with goods like flour, coffee beans, silk rolls, and sugar canes from the various ships and to the warehouses lining the docks. Among the multitude of ships, masts, sails, and people that all crowded my vision, I strained to catch a glimpse of the vessel my brother was aboard.

Ah, there it was, the ship, on the verge of departing from the shore. And I instantly spotted Thomas standing on the deck. He was engaged in conversation with a taller man who appeared to be instructing him in something to do with the sails.

Disembarking from Comet I swiftly secured him to a post. I couldn't afford to leave him unattended so I hurriedly tossed a golden coin to a bewildered-looking man whose rather disheveled appearance suggested that he had just roused from slumber or perhaps stumbled out of one of the nearby taverns. "Watch my horse, would you? I'll have another one of these for you when I return."

I started sprinting towards the pier. Panting, I reached its edge where two men were loosening the final ropes that kept the ship tethered. The anchor was already halfway raised. I was late, but not quite too late.

"Thomas, please! Thomas Graves!" I continued shouting until he heard me, slowly turning with surprise on his face.

"Gabriel!" he called back, startled to see me.

"Thomas, don't leave!" I wasn't a fan of the sheer desperation in my voice, but right now, there was no remedy for it. "Don't go! I've a feeling that something terrible is going to happen if you do." Well, lots of terrible things.

Furrowing his brow, Thomas called back, "I'm sorry, Gabriel, but I've made up my mind."

"If you leave now, I may never see you again." My voice cracked on that last word. "Give me just an hour to convince you. Turn around. There will always be another ship."

If only he'd turn around, I resolved, I would tell him the truth - unbelievable as it was. I'd give him the choice between heading out to sea, of heading to China where he would encounter the sea witch, or of sticking with me here until I could give him the immortal blood.

Thomas appeared uncertain, as if he wavered in his decision. "One hour, Thomas. And if you still want to go, I'll let you. It's not too late."

"But it *is* too late." His voice was now fading as the final ropes were pulled in. I attempted to grab hold of one, but my strength was nothing against the force of the entire ship. Reluctantly, I let it rush through my fingers and disappear into the water. If I tried to hold on, all I would achieve was being pulled into the river.

"Thomas, I would do anything!" My voice trailed off as the ship drifted further away. Thomas still stood on the deck, gazing back at me with a sorrowful expression. It seemed he longed to explain his reasons, knowing that I wouldn't understand.

If only I had been in possession of my vampiric abilities, I would have hypnotized and forced him to turn around. Now, instead, we would be separated by vast oceans of time. When I saw Thomas again, he would be greatly transformed.

If only I could have made him stay, I could have turned him into a vampire, and then he would never become encumbered by those monstrous tentacles that would make it impossible for him to conceal his true nature. As a vampire, it would be relatively easy for him to blend in with humans, as long as he was cautious and adept at disguising the traits that would alarm them. It was a reality I couldn't make him grasp. And now, in any case, it was too late. Trying to catch my breath, frustration surged through me, and I clenched my fists.

At least when I returned to where Comet was tethered, I found him still there, alongside the man I'd paid to keep an eye on him. I reached into my coat and absentmindedly tossed the man another gleaming gold coin.

"Thank you, sir, thank you!" He was sincerely delighted. His eyes, which were the same indeterminate brown-green color as the Thames, shone with gratitude.

As I prepared to mount my horse and ride home in defeat, the man stepped out in front of Comet. He lifted his broad brimmed hat to reveal a head of lank, hay colored hair, and with a slight bow he introduced himself, "I'm Jasper Runner, Sir."

"Gabriel Graves," I said, without much enthusiasm. I was ready to leave.

"Please wait a minute, Sir. If you ever need me to do any other favors or work for you, I'm at your service."

I paused.

Did I need an assistant? It was true that I lacked vampiric abilities, but I did possess wealth, and money was a form of power, too.

The Gabriel of 1665 wouldn't have entertained the idea of paying a stranger two gold coins to watch a horse for a few minutes, nor would he have considered hiring this man as his assistant. But the Gabriel of 1665 had been short-sighted, whereas the man I had become was not.

"Well," I said, "actually, you may come and work for me. Go clean yourself up, have a meal, and then come to Graves & Sons in Bride Lane, off Fleet Street."

I inhaled a deep breath, filling my lungs with air as I straightened my shoulders. Despite the bright sunlight, I felt like Gabriel again, Gabriel the vampire.

Jasper seemed elated, thanking me as he backed away, assuring me that he would present himself clean and sober at Graves & Sons in a matter of hours. With that, he ambled off into the bustling crowd.

So much for attempting to change the course of history, huh? Thomas, it seemed, was destined (or at least determined) to become the octopus-like sea monster that he became. In his own way, he'd placed his bet. And perhaps - I hated to admit this, even just to myself - leaving for China was a surer bet than the alternative. Indeed, what proof, what certainty did I have that the vampiric blood would soon be mine?

At least, with Thomas out of the picture, I could now devote all my attention to Elizabeth and to securing immortality for us both.

CHAPTER

FIVE

My first encounter with my vampiric patrons, the Elysion twins, occurred sometime around 1640. I'd been seven or perhaps eight years old. They had stepped into Graves & Sons on a warm summer's evening, like characters from a storybook, both beautifully dressed in white and black, their clothes, two tapestries of lace, velvet, and silk. I remember being particularly fascinated by Isadore's doublet - a richly embroidered, fitted jacket that was popular among noblemen at the time.

It was clear at a glance that they were wealthy beyond the reach of anyone I'd ever known. I knew instinctively that Isadore and Isadora were extraordinary, but not in what way or what it meant. All of the signs of vampirism - poreless skin, fingernails gleaming like transparent glass, eyes that seemed to glow in the gloom - I read them not as signs of danger but of power and beauty.

And the twins were beautiful, with curls that seemed carved from dark mahogany framing their faces and skin so perfect it seemed more like porcelain. They were like a male and female mirror image of each other, both with the same large, unnaturally glowing hazel eyes with flecks of gold and elegant Grecian noses. But while Isadora's hair fell in a nearly black waterfall to her calves, Isadore's was short and reminded me of a dark halo.

My father had greeted them in an equally reverent and welcoming tone, and I'd noticed him straightening his shoulders as the two vampires crossed the threshold to his humble shop. We didn't get wealthy customers like this every day, or every night, as it happened to be. Outside, a summer drizzle had whispered against the windows, its scent mingled with a foreign aroma that had none of the earthy scents of humanity.

As my father led the twins towards the display of coffins, I followed a step behind, clutching the ledger to my chest.

They'd approached the task of ordering their coffins with an air of choosing finery for a ball. While my father took their measurements, I was finding it hard to concentrate on writing everything down.

The vampires had turned their attention to me, their smiles holding a glint of amusement at my open-mouthed fascination.

"And who is this?" asked Isadora, holding out a hand towards me that was as pale and smooth and perfect as marble. I didn't dare to take it, although this was out of reverence, not fear.

My father, beaming with pride, said, "My eldest son, Gabriel. He has recently started apprenticing here with me."

She smiled, and it was like dawn breaking. I noticed that her teeth were very small and pearly white. "Gabriel?

You must be proud of the work you do here, helping your father craft such fine resting places for weary souls."

I mustered my courage to speak. "They're places where souls can rest, but perhaps also where souls can be reborn." It was my child's imagination speaking, but the twins seemed to like this idea. Isadore's eyes glinted with silent laughter. "Oh, you believe in the hereafter? That's perfectly marvelous!"

"I believe," I said, sensing that these strange people would be able to sympathize, "there is much beyond our understanding. Other lives and other worlds. If there is an afterlife, I don't think it looks like what it says in the Bible."

My father shifted uncomfortably but the Elysion twins seemed to approve.

"Indeed," Isadore's voice was a soft echo, almost wistful "There are many mysteries that most will never even begin to uncover in their lifetimes. Maybe you'll uncover some of them. Something tells me you'll try. And we like that, don't we, Isadora?"

"We do."

Since that first meeting in the shop, Isadore and Isadora had intermittently returned over the years. They weren't frequent visitors. But whenever they did appear, they ordered the most beautiful and elaborate caskets and coffins. Each of their custom orders was a challenge to the skills I was slowly but surely developing. As I continued leveling up, they never failed to notice and praise me for it.

The Elysion twins never aged, not even by a minute. Each appearance felt as if they had momentarily stepped outside and then reentered the room. Their attire was the only aspect of their appearance that varied with each visit. I grew up while they remained unchanged.

By 1665, the Elysion twins had been patrons of Graves & Sons for twenty-five years. My father appreciated their patronage, but over the years he had grown increasingly weary of them and their never changing, never-aging ways. The fact that they only ever appeared at night, usually delivered to our stoop in a black-lacquered ornate hearse pulled by ghostly white horses probably didn't help. Not to mention, what were they doing with all of those caskets we'd made them?

I never feared Isadore and Isadora, but rather looked forward to each of their visits. As I grew from childhood into adulthood, I too became convinced that the Elysion twins weren't human. What they were, I didn' know. But just as I had from that first meeting, I sensed that they were part of a magical and exclusive realm. A realm to which I, of course, desired to belong.

In the end, I believe it was my artistry and lack of fear that swayed them to bring me into their realm. And now I had to put this theory to the ultimate test.

I SPENT THE DAYS FOLLOWING THOMAS' disappearance helping my father in the shop. Truth be told, I was grateful for the chance to relive these everyday moments that had long since faded from my memory. Still, beneath the surface, my anxiety churned.

We received numerous customers ordering coffins for dying or already deceased loved ones. Every conversation revolved around the Black Death.

With the plague creeping through London and nearing its peak, I knew that the Elysion twins would soon be making an appearance, and I elected to wait for them. I knew where they lived, but I couldn't very well turn up on their doorstep, claiming to have traveled back in time and demanding the blood. No, it was better to wait for them to come to me.

And as it turned out, my intuition was right. On the fourth night after my arrival in 1665, the doorbell rang in the shop, and Isadore and Isadora entered, both of them as unruffled and untouched by all the human misery around them as ever. My heart skipped several beats; Never in my life or in my afterlife had I been more relieved to see them.

"Gabriel," greeted Isadore with a voice smooth as the silk of his cravat, "can we rely on your skill once more? Isadora has come up with a wonderful, a simply terrific idea!"

As he stepped across the threshold, holding the door open for his twin, his beauty and grace stood out as ever against the backdrop of the grimy, unsanitary streets and buildings of the 1600s.

I'd long since been given permission to address them by their first names, and that's how I greeted them now. "Isadore, Isadora!"

I rushed forward. I wanted to hug them, to shake them, to demand an immediate transfusion, but instead I stopped in the middle of the floor, splaying my hands in a gesture of welcome, "How I have been looking forward to seeing you both here again. You must tell me all about your creative visions, Isadora."

I supposed a small part of me had been afraid that going back in time to be turned into a vampire could mean that perhaps Isadora had experienced time differently and things might not unfold in exactly the same way. But here they were, sweeping all of those grim possibilities aside.

"Gabriel," Isadora said, coming towards me and holding out her hands, which I took and kissed lightly. She was, of course, wearing gloves, the age-old trick employed by vampires to hide the coldness of their touch from mortals.

"You look resplendent," Isadore commented, stepping out from behind his sister and extending both of his hands to shake mine. It was a rigorous shake, but I knew he was holding back a significant portion of his strength.

After spending several hundred years as an immortal, I viewed Isadora and Isadore with the same admiration I had as a mortal, but also with the knowledge that I knew something they didn't. The Isadora I was engaging with now in 1665 hadn't yet experienced the future, but I had. I knew what the 2020s looked and felt like, what technologies were available to us, and what developments had happened politically and socially. The Elysion twins I was looking at now only knew the world up to and including the 1660s.

Of course, I was still in a fragile human form while they were in powerful and strong immortal bodies. And the fact remained, I needed what they had - I needed the blood.

"It is good to see that you're keeping well in these dark times," Isadore enthused. "Isn't that right?" He turned to his sister. Isadora nodded, her long mahogany hair shimmering around her and catching the light of the oil lamps. The twins often did this; one of them would make an observation or a statement, then turn to the other for confirmation.

"How is business? You must tell us honestly. We don't like the idea of your family struggling," said Isadore, looking into my eyes as if searching for a hidden truth.

"For now, business is booming," I waved towards the counter, where vials and posies and other alleged cures for the plague were on display. "But that could very soon change. If the plague keeps growing at the rate it is now, who knows, there might be no need for coffins, only for deep graves."

"Well, we can't have that," Isadore commented.

"There'll always be a need for finely made caskets, as long as my brother and I are around," Isadora assured me.

Isadore hastened to add, "Which we promise to be for quite some time."

"We are all worried, of course," Isadora said. She gave me what was almost an apologetic smile. "And the truth is that no one can know the future. There are so many wonderful places, so many businesses that we are patrons of, so many friends, so many loved ones - all of them in grave danger. Pardon the pun."

"You have always been pardoned, Isadora. I must say, I truly admire the courage both of you possess. I've always immensely admired both of you, since the first time you entered here. And over the years, this perception has only proven more and more correct."

From my personal experience, I knew that flattery often works, even on those who have lived for centuries or millennia. The ego still craves validation.

"Or perhaps you flatter us," said Isadore with a laugh, patting me on the shoulder. "But now, let's get down to business. We're here to acquire a new set of caskets, and we have a rather peculiar request." He exchanged a mischievous glance with his sister. "We would like them to feature scenes and figures of the Black Death, as well as the wings you see on the bills of mortality posted in the squares and on the doors of all the churches. I know it may seem macabre and lacking in good taste, but if executed beautifully, they would be like works of art. And we believe having them prepared in case we succumb to the terrible disease would provide us with some comfort."

The twins often shared similar stories and explanations whenever they ordered new caskets and coffins, always for themselves. Despite their cheerful dispositions, they claimed to constantly worry about mortality and the looming specter of death. I suppose they found enjoyment in having coffins that reflected the spirit of the time, the current boogeyman, if you will. And my philosophy on this had always been, hey, as long as you pay me, I don't care what floats your boat.

"I won't judge my clients' tastes," I assured them. "In fact, I have to say I love the idea. Moreover, I'm confident that I can create coffins more exquisite and captivating than any you have ever seen." This was true. Of course mortal hands lacked some of the strength and agility that their immortal counterparts possessed, but the mortal man I was now had the advantage of hundreds of years of coffin building experience. The Elysion twins had no idea that the Gabriel Graves they were looking at now was a master craftsman, very likely the finest coffin builder in the world.

"That's what we like to hear," Isadora exclaimed. "You always manage to impress us, Gabriel. In fact, I must confess, you have surpassed your father's skill and craftsmanship, and it has been evident for quite some time."

"Thank you," I acknowledged her compliment with a modest inclination of my head. "If only I could work even more efficiently to keep up with the rising demand. Everything would be perfect."

The twins exchanged a meaningful glance. I suppose they had either discussed or were already considering the possibility of bestowing the dark gift upon me. It pleased me to sense this. I didn't expect them to turn me tonight, but their demeanor boded well.

We went through the customary motions of Isadora

selecting the woods, finishes, details, carving styles, and lining materials for the caskets, disregarding cost as always. I never truly knew Isadora and her brother's origins or their true age, but I was certain they weren't English. By the time of the Great Plague, they had likely roamed the world as immortals for a considerable period of time, amassing immense wealth in the process, as vampires tend to do.

The Elysions resided in an opulent villa located in the prestigious Knightsbridge area, and their membership in London's upper echelons was a matter of course. I suspected that a significant portion of their wealth came from their friends, who also served as their victims, allowing them to maintain their lavish lifestyles. I meticulously noted down the details they described for the new caskets, such as the carving of winged skulls on the lids and sides.

"You know," I said, once I was sure I'd captured every facet of their wishes on paper, "I've heard that many of the city's wealthy have already fled in anticipation of the plague worsening. So why haven't you?"

Isadora laughed, her eyes sparkling. "We've considered it, but in the end, my brother and I simply love London too much."

"If this ship goes down, so will we." Isadore winked at me as if sharing an inside joke. "Remarkable," I said. "Most who can afford to do so are packing their bags as we speak."

"Very true," Isadore agreed, after sharing another conspiratorial glance with his sister, "But some things are more important than matters of life and death. And as you can see, if we do end up contracting the plague, we will have our caskets ready."

"How long do you need to prepare these caskets?" asked Isadora.

I pondered the question. How long would it take to craft, prepare, and polish two exquisitely made caskets? They would have to surpass anything I had achieved in my mortal life, impressing them to the point where they believed I deserved to join their bloodline. It was a tall order.

"Give me a week." I was tempted to offer an earlier deadline but wanted to ensure I could fulfill their expectations.

"Very well," Isadore said, lifting an eyebrow. "We will return in a week's time to collect your creations. You won't let us down, will you, Gabriel?"

"Never."

In the next week, I would have to pull off a medium-sized miracle. The caskets I created for my patrons would have to display the finest craftsmanship of my existence, both mortal and immortal. If I could accomplish this, Isadore and Isadora would have no other choice but to reward me with something infinitely more precious than gold.

Right?

SIX

Beyond the doors of Graves & Sons, the grip of the plague was tightening. We had no shortage of customers, only of time. My father had his hands full with the mounting workload while I toiled away on the caskets for the Elysions whenever I could steal a moment.

My hands aching, I stood back now to admire them in the golden late afternoon light filtering through the workroom's singular grimy window. It was a terrifying time to be a Londoner, but my full concentration was here, on the work in front of me.

I'd spared no expense, procuring the finest mahogany and the most luxurious silks. Life in London was simple in many ways for the average man, but in 1665 English ships were bringing home exotic wares from all over the world every day of the week. All one needed to do was go to the harbor and strike a deal with a ship's crew before their wares made it to the shops and were marked up twice or tenfold.

I'd thrown all of the riches I'd brought from Villa Graves into the materials, and I'd slipped quite a few coins from the family's till just to make it up. If only I'd have known that I would be confronted with having to craft these caskets there was so much more wealth I could have brought. Gold and silver bars, real diamonds. But never mind.

The caskets' elegant forms were already completed while a visual saga of the Plague's grim crusade was starting to emerge on their lids and sides. Coaxing the little dancing skeletons from the fine wood also provided me with a source of stress relief. Stress truly feels corrosive in a mortal body - it is like an acid coursing through its tissues, wearing them down.

The creak of the shop door interrupted my thoughts, and my father's slight shadow fell into the workspace. Right away, I sensed that he was in an unusually gloomy mood. I suppose I couldn't blame him - one of his sons had run off to join a crew of pirates, as I knew and my father suspected they were, and the other was spending his time obsessively working on two extravagant caskets while the orders for simpler ones were piling up. Dwight was old enough to start apprenticing, but due to the plague, we preferred to keep him upstairs, where his only responsibilities were to help his grandmother and aunt prepare the plague cures and posies.

"Gabriel." My father's voice sounded like the evening tide, tired and worn from crashing against ragged shores. "We need more caskets, plain and ready. We've got plenty of pinewood waiting to be used up."

"I'm well aware, Father." The words came out a little more forcefully than I intended. My eyes were still locked on the caskets in front of me. "But these are more important than any number of pine coffins."

My father stepped closer, his eyes squinting in the low light. "They're for the Elysions, I take it?"

I nodded. I knew that my father would gladly accept their money but had come to prefer not to interact with or even refer to Isadore and Isadora. He feared them, and out of consideration I'd been covering up the caskets with sheets whenever I wasn't working on them. They'd stood there like two ominous shapes, and I had no doubt my father had noticed them.

"They're remarkable." He leaned in close, admiring my handiwork. He reached out his hand, but instead of sliding it over the lid of one of the caskets, he kept it hovering in the air above it, as if he was worried about what might happen if he touched it. "You've far exceeded my skill, that much is clear."

His admiring tone made me glow with pride, despite my annoyance at being interrupted.

"But," he continued in a tone that was gentle but firm, "we have to focus on survival. Remember, we cannot dine on the indulgence of fine woods or the luxury of silk."

"Of course. But Isadore and Isadora are going to pay a king's ransom for these. Believe me, when the Elysions come to collect, these two caskets will more than make up for the twenty simple pine coffins I could've built in their place."

"No, Gabriel, listen to me." My father was shaking his head, "We cannot afford to gamble on the nobility's whims. Our primary focus should remain on our most reliable source of income, and you know what that means; serving the community of St Bride's with well-built, coffins that our neighbors are able to afford. With the plague raging, devouring entire families in a matter of days, what we need, son, are pine caskets. I want to see them stack up as many and as fast as possible."

The frustration that had been simmering within me came to a boil. "Me focusing on getting these ready is not a risk, Father; it's an assurance. The Elysions can lift us out of this pit of scarcity, of endless pine boxes."

"The simple pine boxes you're railing against is what sustains us. Your extravagant ways could very well drain us. Yes," he held up a hand to halt my impending interruption of his flow of words, "I've noticed you dipping into the till. I admire your desire to impress the Elysions, but-"

I froze. I didn't want to see, but I saw it - the tell-tale ring of roses on his hand. "Father," my voice came out a whisper, and then in something that was nearly a roar, "your hand!"

As he looked down at his hand and the plague tokens that marred it, we both fell into a damning silence. He broke it by letting out a hollow laugh. "It seems like the Black Death has laid claim to me."

My heart leaped into my throat, pounding wildly like a wartime drum. I was at a loss for words. As I shook my head in disbelief, I realized that I was trembling slightly. Even my legs felt unsteady, and I had to brace myself against the workbench in front of me. Seeing the tokens on his skin still hit me with the force of a wrecking ball. How could this be? This wasn't supposed to happen! My father was destined to succumb to pneumonia two years after the plague. Wasn't he?

My father straightened up and gestured towards the caskets. "Finish these, Gabriel. For the Elysions, for our family. But then you must promise me to get on with building pine caskets. Many more will be needed in the coming weeks and months, I'm afraid."

I could only nod, my throat tight.

"I'll retreat to Thomas' quarters, at least now they will not stand empty. Tell your mother and your sister, and Dwight, not to come near. And there's another thing you must promise me." My father turned to me, piercing me with his gaze.

"Anything, Father."

"You'll protect our family no matter what happens. You will not let any harm come to your mother, to Dwight or to Elizabeth. Especially not Elizabeth, who you know I worry about most of all. I need to know she is going to have a protector once I am no longer here."

"I promise. But father?"

"Yes?"

"You may recover." And this was true. Some who contracted the plague did survive. With proper care, why couldn't my father be among the fortunate ones?

"I may, son. I may. Goodnight."

With a lump in my throat I watched my father leave through the darkened door. Suddenly, he looked smaller and more frail to me than he had when he walked in. I turned back to my work, picked up the chisel and wooden hammer with hands that I was willing not to tremble. Soon, I'd refilled the workshop with sounds of the tools against the wood as more and more skeletons emerged from its dark surface.

As it turned out, my father wasn't the only one who'd contracted the plague. Dwight, who was meant to be untouched by the deadly miasma and treacherous vapors of the Black Death, was also marked by the tokens, those little silver pennies of raised, gangrenous flesh I'd seen on my father's arms and hand.

I'd taken every precaution upon my return to 1665 to ensure the safety of my family. I'd taught them modern hygiene practices and ensured we were well-stocked with essentials like soap and vinegar for cleaning ourselves and our surroundings. I'd kept Dwight occupied upstairs, working alongside Elizabeth at the kitchen table, crafting various remedies and little boxes filled with cloth soaked in vinegar, meant to protect people from the noxious fumes. Still, it seemed my efforts had fallen short. Dwight, who was supposed to traverse the centuries with me in vampiric form, would suffer the same fate as my father. And whatever that was going to be was anyone's guess.

It was agreed that my father and Dwight would take over the attic, and that I would move downstairs into Dwight's tiny, narrow bedroom, which was really nothing more than an alcove in the wall. My mother and Elizabeth were both desperate to tend to our two injured soldiers, to offer comfort, but I adamantly forbade them from entering the attic. Though there was no lock on the attic's trapdoor, I emphasized that it might as well have been there.

I kept working on the Elysion's caskets deep into the night. Several times I went upstairs to pour myself a glass of water, and each time I saw Elizabeth perched on the ladder below the trapdoor, reading aloud from one of the only books our family owned, a precious printed collection of Shakespeare's plays.

"FATHER?"

It was the morning after the devastating discovery of

plague tokens. Once again I rapped on the trapdoor leading to the attic, louder now.

"Father?"

When no response came, a chill crept through my bloodstream. Why the silence? I'd certainly knocked and called out loud enough.

I mustered the courage to enter the attic, grateful that my mother and Elizabeth were both still asleep. The trapdoor creaked as it swung open. I wasn't breathing.

The attic was heavy with a sickening odor, despite the slightly open window.

I stumbled toward my father and Dwight. Both were lying motionless and still, Dwight tucked into Thomas' bed and my father on the wooden floor next to it.

Panicking, I knelt down and shook Dwight's shoulders, hoping for any sign of life. But no, his small body shook limply, his ash-blond head lolling from side to side without resistance. Slapping him hard across the cheek only yielded lifeless silence. I should have known; his skin was grayish-green.

My father, too, was gone.

On the table beneath the street-facing window, I spotted plates and cups from the previous night, which I eyed with suspicion. There was an odd scent emanating from the tea cups - a scent I recognized as arsenic.

Arsenic, a common remedy sold by unqualified apothecaries, was often promoted in small quantities as a plague cure. It appeared my father had kept some hidden away, perhaps in preparation for the possibility of the plague infecting our family. Now, it seemed he had taken matters into his own hands yet again, poisoning both himself and his grandson to spare us the burden of their suffering.

I shouldn't have slapped Dwight with my bare hand,

but I compensated for it by pouring the contents of a bottle of gin I found in Thomas's cupboard over my hands to disinfect them. Then, ashen-faced, I retreated back to the trapdoor, down the ladder and into the hallway where Elizabeth now stood. I turned to her, stricken.

"Elizabeth, do not go up there." I swiftly closed the trapdoor, hoping to shield her from the sight of our deceased father and nephew. "Let's not tell Mother yet."

Too late. Marie Graves, summoned by our distress in a way that only a mother can be, appeared at the end of the hallway. When she saw us, she must have instantly read on our faces what was wrong. Elizabeth ran to her as she crumpled to the floor.

Treacherous tears were stinging my eyes, but I fought to maintain my composure. Someone had to remain strong, and it had to be me.

"Listen," I said, "they're gone - there is nothing we can do for them. But we can still protect ourselves. If anyone finds out what has happened here, our household will be marked, and we will fall under the control of the authorities. Moeder," I spoke to my mother now in her native Dutch, using the gentlest voice I was able to summon as I knelt down beside her and took her hands, "go to your bedroom and stay there until we return. It is best if you don't know what we do with the remains. Elizabeth and I will handle this."

My mother shook her head, but she didn't protest when Elizabeth and I led her back to her bedroom and tucked her into the bed.

I didn't want it to be this way, but I knew what had to be done.

Elizabeth and I entered the attic together. We gently covered the lifeless bodies with blankets before carrying them downstairs and into the shop. Here, we laid them side by side on the floor, resembling two shrouded caterpillars.

"What now?"

I met Elizabeth's wide-eyed, terrorized gaze - she was looking to me for guidance. She was just a kid, and my heart ached for her. I would have preferred to handle this on my own, but because time was of the essence, I needed her.

"Now we bury them in the shed."

From Elizabeth's expression it was clear that she wanted to protest, but she didn't have a better alternative in mind.

"It's only temporary," I added.

We ventured into the courtyard. I hoped to high heavens that none of our neighbors were watching us, but there was no way to be certain. It was just before sunrise, and the entire neighborhood would soon be awake.

We entered the stable, and I led Comet outside. Then, shielded from prying eyes, I began to dig a deep and sizable resting place.

"How can they simply be gone? I can't accept it."

Well, neither could I, but what mattered was disposing of the bodies.

"We shouldn't be burying them here, like this." Elizabeth sobbed, but she still grabbed the other shovel hanging on the wall of the shed and started digging next to me.

The sound of dirt hitting dirt reverberated as we buried our dead.

SEVEN

The caskets were finally complete. I'd poured my heart and soul into them, I'd dedicated every ounce of my being to their meticulous carvings. Beautifully rendered scenes of the devastating plague covered every square inch of the gleaming wood, and on the inside, the caskets were upholstered in rich, chinese silk, one in black and one in white, both with a pattern of herons. I've always been partial to chinoiserie.

I stepped back, a sheen of sweat glistening on my brow. Pride welled up within me. It had been a long time since I'd experienced such a profound sense of accomplishment. I suppose being mortal wasn't all bad - at least not in this particular moment.

Gazing at the two magnificent creations resting on the workbench before me, I marveled at what my sluggish and weak human hands had wrought. These two caskets, in my own humble opinion, surpassed any previous work I had ever undertaken. Throughout my centuries of existence, I'd honed my skills and perfected my artistry. These caskets fit for royalty - fit even for Isadore and Isadora.

74

Now I just needed my two vampire patrons to actually show up and claim them. They knew that I was skillful, yes, but when they placed their commission they would not have been expecting anything like this. They would have no other option than to be swept off their feet. Ah, the reverence they would feel the moment they stepped into the workshop and laid eyes on these works of art! They would understand, or so I hoped, that I'd reached the pinnacle of my human prowess. Only the vampiric transformation could catapult me into higher echelons of experience and possibility.

"Jasper!" I called out for my assistant to come and admire the caskets, but there was no response.

Strange. I thought that he would be right next door, sweeping the floors of Graves & Sons as I had instructed him.

It took real effort to tear my attention away from my beautiful creations, but I managed it, and then I turned towards the shop.

It was empty - neither Jasper or any customers were in here. The premises of Graves & Sons were small enough that I could take it all in at a glance. Still, I made a point of letting my gaze move slowly and meticulously from one darkened corner to the next, but no, he wasn't here.

It wouldn't surprise me if the the man had fallen back on drinking. These were hard times, and people had different ways of coping. Not that I was going to buy any of his excuses for not attending to his duties.

Not that there was much to do. We didn't have many customers at this point; the plague was simply too rampant, and many no longer had the time or the resources to give their dearly departed a proper burial. For the most part, both the dead and the dying were left to the mercy of plague doctors and their macabre rounds.

But what was this now?

The back door stood ajar.

I went over to it and pushed it open, hoping to catch a glimpse of Jasper. He might have stepped out for a breath of fresh air or, more likely, a sip of a clandestine liquor bottle which I'd seen him hide in one of the scraggly rose bushes. But the courtyard was empty, not even a whisper of Jasper's presence.

Comet's shed, which I quickly checked, was empty too. And I mean empty. Comet was gone.

With a growing sense of worry, I made my way back up to our family quarters. The scent of herbs wafted from the kitchen where I found my mother leaning over the narrow table, bundling sprigs of rosemary and thyme. She was dressed in dark grey and green instead of the traditional black that would signal her mourning. I knew that she resented having to hide her grief and its true cause at least as much as I did, but I had at least managed to convince her that there was no other way, that being open could bring with it a wave of consequences over which we would have no control.

A pile of completed posies and herb bundles were stacking up on the table next to my mother's elbow. I wasn't too convinced of their effectiveness as plague cures, but at least they weren't harmful, unlike some of the snake oil that was being peddled - like, say, the arsenic that had expelled Dwight's and my father's souls from their bodies.

"Moeder, have you seen Jasper by any chance?" My voice cut through the methodical rustling of leaves.

Her concentration never broke and her hands never ceased their work as she replied, "Oh, not since this morning. He looked rather worse for wear, if you catch my drift. I made him a cup of coffee."

A cold dread settled in my stomach, spreading its icy tendrils through my limbs. "And when was this?"

"Oh, I don't know. Around eight or nine, I should think. Hours ago. Gabriel, you look so worried, is anything wrong?" She looked up from her work finally, her features twisting with concern.

My newly hired assistant had vanished, hadn't he? And if my rapidly growing suspicions were true, the scoundrel hadn't just shirked his duties but also what moral backbone he might have been in possession of.

Without explaining things to my mother, I raced back downstairs and into the workshop. I'd left my coat and the coin purse that should have been heavy with the day's earnings. I thrust my hand into its emptiness, my pulse beating in my ears. Gone.

Then, the air seemed to grow thin. What if money wasn't all he'd stolen?

I rushed into the courtyard, my hand instinctively patting all of my pockets in search of the vials of ectoplasm. Where the hell were they?

Finally, I discovered the vials safely tucked away in their hidden pocket. A powerful surge of relief came over me. My assistant's sole motivation had been money, oblivious to the significance of the mysterious vials. The fool!

Of course I was a fool, too, for having hired and trusted him.

I was crossing the courtyard, heading back towards Graves & Sons when a sense of unease prickled at the back of my neck. I could feel someone's piercing gaze burning into the back of my skull.

Spinning around on my heel, I found myself eye to eye

with Ethel Nesbit. Her wrinkly neck was craned, her eyes burning with ill-disguised curiosity. I met her gaze head-on above the fence that separated her backyard from ours.

"What has you so disturbed, Gabriel?" Her voice was so sugar-coated it was porous.

I sighed, lowered my shoulders. "Oh, it's nothing to concern yourself with." I sounded weary, even to myself.

"I watched you rushing to and fro. Like a decapitated chicken, Gabriel." Her wiry, white eyebrows rose as high onto her narrow forehead as they would go. "Something must have unsettled you."

And you would love to hear all about it, wouldn't you? If energy vampires were a thing, Ethel Nesbit would be the textbook example.

"Well, I have good reason," I replied, making the snap decision to tell her the truth, but of course only a small fraction of it. "It seems that my assistant has made off both with my horse and with the contents of the till."

"You should alert the authorities, then," was the widow's tart advice. Her dark eyes gleamed with glee as they roamed over my face, taking in my distress. I imagined that she stored moments like this in some special compartment of her mind, and that she pulled them out to warm herself by in the cold winter months.

I shook my head. "The powers that be have bigger fish to fry at the moment, wouldn't you say?"

She didn't respond, just watched me suspiciously. Whether she believed me or not mattered little to me at this particular moment. Just like the elusive authorities - most of which, by the way, had fled London to keep themselves and their families out of reach of the Grim Reaper - I, too, had bigger fish to fry.

"You were patting your jacket. Has anything gone missing from its pockets?"

It wasn't really a question I was prepared to answer. I gave the widow a forced smile. "I have business to attend to, Mrs. Nesbit, if you don't mind."

She did mind, but what could she say? She frowned, as seemed to be one of her obnoxious habits. "Very well, Gabriel. But let me make one thing clear; I consider myself the guardian of this parish. While others are busy enriching themselves in the midst of tragedy, I am doing my humble bit by keeping an eye out for the devil's assistants. I can always sniff them out, Gabriel. Even the ones that look the most like angels, so just remember that."

"I'll keep it in mind."

As I reached the entrance of Graves & Sons, I couldn't resist stealing a glance towards Widow Nesbit's window. There she was, peering at me with an indeterminate mix of suspicion and what was probably delight.

I had to be careful. I might not place much stock in her mad ramblings, but others might. I had to admit that she was a respected figure. Her perception of me potentially held the power to shape the community's perception as well.

Did she suspect something peculiar about me? I pushed such thoughts aside as I reentered the shop, where long, late-afternoon shadows were now crawling along the floorboards.

I needed to focus on this evening.

With the vials nestled securely in my breast pocket, I set to work once more. Pine coffins, like I had promised my father. Now that Isadore and Isadora's caskets were complete, I might as well craft a few of these to kill the time.

As the sun finally dipped below the horizon, I covered the two caskets with a large piece of cloth, ready for the great reveal. I even went out to gather a fresh bouquet of flowers growing near the muddy banks of the Thames. With the sickness seeping through the streets of London, no one else seemed to be concerned with flowers anymore and there were plenty to pick from. Sweet honeysuckle and lavender, which I arranged in a vase on top of one of the work-benches. Tonight was the night! Isadore and Isadora would collect their caskets - and I would welcome my reward.

And then there was nothing to do but wait. I paced and paced as twilight gave way to a starless night.

At long last a knock at the door shattered the silence, jolting me from my reverie.

But it wasn't the elegant figures of my once-and-forever makers that stepped across the threshold of Graves & Sons. Instead, it was an inconspicuous, olive-skinned, dark-eyed stranger wearing simple attire.

"Gabriel Graves?" The man took a few somewhat hesitant steps into the room, as if uncertain of whether or not he was welcome. Who was he and what did he want? I supposed he might be a customer, but really I just wanted him out of here so that I could concentrate fully on my patrons, when they arrived. I remained in the doorway to the workshop out back, regarding him with a dark look.

"My name is Jonathan Spriggs. I've been sent here on behalf of Isadore and Isadora Elysion."

Ah, so they had sent a courier to collect. I'd imagined that the Elysion twins would come here to collect the caskets themselves, but I knew that they had servants, and that they were busy people, so to speak. They didn't owe me making a personal appearance.

Pushing my disappointment aside, I bit down on my lip. Out of habit, I stopped myself mid-motion before remembering that I didn't have fangs to worry about. A sad state of affairs that it now seemed unlikely was going to be rectified tonight.

"I'm terribly sorry, Mr. Graves, but my employers will not be collecting their order tonight."

"They won't?"

My heart sank further, a heavy weight settling in the pit of my stomach. "They're going to be delayed?" I resented the desperate hope that ran through my words like an undercurrent.

"Yes, quite. They've departed for Italy. They left just a few hours ago, but they have plans to return to London in a month's time. And no, before you ask, they gave no specific date. They never do," he added with a good-natured laugh. A month?

Those words hung in the air, pressing down on me with a crushing and almost tangible weight.

Whatever happened to Isadore's notion of going down with the ship? I'd devoted every ounce of my being to their request, to our meeting. I'd pinned everything on it. Didn't the twins understand how precarious my situation was? How could they be so flippant? Had they no empathy for how very mortal I felt?

Suddenly it struck me; of course they didn't. I wouldn't have, either, in their position.

The courier, Spriggs, looked down and refused to meet my burning gaze. "I sense your disappointment, Mr. Graves. I am sorry. The message stated that they regret the delay but assure you of their commitment to collecting the caskets as soon as they're able."

Oh, I'm sure. This stranger's words carried no weight. I felt left to the whims of fate.

"May I take my leave, Mr. Graves?"

"By all means!" I couldn't wait for him to get out of here, so I could be alone with my storm of tumultuous thoughts and emotions. If he reported back to Isadore and Isadora, as indeed he might, I didn't want him to have picked up on any resentment, any animosity brewing within me.

But it was definitely there. I'd always adored and appreciated my makers. It goes without saying that, without them, my vampiric existence would not have been possible. But being made to wait - being treated like just another mortal on their path - this didn't sit well with me at all. I wasn't used to being dismissed, and I have to say that I did not like it one bit.

CHAPTER

EIGHT

By mid-August, London had descended into a precarious balance between chaos and control. Government officials, many of them now giving their orders from a safe distance in the countryside somewhere while the disease tore through the capital's lower classes, had manipulated the mortality records to downplay the severity of the disease for months. For a while, the falsified lower figures had prevented the spread of panic and the need for even more draconian measures to be imposed. But as summer reached its peak, the plague exploded like a volcano whose destructive force soon engulfed every corner of the city.

The scale of catastrophe was undeniable, and so harsher restrictions were enforced. Venues that had once filled London with music, puppet shows, gambling, and dancing were forced to close their doors. Animals were suspected of carrying the contagion, and because of this, livestock animals and pets alike were slaughtered by the thousands. The court had fled to Oxford, but distance was no hindrance to them appointing search teams whose task it was to identify plague victims and separate them from their families. In a surprise to precisely no one, their raids mostly took place in London's poorer parishes. Wherever plague tokens were found, homes were marked with a red cross above the door. Watchers were then stationed outside. Their job? To prevent anyone from escaping whatever fate awaited them behind the red-marked door.

Of course, there were cases of desperate individuals who managed to evade their captors, usually through violent means. While all of this was going on, pest houses (or plague hospitals if prefer to think of them as actual medical establishments, which they most certainly were not) sprung up like mushrooms all over the city.

Most notable among these was the Clayfield Pest House. Spanning five acres, its reach extended beyond St Martin's to encompass neighboring boroughs including St Bride's. It was in this unsettling environment that Malm Westminster had offered Elizabeth work as a nurse. And unfortunately, after the death of Dwight and our father, she insisted on accepting it. I tried to talk her out of it, believe me, but despite her mild demeanor, Elizabeth could be both stubborn and immovable once she made a decision. And she decided to be a nurse. All of my warnings, pleas and somber promises fell on deaf ears.

When the day of her first shift arrived, Westminster himself came to collect his prize. It probably won't surprise you to learn that he had quickly risen through the ranks at Clayfield - that he'd more or less crowned himself its head doctor.

I can't say that I was happy to see him as he strode into the courtyard behind Graves & Sons, taking his long and heavy steps. While the dark cloud of the plague seemed to make most Londoners shrink, it had the exact opposite effect on Malm Westminster. He radiated confidence and good cheer.

"Gabriel Graves," he called out in his loud, booming voice. "How are you holding up?"

"Westminster," I responded in a polite but clipped tone. I did not invite him into the shop. I didn't want this man's energy polluting the air I had to breathe. It was true that I'd sent a courier to his home on Temple Place, inviting him here to take Elizabeth to her first shift at the plague house - but only in the hope that his ominous presence might make her falter in her resolve to be a nurse. I knew that she was afraid of him.

Westminster removed his beaked mask and wiped the sweat from his brow. Despite the early hour I knew that it was going to be a hot day. I could have offered him a glass of water, but I didn't.

As the two of us stood in the courtyard his suspicious eyes scanned our surroundings, peering over my shoulder. Let me remind you that Westminster had spent the past twenty years as a witchfinder. And right now, there was something about him that reminded me of a dog sniffing out a bone.

"I haven't seen either of your dear parents for some time," he finally remarked, his tone laced with just a hint of suspicion. "Not to mention Thomas, or young Dwight."

I shifted uncomfortably but attempted to sound nonchalant. "Dwight and my parents have been taking precautions and keeping to themselves, as have many others."

His eyes narrowed as he asked, "And Thomas?"

"Thomas," I replied with a genuine sigh of frustration, "has seen it fit to take work on a ship and to leave the rest of us to it. Can you believe the gall?"

"I see." Westminster's piercing gaze lingered on me. I knew that he suspected that there was more to this story than what I was telling him.

"I find it curious," he said slowly, his voice dropping low. "The disappearance of most of your family coincides with the worst outbreak of the plague this city has ever seen. One can't help but wonder... well. If anyone in this house had caught the plague, you would tell me, wouldn't you?"

"In a heartbeat." I gave him my most pleasant smile. I could almost taste the sourness of his suspicion in the air and I needed to dispel it. "But as it happens, we've simply been lying low. There's nothing more to it."

Westminster didn't seem convinced. His beady gaze lingering on me for a moment longer. "Be that as it may," he said, his tone guarded. "I find it a little odd. I wouldn't think your father's shop would be able to keep the business afloat without all hands being on deck. But then again, I suppose that's why Elizabeth has turned to me."

I silently prayed that my mother would miraculously choose this moment to come downstairs. Her presence might go some ways towards allaying Westminster's suspicions.

"You claim there's no illness within these walls, yet there's an air of unease that seems to hang about the place." His gaze drifted across the courtyard again. He was feigning admiration for the few flowers that managed to bloom between the stonework. Then he added, without looking at me. "Tell me, has your home been searched?"

I shook my head and shivered inwardly. "We've been cautious, we've given searchers no cause to visit."

Westminster chuckled with a morbid sense of amusement. "Oh, I'm sure," he said, his voice dripping with a knowing tone.

Thankfully, Elizabeth descended the staircase at that moment, followed closely by our mother, both of them wearing light linen gowns with square necklines and voluminous sleeves that let in plenty of air. Soon, though, Elizabeth would be encased in the heavy and restrictive uniform of a plague nurse.

"Marie Graves, what a joy it is to see you!" Westminster's tone was enthusiastic, but not sincere. "Here I was, halfway accusing your son of keeping secrets, as so many families do when they find the plague's fingerprints on their loved one's skin. But I see that you're well."

He grinned at my mother, but I could sense the disappointment in his whole demeanor. He would have preferred to have spotted her corpse through one of the shop windows so that he could arrest me. Instead, now, he would have to leave empty-handed. Except for Elizabeth, whom I had admonished to be careful around this man.

I could still taste the sourness of his suspicion on the air, but at least he hadn't even glimpsed the shadow of my real fear, namely that his attention would somehow move him to look in the stable where, beneath layers of straw and dirt and secrecy, my father and Dwight lay hidden.

"Elizabeth, are you really sure about this?" I asked her one last time, hoping that the unpleasant reality of Westminster's presence had deterred her.

But Elizabeth wasn't shaken. She nodded.

"Well, then," said Westminster, turning to her, "we should make haste. There is much for you to learn and there are many who need us today. Clayfield is already overflowing."

He and Elizabeth made their way down the cobbled

street, his presence a dark cloud by her side. A silent scream clawed at my throat, urging me to call her back, to forbid her from walking with him to the pest house of all places. But I held my tongue. Who was to say whether working at Clayfield was better or worse than the fate Elizabeth had originally suffered, catching the disease as inexplicably as Dwight and our father?

LATER THAT DAY, the bell rang over the door, announcing a visitor. It wasn't the searchers I'd half-anticipated Westminster would send, but rather another plague doctor. This new arrival was taller and leaner than Westminster, and despite his face being concealed behind a beaked mask, I suppose that he was also considerably younger.

"Doctor," I offered him a welcoming smile. "Welcome to Graves & Sons. I am Gabriel Graves. How may I assist you?" It was my usual line, rolling effortlessly off my tongue.

I interlaced my fingers and folded my hands in front of me on the counter. This disarming gesture tended to work well on my mortal, 21st century patrons and I saw no reason why it shouldn't also work on this plague doctor.

The man's voice sounded muffled through his mask as he replied, "Thank you, Mr. Graves."

Realizing that the mask would have to go if he wanted to be heard, he paused and slowly removed it, revealing a man in his mid-thirties, with thinning light brown hair and a prominent forehead. He wasn't someone familiar to me, unlikely to be from the nearby streets where I had spent my life. I knew every face in this neighborhood, and his wasn't one of them.

"Arnold Ellery," he introduced himself. "I'm simply here to see what work you do."

How peculiar. Probably a lie, too.

Plague doctors were typically occupied with visiting homes and removing corpses from the streets, rather than making individual visits to businesses unless, perhaps, they were establishments serving food and drink. Not that many of those were still open.

"Well, sure," I responded, gesturing with open hands. "You're more than welcome to take a look around. This shop was established by my father and uncle nearly forty years ago."

The plague doctor appeared somewhat condescending, scuffing slightly as he strolled through the shop, his hands folded behind his back. He meticulously scanned every detail of the space, his gaze narrowing as he focused on the display near the till that I had just finished arranging.

"So you and your family are coffin makers?"

I nodded. "Yes, indeed. The workshop where we build the finest coffins and caskets in all of London is right out here, appointed to the room behind me."

Ellery's hazel-colored eyes grew narrower as he stood near the till and examined the array of plague cures, apparently intrigued by what he saw. "Plague cures. Are any of these effective?"

"Oh, absolutely," I replied, the consummate salesman. "Graves & Sons pride ourselves on offering some of the finest cures. Admittedly, we prefer to stay away from the more experimental ones. Here, we have a variety of herbs, powders, vinegar-soaked cloths and sponges in skull-shaped boxes, you'll see them right there on the lowest shelf. They can be carried in pockets or held up in front of the noses of those wishing to traverse the plague-ridden streets without falling prey to the disease." This was quite a load of bollocks, of course, but so were all of the plague cures that were being sold. At least I didn't claim to be selling ground unicorn horn, unlike many other shopkeepers on and around Fleet Street. While the cures you might find at Graves & Sons may not have any direct effect on the plague itself, they were guaranteed and intended to lift the spirits and hopefully provide a bit of a placebo effect.

As Ellery inspected some herb bundles before returning them to their place, he commented, "I see that you're not selling anything untoward here, or at least not up front." He glanced at me, his eyebrows rising inquisitively. Ah, so he was here on official business. Go figure.

"If you'd like, I can show you the types of caskets we build," I offered, gesturing toward the workshop out back. "I have a few that are on the way."

"Certainly." A small smile crept onto Ellery's thin lips.

Leading him into the workshop, I started out by showing him the extravagant caskets that I had built for my two undead patrons. Alongside the much simpler pinewood coffins that my father had been so proud of, they were all the more breathtaking. The plague doctor leaned in to look at them in the dim light with a sense of admiration.

"I've heard that my good friend Westminster has hired your sister as a nurse assistant," Ellery remarked as he stood back and straightened up. "I must admit, I do not trust a man who would send his own little sister to the frontlines while he remains hidden in a place like this."

Ellery let the words hang there as he continued his inspection, scanning the workbench and tables as if searching for something specific. An unease had settled over me, but what to do about it?

I startled as the ghost-like outline of Octavia flickered into view over Ellery's shoulder. Finally! Where had she been these past few weeks while I'd been here, struggling on my own?

Ellery was hunched over, rifling through boxes of nails, hoping to find something interesting hidden in there.

Octavia held her finger to her lips as she pointed with an outstretched hand to the workbench next to her. Specifically, she was pointing to the heavy claw hammer lying on its surface among other scattered tools.

After her appearance in St Bride's churchyard and offering me her help she'd been leaving me well enough alone. But here she was, and I suppose what she was offering me was a better solution than any I could think of.

Carefully, I took a step sideways toward the workbench. Ellery was now pouring the contents of several boxes out on the table underneath the thick-paned window.

Silently, I reached out until my fingertips brushed the hammer's handle. The moment I closed my fingers around it, Octavia evaporated.

I cleared my throat. Her silent suggestion had been crystal clear.

"I'm not sure what Westminster has told you about me or what he has implied," I said, hoping to keep plague doctor Ellery, apparently Westminster's acolyte, distracted.

Ellery turned around and took a step toward me, shaking his head. The very atmosphere seemed to grow tense around us.

"Truth be told, Mr. Graves, I am here regarding some concerning rumors."

Oh?

I forced a laugh, hollow as the coffins leaning against the walls around us. "Ah, neighbors and their tales! You know how it is, Doctor. In difficult times, paranoia has ample opportunity to grow unchecked. But whatever rumors you have heard are just that, silly rumors."

Ellery tilted his head, as if examining a specimen that was both fascinating and repellent. "Just rumors? I hope you are telling me the truth. London sleeps not, and eyes are everywhere."

His words sent a shiver down my spine, and a thin line of sweat formed on my back.

"Do you deny," Ellery continued his line of questioning, "that you have been keeping strange hours? That you have been seen standing in the courtyard, right out there, holding a shovel in the dead of night?"

"I am a gravedigger as well as a coffin builder," I attempted, but Ellery would have none of it.

"Tell me, Mr. Graves, where is your father, your brother, your nephew? Neither have been seen by anyone for weeks."

Feeling the tension rise, I clutched the hammer tightly behind my back, ready to act if necessary.

"Well, if you insist on the truth," I began, my voice as steady and calm as I could make it, "Westminster and Widow Nesbit are correct. I have been hiding something."

"Yes?" The plague doctor took a step towards me, seemingly intrigued by what he sensed were the bare bones of a confession. His entire demeanor was alert, and I sensed that he relished the prospect of uncovering a hidden truth. Perhaps he anticipated some reward if he could get me to confess to a crime and expose me to the authorities. "Tell me. You must confess what you've been hiding. If you do, perhaps I can be convinced to help you."

"My father and nephew both succumbed to the plague weeks ago." I lowered my head in rather theatrical defeat.

The admission was the truth, albeit twisted to suit my purpose.

Ellery appeared captivated by my revelation. He took another step forward, eager to extract the details of my crimes.

"They're buried here," I said, "in the workshop, under the floorboards."

His stance shifted slightly, the leather of his plague suit creaking with the movement. "Under the floorboards, you say? A risky choice, Mr. Graves. The law is clear on the handling of plague victims. You have to show me where exactly."

I pointed towards the darker floorboards in the corner of the room, the remnants of the old flooring that existed before the renovations I had helped my father carry out in 1663.

Plague Doctor Ellery approached the place I'd pointed out, kneeling down to touch the floorboards with his hands. This was my opportunity, and I seized it. Swinging the hammer above him, I brought it down with force. The sound of his skull cracking echoed through the room.

Ellery's mouth opened to scream, but only a choked gurgle escaped. I quickly stifled it by shoving a length of torn linen, the type we used in the workshop all the time to clean the tools, into his open mouth and down his throat. He staggered for a moment, trying to get up from the floor, before finally collapsing, his life extinguished. I had never killed as a mortal man and had anticipated that it would be harder. But as it turned out, it had been both easy and swift. Gabriel Graves, angel of death.

But what now?

Blood and brain matter stained the floor as I stood over Ellery's lifeless body. Swiftly, I rolled him behind one of the workbenches so that no prying eyes, not even Widow Nesbit's aging falcon-eyes, would be able to see him through the window. I unfastened his coat and removed it from his frame, which was tall and lean, not unlike my own. I also took his beaked mask and his heavy leather boots.

"Gabriel?" My blood froze to ice at the sound of my mother's voice. She was calling my name, thankfully from the shop floor. "Is everything all right?"

I could hear her footsteps as she approached, her voice muffled by the door.

"Yes, Moeder!" I called out, trying to infuse my voice with an air of tranquility that I certainly did not feel. I could hear the drum of my own heart beating in the sudden, eerie stillness. What had my mother heard?

"I just stumbled over one of the coffins in here. Please don't come in before I've tidied up all of this mess!" My lie, spoken to the door, would be the narrative I presented to any who inquired. Including my mother and Elizabeth.

My mother's footsteps retreated, somewhat hesitantly.

I looked at the plague doctor's mask and coat, and despite my edge of panic, the outlines of a plan was beginning to take form in my mind.

But first things first. For now, I would have to cover up what had just happened here. Burying Ellery next to my father and Dwight underneath the shed felt inappropriate. I didn't want to taint their resting place.

Instead, I'd conceal him beneath the very floorboards I had indicated to him. The grim irony of it rather appealed to me.

I carefully wrapped Ellery's lifeless body in the sheet that I had used to cover my patron's caskets. Then, I made preparations to bury him beneath the floor by removing the floorboards. Using my chisel and other tools, prying the floorboards apart and lifting them up was easy enough, and as soon as there was a big enough hole, I unceremoniously dumped Ellery's body into it.

I pressed the floorboards back in place, but I didn't hammer in any nails. Tomorrow, I would venture out to collect a few ingredients, and when I came back, I would lift Ellery's body back out of the hole and embalm it, using the undertaker skills that no one else in 1665 had even dreamt of. Once this had been done, I wouldn't have to worry so much about the smell.

With Ellery out of the way I scrubbed the floor where his blood had spilled. The water in the bucket turned a murky crimson as I whistled a tune by Vivaldi.

Once the task was done, I sat heavily on a stool, my body and spirit exhausted. The hammer still lay on the table, blood and hair stuck to its shiny metal head. I picked it up and cleaned it before returning it to its usual place.

A bit of an awkward day, but I thought I'd handled it all rather well. With a little nudge from Octavia.

NINE

I n the days that followed, the devastating flames of the Black Death continued to rise. At Graves & Sons, business slowed to a crawl. We'd entered the era of mass graves, just as Westminster had predicted.

And that was quite unfortunate, since the theft of my money and my horse had left the Graves family fortune depleted. It was only a matter of time before we would have to close the shop and I would be forced to work as a gravedigger, laboring day and night to dig the mass graves. Of course, engaging in such perilous work would make me highly susceptible to contracting the plague myself.

At this point, it was fair to say that the initial hopefulness I'd felt when I first arrived in 1665 seemed like a distant memory, fading away with each passing day.

My only hope was the twins.

To them, of course, time was not of any particular essence. All I knew of their whereabouts was that they were still in Italy. I'd visited their grand house in Knightsbridge on several occasions, only to find it empty with darkened windows. The housekeeper could provide no insight on their exact return date, but money was being sent weekly to sustain her in looking after the property during their absence. None of this was of any comfort to me.

Restless and unable to find sleep, I paced the polished floors of Graves & Sons - yes, the very same floorboards underneath which plague doctor Ellery's corpse was happily rotting away. At this rate, it was a small miracle that my agitated footsteps hadn't worn a visible path on the wood.

Suddenly, the sound of the shop bell above the door startled me. It was an unusual hour for customers.

Except, of course, for Isadora and Isadore.

My heart quickened as I halted my footsteps and turned around.

It was them. My hand, almost of its own accord, rose in a gesture that was part welcome, part disbelief. I raked my hand through my long, light blond hair, sweeping it backwards.

"Isadore, Isadora," I managed.

The corners of Isadore's mouth twitched into a smile as he removed his gloves and slipped them into his coat pocket. "You seem relieved to see us, Gabriel. Terribly sorry for the delay. Italy is just so very captivating! You must visit it one day."

Isadora, every bit as timelessly graceful as her brother, remained standing behind him. Her eyes gleamed expectantly when they met mine. "We're excited to see what you have conjured up for us. Are you ready to show us?"

"I wasn't sure I would ever see you again," I said, the relief spilling into my words. I resented the vulnerability they betrayed, but there was no remedy for it.

"But of course, we always return," Isadora reminded me. Her tone was reassuring. "There was never any question about it. And we are only sorry that we had been so delayed, an entire week or perhaps a little more."

Perhaps? A *little* more?

I felt my eyebrow twitch. I couldn't believe their nonchalant attitude towards time. Isadora spoke as if their month-long delay was no big deal, but while they'd been gone I'd lost my father, I'd lost my nephew, and I'd killed a man.

Suppressing my frustration, I made an inclination of my head and shot my patrons a practiced, affable smile. I had to play my cards right. Once I was a vampire again, of course, I might admonish them.

"Your caskets have been ready for you for weeks," I assured them. "And I dare say, they are the finest works that I have ever accomplished. You'll be astonished when you see them, I guarantee it."

Isadore's eyebrows arched in curiosity, and he exchanged a significant look with Isadora. "Well, we would expect nothing less from you. Now, do show us the way."

I led Isadora and Isadore into the workshop where the caskets stood on the central workbench. I'd covered them up with linen sheets, which I must admit had gathered a layer of dust. There had been no telling when the twins would see it fit to return, and so this time they were greeted by dust instead of freshly cut flowers. But that was their loss, I told myself, and I'd better not dwell on it lest my irritation shine through.

I pushed aside some scattered tools and other clutter, eager to finally reveal my creations. As I pulled the cloth aside, releasing a dust cloud into the air, Isadora gasped.

Isadore stood speechless at her side. His dark eyes were fixed on the stunning, writing and dancing figures in the seamless wood. I'd sandpapered and chiseled everything to perfection - I hadn't used a single nail or screw. The twins both ran their fingers gently over my intricate carvings, both of them completely silent.

"These are absolutely magnificent, Gabriel," Isadore finally said, turning towards me. "I knew you were a craftsman of rare skill, but this, well, this has far exceeded my expectations. These carvings, Gabriel, they're the stuff of fantasy, of mythology. I'm more impressed than I can say."

I accepted the compliment quietly while waiting for the greater prize.

"And you crafted these all by yourself?" Isadore's voice was very quiet.

"Of course. Show me anyone in London, indeed anywhere, who could make something like this."

The Elysion twins exchanged a charged glance.

"Forgive me. It's merely that you have bowled me over, Gabriel. I am, for once, at a loss for words."

Isadora turned to her brother, eyes gleaming. "Well, I've got words. These are, without a doubt, the finest resting places we have ever been offered."

Iasodre nodded, his eyes now fixed on me.

A sense of anticipation filled the air, though I might have been the only one able to sense it. After all, it was my life and my immortality at stake, not theirs.

Finally, Isadore opened his mouth again. "Gabriel, you have clearly risen to the task that we set for you. Skill like this deserves to be rewarded."

Yes, yes it does.

I realized that I'd been holding my breath, who knew for how long. Lightheaded, I breathed out, trying to steady my trembling heart as I awaited their next move. They were going to offer me the immortal gift, right now, right here in the workroom. It wasn't the setting I would have chosen, but the location really didn't matter.

In the original turn of events, my transformation had occurred in their abode, months after the present moment. But I saw no reason why that couldn't change. The caskets I had crafted this time around were undeniably superior to the ones I had made before. I had pushed myself further, powered by the skill I'd had centuries to hone, and driven by the knowledge of the reward that awaited me.

A reward that was about to fall back into my lap. It took every ounce of my willpower to stop myself from reaching out my hands in an either beseeching or demanding gesture. But inwardly I was screaming, Give it to me!

Isadore reached into the inner lining of his coat, producing a pouch filled with jingling gold coins. It was a greater stash of wealth than I'd brought with me from the future, enough to provide for the Graves family, what little remained of it, for months to come. But it was just gold, just money. And money is only ever just a beginning.

Isadore courteously placed the gold in my hands. "I know that this is merely material wealth, filthy lucre, and that these beautiful caskets are worth much more than that."

"Can I speak with my brother for a moment, Gabriel?" Isadora cut in.

Isadore looked at her, a little startled, but then he nodded in agreement. "If you will, excuse us. We'll just step outside for a few moments. But we will be back before we leave."

With that, the two vampires exited my workshop, leaving me alone with my thoughts.

I strained my ears, attempting to catch snippets of their hushed conversation in the courtyard, but without my vampiric hearing, it was of no use. I knew that they had to be discussing my fate and the true reward that awaited me. This was finally it, I told myself. My turning was within reach. In just a moment, they would return with their invitation for me to join their bloodline.

Soon, Isadora pushed the door open and the two of them stepped back into the workshop. My mouth was dry, and my palms were moist with sweat as the two of them stepped back into the room. There was a taut string of secrecy between them.

I realized I'd been holding my breath again. I released it, letting my shoulders sink and relax. A slight tremor still coursed through me, and I couldn't fully conceal the storm of emotions and heightened excitement raging just below the calm, cool surface I was so practiced at maintaining.

"Gabriel," Isidore spoke, his voice resonant with a sense of authority. He was often the spokesperson for both of them. "As you know, Isadora and I couldn't be more impressed with what you've accomplished here."

"We also recognize in you a powerful and abundant spirit, a rare desire to transcend the limitations of your mortal life," Isadora joined in, her voice soft yet intense, "These are qualities that you've always possessed, and we have been privileged to see them develop as you've grown into the man you are now. You've always sought to reach higher, and we greatly admire this." Stepping close, she rested her cold, gloved hands on mine, which were warm and bore the marks and calluses from working with the wood.

Isadora's touch was cold and ethereal, like the touch of destiny itself. It sent a shiver down my spine.

"We see in you a reflection of our own past selves," Isidore extrapolated. "We, too, were once driven by a thirst for something beyond the ordinary. We have never aged as you have grown from a small boy into a man. You must have noticed this, am I right?"

I nodded, a lump forming in my throat. Yes, it was happening. This was the moment they were revealing their true nature and their intentions towards me.

Isadora glanced towards her brother again as if seeking his silent agreement to continue. He nodded encouragingly.

"Isadore and I, we are not like any mortal men and women." Isadora's voice was steady and sincere, but there was also a sense of hesitation about the way she said it, as if she perhaps feared that I might react with shock or fear. "In fact, we are not mortal at all. Neither Isadore or myself have been mortal for many a year. We are separate from humanity in a way that is difficult to describe. You've already sensed it, haven't you? Deep down, on an intuitive level."

"I have," I admitted, drawing in a deep breath, steadying myself. "I've always known, on an intuitive level, as you say, that there was something otherworldly about you. But whatever your secret is, it compels rather than frightens me."

I cast an appreciative glance at one, then the other of them. Isadore and Isadora were both watching me with gleaming eyes as if they were at least halfway flattered hearing the truth of their undead existence reflected back to them by a perceptive mortal.

"Your perception is accurate, Gabriel," Isadora said after a brief silence. "Just as we have watched you grow, you have observed us. You've intuited our secret, if not its exact nature, then certainly its presence and its effects. And now, this is what Isadore and I were discussing outside before.

We believe that you have nearly reached the peak of what you can accomplish as a mortal man."

"So do I." I leaned closer, eager for their next words. "I've begun to wonder what I might be able to accomplish if I were dealt a better hand - perhaps a supernatural hand."

She paused, her hesitation filling the air with suspense. My heart pounded and pounded in my chest.

Isadore now stood beside me, placing his hand on my arm. His touch, like Isadora's, sent a chill through my veins. The three of us stood closely together, our foreheads almost touching as our three minds marched inevitably, or so I hoped, towards a shared decision.

"Seeing these masterworks," Isadore gestured towards the caskets behind us, "has confirmed what we have long believed about you, namely that you are worthy of being dealt, as you call it, a better hand.

"And so, we want you to know," Isadora took over in her soft, melodic voice, which she had now dropped quite low, "that we will never let you perish the way so many others are dropping around you like flies. You are infinitely valuable to us and so you must know that you are under our protection."

"This is a promise," Isadore added, "that we do not give lightly."

"But wait! Steady your horses, please." A sense of unease stole over me in a rush. They were speaking of protection in my mortal life, but they had yet to mention the gift of immortality. "I appreciate your gifts of your friendship, loyalty, and protection." I was wording my thoughts carefully. "I'd never take them for granted. But Isadora, Isadore, what more powerful protection could you offer me than simply bringing me over into your realm? Now, I understand that there may be risks and costs involved, but whatever they are, they're perfectly fine by me. I'm willing to risk anything, pay any price to become... whatever it is that you are."

Isadore and Isadora exchanged another one of their weighty mirror-glances, a silent conversation passing between them. What on earth could they possibly be contemplating? I'd earned their blood, and here I was, practically with my mouth open ready to consume it. Why the hesitation? I wanted to scream.

When Isadore finally spoke, his tone was quite solemn. "There are grave risks and costs associated with what you're asking of us. But yes, we do possess the power to transform you completely."

Well, then. Do it! I leaned in. Isadora released a soft sigh. "Becoming what we are is not as glamorous as you may believe," she explained, or should I say fibbed. Being a vampire is, in fact, quite glamorous. It is one of the many cliches about vampires that actually tends to be true, and in my case, certainly is.

"We aren't simply immortal and untouched by the hardships that plague humanity," Isadore took over again, "We carry something unnatural within us. Many would consider us to be monsters." A darkness rose in his eyes, or else a ghost of sadness. "Every night, we pay a heavy price to remain youthful and vibrant. And that price drives us to commit the most horrendous of sins."

"Killing?" I made it a question despite being perfectly aware of the answer.

They both confirmed with solemn nods.

"To sustain our lives, we must take the lives of others," Isadore spelled it out. "There's no way around it."

"We are making a significant admission to you here,

Gabriel," Isadora emphasized, "but we know that we can trust you."

"Regardless, I wish to become like you." My voice was calm, but firm as a rock formation. "As I said, I'm ready and more than willing to bear any cost, to endure any sacrifice."

Isadora regarded me in the same way that an old, wise woman would a naive child. "You possess the heart of a lion and the spirit of a bold demon, Gabriel. Or perhaps I should say a fallen angel," she added in a whisper. "Perhaps, one night, we shall grant your wish. But know that the path you seek is a path of darkness and more sacrifices than you can imagine from where you are standing now."

In my book, sacrificing others is a damn sight better than growing old and dying yourself, but hey, I suppose we all have our different values.

"Since you're so certain that you wish to become like us, you should come with us as we go to the... where should we go tonight, Isadora? The Rainbow Coffee House, The Mermaid Tavern, or perhaps The Devil Tavern again?"

I knew the Mermaid Tavern, a place on the corner of Bread Street and Friday Street east of St Paul's Cathedral that Thomas and I had often frequented together in the pre-plague days. Apparently, the great William Shakespeare had been a regular visitor. But that had been a little before my time. I imagine he probably found much inspiration in the tales told by the pirates and other sailors that were among the clientele. As had Thomas, for that matter. Actually, I suppose The Mermaid Tavern was at least partially responsible for fanning the fires of my brother's wanderlust.

"Let's go to The Mermaid Tavern."

The twins both looked at me, a little startled. They were used to me deferring to them, but despite my mortal state, I wanted to show them that they could consider me their equal - and that I could watch them hunt without raising an eyebrow or breaking a sweat.

Yes, hunt. That was what we were about to do. They were clearly concerned that I was too naive, or perhaps that I would be too squeamish to deal with the reality of having to feast on human blood as a vampire. Well, they were in for a surprise.

Outside, the night was damp and misty - perfect weather for an outing such as the one we had in mind. As we walked along the dirty streets, passing one boarded-up door after another, breathing the rain-filled midnight air, I was starting to feel optimistic once again that tonight was going to be my night. And I knew that as soon as I was cloaked in immortality, the sighs and sounds of death wouldn't bother me in the slightest, because I would be above them.

When we reached The Mermaid Tavern, one of the relatively few public houses that had actually managed to obtain a license to remain open, a thick blanket of mist had crept up from the river and was now blanketing the narrow streets. Ideal for hunting.

As it turned out, we did not even have to go inside; as soon as we rounded the corner of Bread Street, a man, only slightly uneasy on his legs, emerged from the tavern door right in front of us.

In a series of movements so swift that I wasn't quite capable of following them with my mortal eyes, Isadore and Isadora rushed to the man, grabbed him by his arms, and dragged him into the dark, mist-filled alley behind the Mermaid. I followed them as quickly as I was able to, my shoes squelching in the mud.

Yellow light shone through grimy windows above us,

but no one seemed to notice the gruesome scene unfolding in the alley. Isadora and Isidore dragged the drunken man into its deepest shadows.

"Who're you?" the understandably disoriented man demanded in a slightly slurred voice. Of course the only answer he received was the shock of two sharp sets of fangs being sunken into his rather wobbly neck from either side. He yelled in surprise and pain as he fell to his knees in the mud.

He saw me standing there, no doubt outlined in silhouette against the light and the mist of the street behind me. "And who are *you*? Don't just stand there, man, help me!"

Isadore lifted his gaze above the man's neck, as if to challenge me to intervene. Then he lifted his head a little more, tilting it backwards and sideways so that the moonlight illuminated his marble-like skin and the crimson blood staining his chin and his teeth.

I didn't flinch and only lowered my gaze a little as the man's life finally drained away and Isadore and Isadora let him slide to the ground before straightening their postures and wiping their mouths clean.

"We are, as you can see Gabriel, murderous," Isadore said with a glimmer of sadness while his sister, matter-of-factly, disposed of the man's body behind an empty cart. Despite the piercing wounds on his neck, this unfortunate soul would be assumed to have fallen victim to the plague, his death going unnoticed and unquestioned.

Isadore turned his gaze towards me, his eyes filled with concern. "I see that you do not flinch at the sight of blood, but Gabriel, you do not truly want to become this, do you? Now that you have seen what we must do, night after night after night. And so it continues, for all eternity."

Ah, sweet eternity, bring it on! Bring it on right now.

Out loud I said, "I won't deny the... gravity of what I've just witnessed. But still I have no fear of you, or of the thought of becoming like you. Look into my mind and into my heart, as I have no doubt you're able to. You won't find a single glimmer of hesitation. Believe me, I am ready. I could not be more ready to leave my mortal existence behind forever."

Oh yes, please let it be forever this time. Seven long weeks of being mortal again had been more than enough.

"If you're certain..." Isadora began, taking a step towards me, but her brother interjected, reaching out and placing a cautioning hand on her arm. "We know now that you're serious about your desire to become like us, and that you understand what it entails. Still, we have our own moral implications to consider. Making more creatures like ourselves is not something that we can do lightly. It is an immense decision that we will have to take our time to ponder."

I felt as if the air had been knocked from my lungs. In my pockets, my fists clenched and unclenched as I fought hard to remain calm. How much more time could they possibly need? What on earth was there to ponder?

"What can I do to convince you, to ease your minds?" I asked. "I'd do anything - have I not made that abundantly clear?"

"Time, Gabriel. Time to deliberate amongst ourselves. You can trust that we will make a wise decision."

Isadore's words hung in the air, as poisonous to me as the deadly miasma of the plague.

"Is there nothing I can do that will convince you to initiate me tonight? This is my destiny, Isadore."

"Your resolve is admirable, Gabriel, but you cannot hasten our decision."

If only I was alone with Isadora, I thought. Isadore was clearly the one hesitating and holding up my plans. But with him here, I knew that Isadora was going to follow his lead.

I squared my shoulders and met her gaze, then Isadore's. "And so I wait?"

"And so you wait," said Isadore, placing a hand on the small of my back and ushering me back to the street. Here, he looked me in the eye, his features softening slightly at the sight of the disappointment that was no doubt all too plain to read on my features. "But you have my word, we will not let you wait for long, now that we know how you feel, and now that we're convinced that your spirit will not buckle under the weight of what the dark flame requires to sustain itself."

CHAPTER

TEN

I stood in front of the bathroom mirror, examining my own reflection in its beaten copper surface. I was utterly unrecognizable.

Plague doctor Ellery's long black cloak was already draped over my body, and now I carefully adjusted the beaked mask until it obscured my face completely, yet allowed me to peek out through the designated eye holes.

The plan that had taken shape in my mind since last night's disappointing endnote was audacious. In my stolen plague doctor's outfit, I would infiltrate the wealthy homes of Knightsbridge, Bloomsbury and Kensington, and perhaps further afield. I would tread the floorboards of the upper echelons of society, and yes, I would rake into my deep pockets any manifestations of wealth that were small enough to fit there. Theft was a much better prospect than digging mass graves.

Besides, if I could gather enough wealth quickly, I could hasten the day when I'd be able to open the doors of Deep Graves. The night of the grand opening had coincided with my vampiric transformation, and if there was any way to sway the Elysion twins into action, surely recreating that sacred evening had to be the key.

"Gabriel?" My mother's voice interrupted my thoughts, calling through the door.

I lifted the beaked mask just a sliver in order to be heard, "Yes, what is it? I'll be out soon. Just getting changed; I'll be digging graves tonight!" There were gravesites aplenty that I might conceivably be heading out to.

"Very well. Be careful, son. You and your sister - you're all I have left."

"I'll be safe. I'm wearing protective clothing."

"Gabriel, I wanted to tell you. There's a strange smell in the workshop. I think there may be a rat's nest under the floorboards."

My pulse quickened. There was a rat's nest under those floorboards all right.

"I'll take care of it, please don't give it another thought."

The very last thing I needed right now was my mother lifting the floorboards and discovering plague doctor Ellery's decaying corpse. Despite my best efforts at embalming him, I simply hadn't been able to find all of the products I needed and had easy access to in the 21st century. I'd done my best, but apparently I would have to think of a better solution. Not now, though.

I looked at my reflection one last time, steeling my resolve for what I was about to do.

It was still broad daylight as I stepped out of the door of Graves & Sons and as I ventured from there out onto Bride Lane and then onto Fleet Street.

~

By the time I'd reached the streets of Bloomsbury, my steps had grown more purposeful and confident. It was a hot summer's day and pearls of sweat had formed on my brow. But it was well worth it - my disguise was water-tight. No one had recognized me or reacted to me any differently than they would to any other plague doctor crossing their path, that is to say, with a sense of reverence tinged with fear.

I lingered for several long moments on the threshold of the first house I entered as I silently asked myself whether I would be greeted with welcome or with rejection. Of course there was also the chance that there would be no one there to greet me at all, as most of London's wealthy were still out of town.

But as it turned out, no one sensed anything amiss. To the anemic-looking young couple that occupied the first villa, my disguise was a symbol of safety in this time of peril. They actually greeted me with relief as they welcomed me into their opulent home. It was only necessary for me to exchange a few words with them as I dug into my satchel bag and gave them some of the posies and lavender sprigs I'd brought from Graves & Sons. After all, I saw no reason why I shouldn't do a little good, even if my true errand was fundamentally criminal in nature. Yes, I know, I'm a complicated villain.

Back out on the street, encased in my solitary refuge, my mind swirled with thoughts of how the version of 1665 I was living now differed from my memories of it. The overall trajectory of events seemed to follow a familiar pattern, but there were notable differences. The most striking of which was, of course, the untimely demise of my father as well as Dwight.

I was saddened by their deaths, of course. But my feelings of loss weren't nearly as intense and raw as the grief that both Elizabeth and my mother had been plunged into. I'd already grieved and processed both of my parents' deaths centuries ago. The time I'd gotten to spend with them now had been a bonus, like interacting with a pair of beloved and particularly vivid ghosts. And I must admit that my feelings about my nephew's death were ambivalent.

Wait, let me explain. I loved my nephew, absolutely, but the version of him I'd left behind in the present was rather the zombie. And before that he'd been bitter and cruel. It's something that seems to happen to those who've been brought over into vampirism too young. Turn someone before they're grown and they'll grow ever more resentful over the centuries, angry and frustrated that they were never allowed to grow up.

And what would be the implications, the ripple effects of Dwight's death? When I returned to the future - assuming, of course, that I did, would I find him there, or would he be gone? If he was gone, what would Thomas think of it? Would he blame me? Would I even tell him?

"Oh, this is rather interesting. In this non-corporeal form, I can easily hear your thoughts. They're all rather self-centered."

Turning my head sharply to my right and then to my left, I saw Octavia, floating just a few inches from my left shoulder. She was eye level with me, which meant that her feet, clad in white ankle socks and gleaming black Mary Janes, were several inches above the ground. I kept walking, determined not to let her see how much her sudden appearance had startled me.

"The questions you have about the ripple effects when

you tinker with and tear the fabric of time are surely questions for Csilla."

Csilla, my finest fledgling - my only loyal fledgling, I should say - and the medium who had facilitated my journey in time by giving me her ectoplasm. I could really do with *her* help.

"As if I haven't already been of invaluable help to you," Octavia frowned, folding her arms across her chest and pouting. She'd been seventeen when she was turned into a vampire - she was, in other words, an immortal teenager. Elizabeth would be too, if this adventure ended as I hoped. But despite being a year younger, Elizabeth was already significantly more mature than Octavia.

"You've been of great help to me, Octavia, I don't wish to deny it."

"Well, you better not. Not if you want more of it. But why are you wearing this ridiculous and frankly rather smelly costume?"

"Opportunity landed it in my lap, as you well know. You were there. I've simply decided to make the most of it, rather than let the opportunity slip me by. While I'm here anyway, I can't simply sit around with my hands in my lap, waiting for immortality to descend on me, now can I?"

"What do you mean, how is wearing *this* an opportunity?" She wrinkled her little nose in a clear display of disgust. It was plainly theatrical - in spirit form, I doubted that she was able to smell anything at all, and if she was, surely the general stench of feces and pestilence that hung over the city, even the nice parts of it, was much worse than the dark, dank scents of the leather.

"It's not wearing the mask and cloak, per say," I explained rather patiently, "it's the doors they can open up for me. If you'd decided to show up just a moment earlier you would have seen me entering the beautiful villa right over there and being welcomed by its inhabitants. Looking like this, I can enter anywhere I like - except, perhaps, Buckingham Palace. Every door will spring open, every guard step out of his way to allow me entry."

"So what?" Octavia wasn't impressed.

"Well, let me put it like this. Plague doctor Westminster, much as I despise the man, is right about one thing. The Black Death brings death and grief, but it can also be looked at as an opportunity. What I am doing here is taking matters into my own hands by hastening the course of history. Now tell me, Octavia, have you got a better plan? Have you reared your head to offer any special insights or guidance that'll help me regain my immortality faster?" My words were bitingly ironic, but my tone was pleasant and that's what Octavia reacted to when she replied, "Alas, I don't. But I think I understand what you intend to do, and maybe that will be enough to impress the Elysions. Make them understand that you are as ruthless as any vampire. I want to meet them, you know, the Elysion twins. After I've helped you gain access to their blood, you'll owe me at least that."

I halted. We had reached an imposing yet overgrown villa at the end of the tree-lined street. "I'm sure that can be arranged. Actually, Octavia, here's a thought." Indeed, it had only just occurred to me. "If I let you know their whereabouts in the present, won't you contact them on my behalf, explain the situation?"

"You think they'd travel back in time for you as you have for Elizabeth?" She couldn't have sounded any more skeptical if she'd tried.

"Well, probably not." And even if Isadore and Isadora wanted to help me, was there any way for them to influence the decisions of their past selves? I sensed a headache coming on, but it might have been the warmth inside the leather mask. "But perhaps something can still be done. Csilla, as you so astutely pointed out, will probably have some theories, at least. Would you mind- oh."

Octavia, apparently bored of our conversation, was nowhere to be seen. Great, just great. I suppose I was pretty much on my own in this, after all.

I turned back towards the villa. The gates yielded with a gentle creak under my leather-gloved hands as I let myself into the villa's neglected garden. Despite the looming shadow of the plague, Bloomsbury still managed to exude the same quiet charm that has characterized it for centuries. Here in the summer-warm garden, the air was thick with the perfume of cherry and apple blossoms, casting a soothing pall over the urgency of my mission. Pollen dusted the cobblestone path leading up to the door like fine, golden snow.

When I went up to the front door and knocked, there was no response, but the door also wasn't locked. Inside, my footsteps resonated through the hollow expanse of the hallway. Paintings of majestic landscapes lined the wall, and there were several large, real glass mirrors - a rarity in 1665. The mirrors reflected my own strange, masked appearance back at me.

"Is anyone there?" Just as my footsteps had done, my voice echoed eerily in the silence.

To my surprise, a fragile whisper came drifting down from the upper floors. I moved toward the staircase. So there was life yet in this desolate manor.

As I ascended the staircase, the wooden frame groaned under my weight, and the voice grew stronger the higher up I got. "In here," it called out.

I found the source of the feeble voice in an upstairs bedroom. It belonged to an elderly gentleman, his presence as fragile as his voice, half-hidden beneath the heavily embroidered covers of a canopied bed. He had been engrossed in a book, but he put it down as soon as he saw me. But not before carefully marking his progress. His eyes met mine through the mask, seemingly unfazed by the sight of the plague doctor standing before him.

"Hello, Doctor," he greeted me rather cheerfully. "Ellery, isn't it?"

I nodded, realizing that he must have recognized Ellery's hand-sewn mask. And apparently, he had been expecting the plague doctor's visit. The old man's calm demeanor contrasted with the fear that the sight of the mask elicited in others.

"I assure you, I'm not ill," he continued, his voice cracking as he tried to sit up a little straighter against the pillows. "I'm merely old and tired. If you are hungry or thirsty, doctor, you are welcome to help yourself from the kitchen downstairs. And now, have you brought me any medicine?" he asked. There was a glimmer of hope in his eyes. "I do not have the plague, but I do have just about every other ailment and ache you can think of."

I reached into the satchel bag I had acquired from diseased Ellery, I retrieved a small bottle of tincture. I'd swapped it out for the bottle of arsenic, pure poison, I'd found in there. Who knew how many lives I might actually have saved by killing Ellery? It had to be more than a few. The bottle now contained a homeopathic blend of mugwort and lavender, crafted by my mother and Elizabeth in the kitchen above Graves & Sons. This concoction was designed to bring about calmness and induce a restful sleep.

Handing him the bottle, I explained its purpose,

keeping my words brief in case he noticed the difference between the timbre of my voice and Ellery's. "This tincture will help you sleep and ease your worries. It contains mugwort and lavender, along with a few other ingredients I'm not entirely familiar with. I have personally tried it, and I can vouch for its efficacy and for its safety."

He smiled as he accepted the bottle, and right away, he placed a few drops on his tongue and savored the taste. "Not unpleasant at all," he remarked. "It's similar to what another plague doctor gave me a few weeks ago. But that one had a foul aftertaste and, I have to say, it made me feel quite unwell."

While he talked, my eyes darted toward a nearby window and the dressing table standing beneath it, bathed in golden sunlight. On it stood open boxes spilling with jewelry and diamonds.

"Really," the old man was carrying on. "The medicine that the other doctor had me drink made me feel strange, almost as if it contributed to my weakened state." Well, of course.

Actually, Ellery might have been carrying out the same plan that I was now following - only in a significantly more ruthless way.

As the old man lay back in his bed, succumbing to the effects of my mother's sleep tincture, I seized the opportunity. Carefully, I walked over to the dressing table. Breathless, I filled my pockets with the jewelry, all of it gleaming with real silver, diamonds and gold.

When I left the house, my pockets rattling and clanking with the pilfered heirlooms, my thoughts churned with the dread of capture. What if my heavy steps on the staircase had awoken him?

He posed no physical threat, but he might call out, raise

the alarm - imprisonment or even execution would both be on the table if I were caught. And if that happened, I could certainly wave goodbye to all of my plans. But so far, so good. While Isadore and Isadora were contemplating whether or not to help me, I could at least help myself.

And not even I knew what would happen if and when I grew impatient with them. I mean, I knew where they lived. Their villa was only a stone's throw away from here.

A terrible idea hit me like a searing premonition. I envisioned myself, breaking into their villa during the day, opening one of their caskets and quite frankly stealing the immortal blood.

But no, it was too risky and too unlikely to work. Drinking a little bit of vampire blood wasn't going to cut it. For the turning to work and to be complete, I needed to replace every drop of blood in my body with vampire blood. In a modern lab and with modern technology, such a forcible turning might be feasible, but not here, not now. Fortunately for them, I would be on my best behavior and bide my time.

CHAPTER

ELEVEN

"I'm learning something new about you every night you're on this journey."

I'd just stepped back out into the cobbled street and closed the door to the Wig and Pen Club - one of the few public houses that were still open - and now I turned my head sharply to the left, the direction of Octavia's voice.

There she was, her little ghost hovering above the rain-wet cobblestones. She was wearing much the same Victorianesque regalia as the last time I'd seen her, but instead of black Mary Janes, she had a pair of chunky Converse on her feet.

"Octavia, how good of you to show up."

My voice came out muffled from behind the beaked mask, which I was still wearing. I'd contemplated taking it off while I was inside the pub, carrying out my errand of sharing today's loot with Eline Blackburn, Dwight's mother. She worked there as a barmaid, and I knew that she could do with the help. Particularly now that Thomas was no longer around to aid or provide for her in any way.

Not, of course, that my brother's help had ever been

assured. For about a decade, he had drifted in and out of Eline's life as he pleased. And she, for whatever reason, never failed to take him back whenever he felt inspired to pick up the loose strands of their relationship.

Anyway, I'd decided against revealing my identity. It wasn't that I didn't trust Eline, but she was a barmaid, a role which at least in part consisted in peddling the latest gossip and news.

"You have it in you to be kind," observed Octavia, regarding me skeptically. "Even when you don't want anything in return."

"And that is a surprise to you?" I started walking in the direction of Bride Lane. It had been a long, lucrative day, and I was eager now to get home with what remained of the day's harvest. Since slipping into the plague doctor's garb that first time, I have to admit the process of doing it had become rather addictive, and not only because it was hastening my purchase of the future premises of Deep Graves and thus the opening night during which I expected to regain my immortality. There was also an element of thrill.

"I've always thought you were a cold-hearted, villainous bastard," Octavia clarified.

"No doubt your brother told you that, painted me in the least flattering light possible."

"Well, there is that. But also, you stole my body. You were prepared to give it away to someone else to live in."

"Not just to anyone," I highlighted. It was a feeble protestation, I must admit. "And as I've explained, I didn't think you had any use for it. It seemed better that your body should be inhabited by my sister than by no one. I suggest you look at it as the complement it is."

"But you never asked my permission."

"I did not." There was no point in trying to obscure or deny the facts. "I didn't think it necessary, and for that I am... sorry." I realized that I'd stopped in the middle of the street. The rain, just a soft misty drizzle moments earlier, was intensifying. "Really I am, Octavia."

To my surprise, I meant it. In the heat of pursuing my own plans and desperately clinging to the hope of giving Elizabeth new life, I'd completely disregarded Octavia. And what had she done to deserve it? Nothing. It wasn't her fault that her brother was an insufferable immortal brat, or that he'd taken my heart, once upon a time, and crushed it in his elegant fist.

"Can you forgive me, Octavia?" I turned to look at her, pushing the beaked mask back and feeling the cool rain beating against my scalp and running down my cheeks.

Octavia was still there - I'd half expected her to dissolve in order to avoid the uncomfortably heartfelt turn this conversation had taken. At first she didn't respond, but then the shadow of a smile tugged at the corners of her small cupid-bow mouth.

"I don't tend to forgive when someone has wronged me," she said, the words seeming much too mature for her youthful, almost child-like appearance. "But then, I don't think you tend to apologize. So yes, very well, I forgive you."

"LAST NIGHT, I had this strange, disturbing dream. I've not been able to shake it off all day."

I looked up from my dinner plate, where I had been moving my potatoes and boiled broccoli aimlessly around, taking only the occasional bite. We were lucky to have enough to eat, but I had very little in the way of appetite. I suppose I was still mourning my father and Dwight. Besides, the novelty of eating mortal food again had quickly worn off.

Elizabeth hadn't eaten much either, and now she put down her fork and knife and pushed her plate aside.

"And what did you dream?"

Elizabeth had my full attention now. If she had had a nightmare involving the grisly Malm Westminster or perhaps the Black Death personified, I would warn her that either was a bad omen telling her to hang up her nurse's uniform and stay away from Clayfield.

But alas, that wasn't it.

"It was about you, Gabriel." Lifting her gaze, she looked me straight in the eye. It was as if our mother wasn't in the room at all and I was all she could see. "Thomas was there too. At first I was simply floating on a dark and tranquil sea, or floating among the stars perhaps. Then, I was suddenly sucked downward, well, sucked or pulled." She paused her flow of words and placed her slim-boned hand on her solar plexus or slightly below it. "It felt like being pulled by a string. Suddenly I was shooting up into a sitting position, as you do when you awaken startled from a dream. But I cannot have woken up, because what I saw wasn't reality - it was something utterly unreal. And utterly terrifying. I'm shivering now, merely thinking about it."

"Elizabeth, stop this now. It was only a dream."

Elizabeth turned her head slightly to look at our mother, who was rising now from the table and started gathering our nearly untouched plates. "No, Moeder. It was more than that. Let me tell Gabriel what I saw."

"I do not wish to listen to this. It is going to give me bad dreams, too. I toss and turn at night these days as it is. Please forgive me."

"It's all right, Moeder, you're not obliged to listen. As long as Gabriel will hear me out." Elizabeth turned her attention back to me, and I nodded to reassure her. Whatever horrors she was about to relay, they could hardly be worse than anything we as a family had experienced lately. It could hardly be worse than the sights and smells of the dead lying here and there in the road, or the sounds and moans of the sick and dying at Clayfield.

"Go on," I encouraged her. "I'm here for the duration."

"I, however, am not. Goodnight. Don't stay up too late, Elizabeth."

Elizabeth waited respectfully for our mother to leave the kitchen and disappear down the hallway. Then she started speaking again, leaning in over the table, her tone low and urgent, "I found myself in a room, or rather some sort of underground cavern. Stalactites and stalagmites everywhere around, as far as the eye could see. Looking down, I noticed that I was half sitting, half lying down in a coffin, made of the clearest glass. The bottom of it was slick with blood. Something felt odd and unfamiliar about the proportions of my body - and when I lifted my hand to wipe my eyes, they weren't my hands. They were smaller, and the fingers were shorter. They were the kind of hands that have never carried out a day's work. You were there, nearby. You were dressed in very fine attire, like a prince. But your shirt was torn and tattered."

My blood had turned to ice in my veins and all of the little hairs on the back of my neck and on my arms were standing up, electrified. I fought to keep my facial expression calm and composed as I nodded for my sister to go on.

"I also recognized Thomas, although he looked different. Monstrous. He had - he had tentacles, like an octopus."

I suppressed a shiver. Could it be that Elizabeth had

dreamt or perhaps remembered that brief moment when I'd managed to draw her spirit into Octavia's body? Yes, I know I've told you that my attempt failed, and it did ultimately, but there had been a brief moment. I'd seen it when Elizabeth, in Octavia's body, had opened her eyes. For a fleeting moment they had been Elizabeth's pale green eyes instead of Octavia's feline, amber-colored ones.

I swallowed audibly. "What more did you see? Who else was there?"

Elizabeth sat back a little, her shoulders hunched. "There were others, yes, but I cannot remember them clearly. I gathered that you had all been fighting before I arrived, or before I awakened. There was so much blood spilt on the ground. So much shattered glass."

"And what happened then?"

"Then, nothing. Then I was gone, and I woke up in my own bed, shivering and crying. I'm saying that it was a dream because I don't know what else to call it, but it was not a dream. It was too vivid and too real."

We both fell silent. Finally I said, "I'm not going to insult you by telling you that it was just a dream. It was, I suspect, a premonition."

"A premonition? About what - that something awful is going to happen to you?"

I paused while choosing my words carefully. "A premonition, perhaps, about what might happen to you. The last thing I want to do is alarm you, but we are navigating through treacherous terrain, and you, well, you've - bravely and admirably, but perhaps not very sensibly - placed yourself on the front line. In harm's way."

Elizabeth frowned, but she wasn't angry. "Someone has got to help the sick and the dying."

"Yes, that's true. I just wish it wasn't you. I promised

125

our beloved Father, shortly before his death, that I'd protect you. If I fail, I'll never live it down." Elizabeth truly had no idea how long a shadow such a failure had cast over my existence.

"Are you seriously thinking of yourself right now, of how it'd reflect on you if I were to catch the plague, if I were to die?"

"Well, yes, but that doesn't mean that I am not sincere. I am, and I love you. What I'm saying is that your death would haunt me forever if it were to happen, and if I hadn't already tried and failed I would forbid you from working another shift at Clayfield. Working in the midst of that inferno is akin to leaving the door not ajar but wide open, with a welcome sign above it, inviting the Black Death to come in."

Elizabeth pushed back her chair and rose briskly from the table. "I thought you understood why I've chosen to work at Clayfield. It isnt's about the money; it's about who I am and what I stand for."

I let out an exasperated sigh. Expressing my concerns to Elizabeth clearly wasn't working - how infuriating that she should be as hard-headed as I. I admired her determination and commitment to what she believed was right, but damn it.

"There's a darkness about you, brother," Elizabeth said quietly, standing back from the table and regarding me with a curious expression. "It is little wonder why there are rumors."

"Rumors?" I rose from the table myself, pricking up my ears. "Please, enlighten me. What rumors are we talking about now?"

"Widow Nesbit has clearly been wagging her tongue to

anyone who would care to listen, and as you know, a certain type of rumor spreads like wildfire."

"Oh?"

"I happened to overhear a rather unsavory conversation today at Clayfield. It was a conversation about our family. Well, mostly it was about you."

I stood silently looking at her, my arms folded across my chest. She continued, "It was just one conversation, between two of the other nurses. I heard them whispering that our family remains oddly untouched by the plague. One of them mentioned Widow Nesbit and her theory is that it is because we're involved in some form of necromancy, and that this has all been initiated by you."

"Sounds like Ethel Nesbit has been rather busy - Clayfield is far."

"In a way, that might be the most concerning thing of all. If these rumors have been circulated as far as Clayfield." She didn't finish her sentence; she didn't have to. We both knew that this didn't bode well.

"Ethel Nesbit is unpredictable," I remarked. "Promise me that you will not talk to her, that you'll give her nothing to work with. Even a sentence she'll worry at like a dog with a bone. She won't let it go. Even the tiniest morsel is enough to keep her going, to keep her interested in us for weeks. Our best hope when it comes to Ethel Nesbit is for her to forget about us."

Elizabeth nodded, her eyes big as saucers.

"Mother has been talking to her regularly, over the fence. She feels sorry for her, says she's old and lonely."

"Well, that has to stop. Just like the flames of any fire, those wicked rumors will eventually fizzle out, as long as we don't feed them. We live in a time in which malicious gossip can all too easily lead to grave accusations. And grave accusations could, under the right circumstances, lead very quickly to the gallows."

It wouldn't be the first time that a toxic tongue had led to a death sentence. It was the mid 1600s and sporadic witch hunts still occurred. News of them throughout Europe reached our ears often enough. And up until recently, Westminster had been making a rather good living as a witch finder - an expert, if you will, in turning feathers into flocks of hens.

"I know," Elizabeth reassured me, "If only Father was still with us. If only he made an appearance, it would put a stoop to any speculation."

If only. Alas, the corpses of Dwight and our father would already be horribly decayed - there was no point in even entertaining the idea of digging them up and attempting to stage some sort of... masquerade for the sake of quelling rumors.

I made a decision right then and there. It was a risk, but it was a risk worth taking. Sooner or later, Elizabeth would come to know my secret plans, anyway. Why not reveal at least one snippet of what I was up to? It might maker her grow more sympathetic to my point of view.

"Well, Father isn't here and he can no longer help us," I said. "And yet we're in a better position than you realize. Elizabeth, I have decided to show you something, to confide in you. Perhaps after I have shown you what I am working on, you can reassure our mother that I have got all of this in hand."

The look on Elizabeth's face was somewhere between skeptical and critical. "Are you building more extravagant caskets for those wealthy patrons of yours?"

I shook my head no. "Come with me to the workshop."

Downstairs, I knelt down to pull out, from below one

of the work benches, the chest in which I kept the plague doctor's garb tucked away. Elizabeth was watching me intently, I think half anticipating, half fearing what secrets I might have kept hidden within the wooden chest.

"You must promise not to speak of this to anyone," I urged her.

"Of course," her voice was barely a whisper.

While Elizabeth looked on anxiously I opened the lid to reveal the plague doctor's dark cloak and mask. I then unfolded the long leather coat, the apron, the gloves, laying them out on the floorboards for her to see. When she realized what the things were, her face fell.

"Gabriel, why do you have all of this?" She knelt down beside me, gingerly picking up the beaked mask and turning it over in her hand. It looked even more ominous without a face underneath.

"Why do you have this?" she repeated. "Please don't tell me you've been looting from the dead?"

I sighed, bracing myself. "I found it," I improvised. "Perhaps it was left out to dry by a plague doctor."

"But why did you take them - for a thrill?"

Sensing her skepticism, prickling along my skin like an electric charge, I added, "Wearing this disguise allows me to move unnoticed and to gain entry into the homes of the wealthy." I raised my hand to forestall her objections, which I sensed were coming. "That's what I've been doing during my unexplained absences. I've been gathering resources, not for my own benefit, but to secure our family's future and to ensure that you no longer have to risk your life as a nurse. I worry about the very real danger of you falling prey to the plague - and I worry about you in other ways, too."

"You mean Westminster." She didn't even have to reach for the name.

"The way that wolf looks at you makes my blood run cold."

"You're starting to sound more and more like him, actually. Gathering wealth while people are suffering." Clearly torn, her expression was shifting between anger and disappointment.

I stepped forward and gently took her hands. "Please, Elizabeth, try to see this from my perspective. I didn't make this decision lightly. When else do you think an opportunity like this might come along?"

She withdrew her hands. "But what about the risks, have you considered those? What if you're recognized or caught wearing that mask, rifling through someone's home? If that happens, you could lose everything, our family's reputation, and even your life on the gallows, or just as bad, a life in prison."

I nodded. I couldn't deny that her words were absolutely true. "You know me, Elizabeth. I've been extremely cautious. No one has seen me take the mask on and off. No one has recognized me wearing the mask and cloak."

She studied me, her eyes searching my face for reassurance, or perhaps for remorse.

"I promise to remain true to who I am. Nothing can change that. Nothing can shake my foundations. But do you understand the agony I feel sending you to the plague house each day?"

"But I'm doing God's work, and I feel there's a guardian angel watching over me," Elizabeth protested, and it was obvious from her tone and the look of conviction on her face that she really believed it. I bit my lip. Her only guardian angel was me, and I knew that the luck that had been keeping her safe so far wasn't going to last.

"But don't you see?" She sighed, some of her anger dissipating, "No matter how much wealth you might amass, I won't abandon my role as a nurse. You might be willing to compromise your morals, but I am not."

It struck me that my younger sister was, in some ways, stronger than I. I'd succumbed to temptation, hoarding gold and riches with the desperation of a starving man while Elizabeth had been helping plague victims.

"Father Dalmane once told me," I said, hoping to bridge the sudden gulf that seemed to have opened up between us, "that in turbulent times, the boundaries between right and wrong can blur, leaving us all to navigate a rather murky terrain with all the wisdom and compassion at our disposal. I'm doing my best Elizabeth. Even if I make choices you wouldn't."

Elizabeth's disappointment still lingered, but some of the sting seemed to have gone out of it.

"I assume you're not planning on giving this up," She arched a single pale eyebrow gracefully. I shook my head.

"Absolutely not. Persisting with this is the only clear path I see to elevating our circumstances. I'm as powerless as anyone to control the merciless plague, of course, but I can counter it with my own form of ruthlessness."

Elizabeth took a deep breath. "I won't betray your trust," she said softly. Her eyes still carried a trace of disapproval, though. "But we clearly don't see eye-to-eye on this."

"I know," I responded, carefully pushing the trunk back under the workbench.

But just you wait. We will, as soon as the vampiric blood is coursing through your veins.

TWELVE

lizabeth's words rang in my ears, echoing with a weight that I couldn't shake off. She had chastised me. And yet I had no intention of stopping my raids. The following afternoon, I was at it again.

Walking the dimly lit streets, I couldn't help but feel a pang of guilt, knowing that while Elizabeth was risking her life to tend to the sick, I was preying upon the vulnerability of the wealthy, like a hyena picking over the bones of injured lions. But then again, maybe our different efforts added up to a sort of cosmic balance.

The familiar cobblestone streets guided my steps as the shadows lengthened around me, leading me to a destination that had long since etched itself into my subconscious.

Before I'd allowed myself to formulate why I was going this way, I found myself standing at the imposing front door of the Elysion residence. Constructed from pristine white stone, it gleamed in the dim twilight which had already descended. The front of the villa was lined with a series of tall, elegant columns, like those of a Roman temple, all covered in acanthus leaves and scrollwork. The heavy, double-wide wooden door at the front seemed like an impenetrable membrane, shielding their fantastical realm from the mundane, pestilence-ridden city.

The twins had made it perfectly clear that they needed time to reflect, but it was as if some invisible force had brought me here to their doorstep tonight. It wasn't an explanation they were likely to buy, of course.

I was only barely able to resist the urge to walk all the way up to the front door and boldly knock. But tempting as it was, the thought of bursting in and demanding that my request for immortality be granted right away, I knew that such a decisive approach might accomplish nothing more than driving my goal farther away from me.

As I stood there, indecisive at the gate, something stirred behind one of the fine and lightly billowing lace curtains. Moments later, the front door's knob turned and Isadora appeared in the doorway.

She was looking straight at me - there was no doubt at all that she'd seen me. And despite the beaked mask still covering my face, I had no doubt at all that she knew it was me. Ah, how I missed being a vampire, missed those refined senses picking up on unnumbered tiny clues that the narrow beam of dull human consciousness simply ignores.

I raised my gloved hands and placed them on the iron gate, and she nodded, extending a silent invitation. I pushed the gate open and stepped through it. She didn't move, but waited for me to join her on the terrace. As I ascended the steps, I pulled off the beaked mask and stuffed it under my arm. No one was in the street behind me - no one saw.

"Gabriel." There wasn't even the faintest glimmer of surprise in her voice. "I didn't know you had plans of entering the medical profession, such as it is at the moment."

"Well, neither did I. Not until I saw an opportunity that was too good to pass up."

Tilting her head slightly to one side, she looked up at me from underneath the lacework of her long, jet-black eyelashes. Her expression was inscrutable. She and her brother were both very good at that. "You've always been an artist, Gabriel, but I see that you also have something of the adventurer in you." Just like her face, her tone was impossible to read. No doubt she knew, without me needing to tell her in so many words, precisely what I was up to, wearing my plague doctor's garb. If need be, I could always show her the contents of my pockets.

"Desperate times call for desperate measures." I said, not actually remembering whether this turn of phrase was in circulation yet in 1665. But it didn't really matter - it conveyed what I wanted to say. "I'm capable of evolving with the times. And isn't it true that only the most adaptable will survive and even thrive in tumultuous times? You've lived through many years; you must know."

I spoke to her not as a desperate mortal beseeching a powerful vampire, but as an equal. At least, that is what I was aiming for.

"I think you're very right about that," Isadora agreed. "My brother and I have had to adapt many times over to new circumstances. We've learned how to embrace the new without abandoning the old - I believe that is key. If you have a strong, solid core, and a malleable outer shell, you'll always find your way. But I'm forgetting my manners. Would you like anything to drink?"

Was this the immortal blood being offered at last, or was Isadora simply playing the gracious hostess?

"Absolutely."

Isadora turned and called in through the still open door for a servant. Moments later, an Indian maid appeared with a glass of water, a pot of richly spiced tea, and a jar of cookies on a silver tray. She placed this on a wrought-iron table that stood on the terrace, and Isadora and I took our seats around it. Isadora, of course, didn't need water or tea, or any other refreshments. But she still watched me expectantly as I politely picked up one of the crumbly cookies, just as I might do when sitting across from a prospective client in my mahogany clad office at Deep Graves.

I nodded my appreciation to the servant girl, who shyly retreated back into the house after filling two china mugs with steaming hot tea.

"Kavya. She's new," Isadora explained. "She's only recently arrived from India and she barely speaks any English yet. Our previous staff all contracted the disease." She sighed at the inconvenience of it. "We've had to quickly replace them. All the new staff are still learning, so I do hope the tea and cookies are to your tastes."

I chewed on my cookie and looked up at the distant stars. In 1665, it was still possible to see the stars at night even in the heart of London.

"They're delightful!" I declared. "I wish you could have some."

Isadora shook her head. "You know I don't require that kind of sustenance. But watching you eat is how I will relish them."

"Say, Isadora, you've never told me how you and Isadore came to be what you are. Night demons, upiors."

A gentle breeze stirred the old oaks in the garden, carrying with it the scent of wisteria.

"Would you really like to know?" Her eyes narrowed,

135

and I nodded, urging her to go on. I'd admittedly never shown much interest in my two patrons' personal histories before, and perhaps that was my mistake. Letting Isadora tell me more about herself and how she came to be a vampire might make her feel closer to me - it might also reveal something important, perhaps something that I could use. I didn't quite know what I was after, but I was sure I'd recognize it if I found it.

"You know that Isadore and I are twins," Isadora started, her voice as soft as the moon's glow as it drifted towards me on the cool evening air, her hands intertwined in her lap. I could see the tension in her as she navigated the presumably intricate rootwork of her past, searching for a suitable place to grab hold and begin. "We were born in Repùblega de Venèsia, the sovereign state and maritime republic of Venice, in 1505."

She paused and looked up from her hands. She was clearly anticipating my reaction.

I merely nodded and gestured for her to continue while stuffing another cookie into my mouth. Hearing that she and her brother had been born in 1505 didn't startle me at all. In fact, I would have guessed that the two of them had walked the Earth for longer than that.

"You accept my words," she said, and it was a statement of fact, not a question.

"Of course," I said. "I trust you. I don't think you have any reason to lie to me."

This flattered her. I could see it in the small smile that curled the edges of her lips.

"But your name," I pointed out, "Elysion. That's not Italian."

She shook her head no. "Our family was originally from

Greece, but they settled in Venice before we were born. Venice was already a very wealthy city when we were growing up. Our family were part of that bustling activity, involved in trade, and as a result Isadore and I both had more than we needed. Our parents were fairly liberal. They allowed both of us to develop our artistic interests and talents. We had an older brother, Apollon, so the responsibility for learning about business and trade rested on his shoulders, not my brother's and certainly not mine. Isadore and I were inseparable throughout our childhood. It was only when we grew up that our paths diverged. Isadore, fascinated by the world of art and the power it held, left his home behind to travel to the great cities of Florence and Rome, the beating heart of the Renaissance. The moment he set foot in those cities," Isadora's voice lilted, taking on an almost reverent tone, "was the moment his life truly began. It was as if he had been a bird trapped in a cage, and suddenly, he found the door open. He sent me many letters describing the city, with its sprawling piazzas, the mighty Duomo, the River Arno. He was fortunate to be taken under the wing of some of the greatest artists of the day. Botticelli, Ghirlandaio, and Perugino – these were his mentors. Even Leonardo let Isadore have a glimpse of his workshop."

Her eyes glimmered, as if Isadore's accomplishments were her own. "But mostly it was Botticelli with his fascination for beauty who taught Isadore to seek it in the most unusual places."

"And what about you?"

Isadora's eyes darkened, and her voice turned soft, almost quiet. "I had to stay behind and get married. Alas, to a much older man who I didn't love. His name no longer matters. Really, during the short, difficult and fruitless years of my marriage, I lived vicariously through my brother's letters and I relished in his growing talents though my own were stunted. Isadore spent days and nights soaking in the wisdom of the masters, learning, observing, and slowly carving out his own unique style. He painted from dawn to dusk, often in a frenzy, forgetting about the world outside the studio. Even, at times, forgetting about me." A note of bitterness or perhaps resentment crept into Isadora's voice.

"When he returned to Venice after his years of apprenticeship, Isadore was changed. No, he wasn't an immortal yet, but his art was no longer just his passion. It had become his identity. And it was his art that led him to Minuetta, and to the fate that awaited him, and well, both of us."

Isadora continued with a note of sadness seeping into her voice. "Minuetta was, as I am sure you have guessed, a night demon, captivated by Isadore's talent. She commissioned him to come and paint the walls of her villa on the island of San Michele. But as you can probably guess, she wasn't honest about what she intended to do."

A shiver crawled up my spine, the air around us turning colder. I knew where this was going. I saw Isadore, the artist, lured into a world he never wished for.

"Sensing something amiss, I followed Isadore to the island," Isadora's voice dropped to a whisper, her hazel eyes now clouded with age-old anger and frustration as she looked through the mists of time and into her own distant past. "When I reached the grand villa, I found Isadore already on the brink of death, his humanity already slipping away in a rush of blood. Faced with the loss of my brother, I did the unthinkable, Gabriel. I beseeched Minuetta to turn me too."

"And she obliged," I said.

"Yes. From that moment on, we were reborn into the world of darkness. The world into which you seem intent on following us." Isadora's words lingered in the air.

"Despite the tragedy of the tale you've just shared with me, I'm still intent on it," I said. I wanted to leave no doubt on the table, so to speak. "I've resolved to become a vampire, a night demon. Nothing, but nothing is going to change my mind. Don't you see?"

"It is Isadore who is dead set against your transformation," Isadora suddenly revealed, leaning forward. I immediately sat up a little straighter in my wrought-iron chair, all of my senses now fully alert.

I'd known, sensed somehow, that something interesting was going to come up in this conversation, something that I could use. I'd been right; this was it. So Isadore had been dead set against them turning me. What had ultimately changed his mind?

Out loud I said, "Why is that, if I come to the darkness of my own volition?"

"Because," Isadore's voice cut into my flow of words. He was suddenly standing at the table, directly between us. I hadn't heard the door open, had not sensed him approaching. Quickly I suppressed the very real urge to leap out of my seat like a damned rabbit, or should I say, a damned mortal.

"The dark flame," Isadore went on as he let his gaze move from me to Isadora and back again while his elegant hands - artist's hands - were splayed on the table, "robbed me of my most valuable gift. Leaving my humanity behind meant leaving my right to participate in the human endeavor of art. And you too are an artist, Gabriel." His dark eyes locked with mine beseechingly. "You're much more than a craftsman. I wouldn't take that away from you."

"Isadore," I greeted him, as a dark realization settled heavily on my shoulders. By outdoing myself, my going above and beyond in my creation of the Elysion twins' Black Death caskets, I had impressed them just as I'd intended - but I had also impressed Isadore with such talent that he had become reluctant to snatch me out of my human existence. Now I understood, and my blood ran cold in my veins. I might have fumbled my plan to change the course of history for the better.

"But I don't see it the same way you do," I protested, my words feeble in my own ears. "Becoming a vampire won't stop me from creating, it won't cool my appreciation for beauty. On the contrary, it'll set me free to pursue my talents and realize my potential in a way that being constrained by my human form and lifespan simply won't allow."

Isadore looked perturbed, as if he had never before entertained this decidedly more optimistic perspective.

My voice grew in strength and resonance proportionate to my conviction as I went on, "You, too, could continue creating, Isaodre. I mean, why not? You can pick up your brush again and get back to your craft. Surely your eye for beauty hasn't weakened as a result of any perceived crime or sin you've committed."

"Well...perhaps not."

Powerful, conflicting emotions danced over Isadore's features. Anger, hope, confusion. Finally he simply hunched forward and allowed himself to sink down into the third chair at the table. "Gabriel," he murmured. "What if you're right? This is something I haven't allowed myself to consider. But no, it isn't possible."

"But what if it could be, Isadore? I am asking you to just imagine it."

A new glimmer of hope stirred in my chest. If I was able to change Isadore's perspective, I would have given him an immense gift - a gift that demanded a proper reward.

THIRTEEN

S hadows chased each other over the stern-looking facade of the Clayfield plague hospital as I approached it. Like many of the buildings that have been erected during the 20th and 21st Centuries, Clayfield had been slapped together in haste in order to serve a need, without, it has to be said, much consideration given to aesthetics. The bare walls, the paneless windows, and the unadorned front door with its heavy lock were all testimony to this tragic fact.

Last night's conversation with the Elysion twins had turned out rather constructive. I'd learned that Isadore was the bottleneck, and that his reluctance to offer me the blood had to do with his own qualms and sensibilities. I was furious of course that Isadore would deny me the gift of immortality, simply because he was struggling to consolidate his vampiric nature with his creative gift. I mean, how selfish does one vampire have the right to be?

At least I'd left there feeling confident that I'd succeeded in planting a seed in Isadore's mind. A seed that I was fully committed to keep feeding and tending to, until it bore fruit.

But now to the matter at hand. I was here to collect Elizabeth after one of her many long and arduous shifts. And, as a secondary motive, I rather hoped that showing my face and smiling affably to a few of Elizabeth's colleagues and patients might help to stamp out any of the unfortunate necromancy rumors about me that were in circulation.

This wasn't the first time the rumor mill of St Bride's and neighboring parishes had been abuzz with my name. This month it was necromancy, and at various points throughout my mortal life, it had been the implicit crime and devastating moral offense of homosexuality. I had never been careless enough to feed the rumor mill a shred of tangible evidence, but that was of very little consequence.

To this day, I still like to take a sort of aloof but direct approach to dealing with rumors. You cannot stop them from cropping up, but you can go out there and amass a proportionate amount of goodwill to balance them out when they inevitably do. Being a well-known figure around the neighborhood seems a formidable cloak of invisibility and protection.

Of course, the moral offence that could potentially warrant my execution in the 21st Century is vampirism. If it isn't one thing, it's another, know what I mean?

I watched as the locked door leading into the hospital creaked open, revealing a glimpse of bustling activity as a tall and rather bony plague nurse left the building. Framed by the door, I could see more nurses hurrying back and forth, their faces drawn with varying degrees of exhaustion. They were all wearing long gowns as well as hoods and gloves made of heavy fabric designed to cover as much of the body as possible. Not for the sake of modesty but to prevent the disease from making contact with the wearers' skin.

As the departing plague nurse stepped out, I slipped through the door. Reaching into the inner pocket of my blazer - yes, the very same that I had brought from the future and which had become rather the symbol of comfort to me; one of the only tangible reminders I had that my immortal existence and all of the trappings that came with it were not mere figments of my imagination - I withdrew a small skull-shaped silver box from its depths. Clicking the skull open, I pinched the cognac-soaked sponge it contained between thumb and forefinger and held it to my nose. It helped filter out the stench of disease and human filth, but only to a point. I started walking through the dimly lit corridor.

The horrible odor grew in intensity, as did the sounds of human misery. Makeshift beds crowded the hallway, each occupied by a soul caught in the grip of the Black Death. There were more plague victims here than there were beds, of course, so some of them were simply crouching or lying down in the shadowy corners.

As I moved past the beds, I took great care not to as much as brush any of their inhabitants with a corner of the cape I was wearing this evening - a long, billowing, bottle-green affair that was sure to help me get seen.

I deliberately avoided looking any of these poor victims in the eye as I strode past them. Now, I may not be the most compassionate creature that ever walked the earth, but seeing all of these lives reduced to this, to such indignity, stirred my sense of indignation, and yes, it even tugged at my heartstrings a little.

As soon as I reached the hospital's main ward, I spotted Elizabeth. She was bent over a patient, removing leeches from the woman's pale and papery skin. As she detached a leech with a wet sound, a few drops of blood ran down the woman's arm. They were the only color inside this damned place.

The sight of blood should have ignited a spark of excitement in me, but instead, I stood there unaffected by the crimson fluid. I was even mildly disgusted by the slurping sounds the leeches made.

I made my way towards Elizabeth, whose grace, poise and soul-deep compassion had never shone as brightly as in this god-forsaken place. If I'd shared Isadore's perspective on things, I wouldn't have been able to even entertain the idea of replacing her dazzling, human light with the dark vampiric flame.

Elizabeth had finished the procedure involving the leeches. She placed the little bloodsuckers in a jar before turning to her patient again to tend to the wounds their hungry little mouths had left behind.

Stepping forward, I caught her eye. She lit up, beaming proudly at me as she removed her gloves and placed them in a nearby basin.

"Elizabeth," I said, stepping fully out of the shadows. "Are you ready to go?"

The patient, a husk of a woman, probably in her forties, had been lying impassively blinking up against the dim light falling through the windows far above. But then her eyes landed on me and a flicker of something like understanding passed through them.

Her face contorted and her already sunken cheeks hollowed even further as she lifted and pointed one trembling skeletal finger at me, croaking, but all too loudly,

"This man, he isn't human! He shouldn't be here! He shouldn't be in here!"

Elizabeth, startled, turned to her patient again. In a soft tone of voice she attempted to calm her down. But it was to no avail, the woman having already erupted into blood-curdling screams that ricocheted off the walls of the plague house. "He isn't human!" she kept repeating with increasing urgency, "Someone get him out of here! Get him out!"

The screamed accusations sent my heart beating like a hammer in my chest. What madness, or what absolute clarity, had gripped this woman?

I quickly stepped backward into the shadows, hoping that creating some distance between us would calm the hysterical patient down, but instead, she was practically convulsing in terror, bucking against her bed in the most theatrical manner imaginable. A beaked doctor, several nurses, and two men that might have been wardens or guards all came running from different directions. The guards held the agitated patient down against the bed while two of the nurses wrapped sheets around both her body and the bedframe.

So much for stilling the rumors; it seemed I had doused them in gasoline instead.

As soon as all of the others moved in, Elizabeth gracefully and wisely extracted herself from the situation and came walking towards me, her unsettled feelings stamped all over her face.

"Gabriel," she sounded rattled. "I'm not sure what happened. I suppose agitation and fear can play horrible tricks on people's minds."

"Clearly," I said, trying not to let her see that I, too, had been shaken by the patient's outburst. I sighed inwardly.

The patient's screams still reverberated in my ears, and worse, throughout the entire building, as we made our way toward the exit.

We were about to leave Clayfield through the same odious corridor I'd arrived through only moments earlier when Malm Westminster came into view. He was without his usual plague doctor mask, which he held folded in one large hand as he moved with purposeful, heavy strides.

Trailing him were four acolytes, or I suppose I should call them assistants. They were maneuvering two heavy carts laden not with corpses, but with gravely ill patients whose moans echoed eerily through the corridor. On their faces I saw emotions ranging from confusion to despair, and I'm fairly certain more than one was oblivious to their destination.

Spotting us, a leery grin immediately spread across Westminster's face, his eyes glinting mischievously. He motioned for his assistants to continue, and they hauled their sorrowful cargo deeper into the building.

Westminster blocked our path to the exit by quite literally placing his own large frame in the doorway. The door was still ajar, and a light breeze of blessedly cool, relatively clean air was blowing in from the world outside.

"Ah, Elizabeth," Westminster was blatantly ignoring me. "Are you leaving so soon? I had so hoped to speak with you before your shift ended."

"And why is that?" Elizabeth's tone was polite enough, but her eyebrows knitted together and her arms were folded across her slight chest. When she didn't like someone, it was always perfectly obvious.

But not to Malm Westminster, whose dark eyes, sharp and intrusive, lingered on her. He was openly appraising her as best he could manage it given the cumbersome nurse's uniform that she was still wearing. "I wanted to express my admiration," he said, "for your dedicated work here. Let me get straight to the point. Seeing how... tenderly you care for our patients makes me wonder what a fine wife you would make."

Westminster's words hung thick in the air, charging it with a palpable tension. Elizabeth was visibly affected, but she faced him head-on. "My personal life, Westminster, is none of your concern." There was a steely edge to her tone.

Undeterred, Westminster picked up his red thread, "Perhaps we could discuss this further at another time. For now, I simply wanted to pay you a compliment and share my thoughts. That is no crime, is it?" He flashed her a lecherous smile that also happened to reveal newly golden teeth gleaming in his upper jaw. Whether these lavish replacements for his original canines were due to rot or wanting to make a bit of a statement was a little unclear.

Either way, the audacity of Westminster's comments and demeanor irked me and I had allowed both to go on for long enough without comment.

"Westminster," I said, my tone of voice civil, but for the first time in any of our exchanges I was allowing an undercurrent of threat to emerge in my words as I stepped up right in front of him. "I recommend that you watch your tongue, not to mention your traveling eye. Elizabeth, if it wasn't already perfectly evident, is not in the market for a husband, certainly not for someone more than twice her age."

Unfazed by the coldness of my words, Westminster's grin only broadened. "How endearing," he remarked, taking a deliberate step closer, his voice laden with self-assured arrogance. "Gabriel, your parents have raised a remarkable young woman in Elizabeth. But she can't remain sheltered under their roof indefinitely. To do so would be akin to stifling a blooming plant by denying it fertile soil. A rare gem like Elizabeth deserves to thrive in conditions suited to her potential. Moreover," he continued, his beady eyes gleaming, "with all those unfortunate rumors of necromancy looming over your family, it might be wise to consider securing her future sooner rather than later. In her current pristine state, her allure is at its peak, a concept perhaps beyond your grasp."

Biting back my anger, I responded, "Rumors are just that, Westminster - ephemeral whispers that fade when nothing is found to support them."

This, of course, wasn't true. As a former witch finder, Westminster had gotten plenty of men, women and children alike, drowned, hung or burned at the stake, all without a shred of anything that could pass for real evidence. He hadn't needed anything as crude as that; not when all he had needed to do was stoke the flames of the fear and superstition that were already burning bright in British minds all up and down the country at the time.

"Sometimes, Gabriel. But there are times when rumors etch themselves indelibly onto one's reputation, much like a stubborn stain on a garment that simply refuses to come out, no matter what you do." As he leaned closer, his eyes sparkled with self-satisfaction. "Surely you grasp the delicate position your dear little sister is now in. Tales of witchcraft and necromancy could tarnish her good name, potentially limiting her opportunities in life. I'd venture to say that a gentleman like myself might not just be a suitable match, but perhaps the best she could aspire to. I'll be sure to discuss my intentions with your parents. I imagine they'll be quite taken with my suggestions."

"I'd rather you didn't," Elizabeth interjected. Westminster glanced at her, his expression a curious mix of lasciviousness and surprise.

"But my dear Elizabeth, you're far too young to discern what's best. And your brother? He's just as clueless. Still unmarried and without offspring? Well, we all know what that means."

My patience was wearing thin. "Be careful, Westminster."

"Oh, should I be afraid, Graves?" Westminster's tone was mocking. "You'd do well to remember where you stand. You're in my domain." He gestured broadly, perhaps referencing the plague hospital or, more broadly, the era in which we found ourselves. Either way, I got the message.

I considered wiping the smug look off Westminster's face by planting my first in his mouth and hopefully knocking his new gold teeth loose.

But no, no, that wasn't wise. The short-term satisfaction it would bring me was, if only slightly, outweighed by the potential consequences. It seemed I had already made a bit of an enemy of Westminster. I was in no rush to cement our standing.

Elizabeth's anxious eyes, which had regarded Westminster with disdain throughout our exchange, now settled on me. Her reassuring hand gently touched my back.

Taking a deep breath, I managed to force my anger down. I reminded myself that, unbeknownst to Westminster, I had an escape route in the works. An escape route that would ensure that Elizabeth and I would never have to be at his mercy.

"Thank you for the conversation, Westminster," I said, slipping back into an infallibly polite tone that I knew he would find infuriating. "However, we really must be going.

Business is booming at Graves and Sons, as you can well imagine."

Westminster bowed slightly, his sardonic smile wavering. He had hoped, I sensed, that I would lose my temper. He was trying to provoke me, even now. But I knew better than to engage.

As Westminster finally stepped aside so that Elizabeth and I could step out of Clayfield, I could feel the weight of his gaze, like two piercing coals, burning into the back of my skull. The man hated me. I could only hope that he was too busy to do anything about it.

FOURTEEN

The moon hung high in the night sky, casting its silvery light over the city. I stood in the shadows outside Westminster's opulent residence on Temple Place. It was near the river, in a prestigious area not far from Bride Lane, but rather a lot more upscale. The dark waters of the Thames were just out of sight, but the light breeze and the muddy smell of river water were reminders of the proximity of this place to the river.

I'd tried to talk myself out of this, but only briefly. The part of me that resented Westminster and wanted to put him firmly in his place was simply too much of a smooth talker.

I burned with a desire to teach Malm Westminster a lesson he wouldn't be able to forget in a hurry. Challenging him directly, any more than I already had done, was out of the question. It was simply too risky. Still, it was time to turn the tables, to show him that his power and privilege did not grant him perfect invincibility and safety, at least not from me.

The heavy iron gates that guarded the entrance to his

home seemed to mock me, but I knew that with a little persistence, I'd be find a way in. After all, this was 1665 and burglar alarms were not even something people could have imagined.

Westminster had no wife and no children for me to worry about. A man of Malm Westminster's caliber had of course not made it to the age of fifty as a bachelor. He'd been married once, my father had told me, but when he discovered his wife in bed with another woman, he had simultaneously discovered her to be a witch. And who knows, had there been no Alexandra Westminster, it might never have occurred to Malm to become a witch finder.

There might be guard dogs or even a servant behind those darkened windows, but if I encountered either, I would treat them to just a few drops, held over a handkerchief over their mouth and nose, of the special solution I'd concocted in the Graves family kitchen while my mother and Elizabeth slept peacefully. It contained just enough deadly nightshade to subdue but not to kill.

Thanks to Elizabeth, I had a good idea of when Westminster would be working one of his shifts - and tonight, I expected him to not return until sunrise. In other words, a luxurious expanse of hours stretched out before me. I was more than happy to forego a night of sleep for the sake of putting the fear into Westminster.

Silently, I crept along the perimeter of the sweet-smelling garden, my footsteps as light as I was able to make them. The fence was tall, but at the back of the house, protruding through the sidewalk and leaning over the fence, stood an apple tree. It could not have been more perfect. Thanking whatever powers orchestrate these kinds of useful coincidences, I climbed up into the branches and let myself drop down softly in the grass on the other side.

Right now was one of those situations where I became aware of how powerful my vampiric gifts usually made me. How I missed them! How unconcerned I would be if I had them.

Nevertheless, I made my way through the garden, ducking under branches and stepping over rotting fruit and fallen branches on the ground that might squelch or crack under my feet and give me away.

The night air was filled with the electric charge of my anticipation, and my heart was pounding forcefully in my chest.

Finding an unlocked thick paned window on the ground floor, I carefully pushed it open. I breathed a sigh of relief when the night remained unbroken, and with a nimble grace that it had taken me weeks to even begin to find in my mortal form, I slipped inside, stepping into the darkness of the villa. I listened for any signs of movement, but so far, so good.

My eyes slowly adjusted to the dimness of my surroundings. I was standing in a well-appointed hallway, with plenty of rather imposing landscape paintings hanging on the walls around me, most of them incongruously featuring scenes of tranquil British countryside and sunsets. Did these paintings represent a different, softer side of Malm Westminster? Clearly, they had been chosen by a man who appreciated beautiful things. But then again, you can appreciate beautiful things and still be a colossal bastard.

Now, my focus honed in on the task at hand - locating Westminster's most valuable possessions. The thought of stripping him of some of his ill-gotten wealth filled me with a sense of glee. Not only would I be adding to my own bottom line, I'd be subtracting from his. It was a rather beautiful concept.

Room by room, I searched, my hands deftly navigating through drawers and cabinets, reaching for what I found of value. And there were lots, because as I've said, Westminster had always been a vulture. Diamonds, gold, and priceless jewelry gleamed in the moonlight as I tucked them away. Anything that was small enough to carry went into my pockets, and once they started filling up, I emptied two sofa pillowcases to use as makeshift bags.

My eyes darted around as I continued my raid through the rooms of Westminster's home. I had a strange feeling in my gut - a feeling telling me that I was going to find something of interest or importance. A man like Westminster had to be keeping secrets, no?

My fingers brushed against the delicate fabrics and polished surfaces of fine furniture and opulent upholstery, leaving behind an invisible trail of my intrusion, but what of it? Things like forensic fingerprint testing were still centuries into the future. How easy crime - any sort of crime - had been in the olden days. It was astounding, I mused, what people in the 1600s had been able to get away with, had they wanted to. It was just fortunate that most people are either too good or simply too lazy to do each other harm.

It was when I entered the master bedroom, done up with lavish drapes and plush furnishings, that my eyes fell on a sight that made my blood run cold. This was accompanied by a sinking feeling in my chest.

On the polished mahogany table by the bedside, amidst an array of trinkets and treasures, lay a delicate lock of hair. The pale golden strands glistened under the soft glow of the moon from the windows.

Time seemed to stand still for a moment as I stared at that lock of hair, my mind swirling with disbelief. This was Elizabeth's hair, it had to be. I didn't even need to hold it up to my own head for comparison - the pale golden luster and the fine silky texture of it clearly matched.

I picked up the lock of hair and clutched it tightly in my hand. Leering at my adolescent sister was apparently no longer enough to satisfy Westminster's attraction to her. And here in my hand I held her very essence reduced to a mere possession. A trophy, or perhaps an appetizer.

How had Westminster acquired this? I imagined him cutting the lock from Elizabeth's head while she, distracted and unsuspecting, was tending to one of her patients. In my mind's eye, I saw Westminster's hulking form looming over her, a pair of glinting shears in his hand.

Fury coursed through my veins and my hand reflexively tightened. Without even thinking about it, I slipped the lock into my pocket. I couldn't leave it here, couldn't let Westminster keep it, simple as.

I was about to leave the bedroom when my eyes happened to fall on a display cabinet standing between the room's two street-facing windows. There was something about its presence that compelled me to take a closer look.

I walked over to it, straining my eyes to see in the dark. Damned mortal eyesight!

Its shelves were covered in what appeared to be little jars.

I leaned in closer. The jars contained more locks of hair. Blonde, caramel, chestnut, copper, black, silver... It was quite an eclectic collection.

How many women's hair had Westminster gathered, and more disturbingly, how and why?

It was possible that he had taken these from plague

victims, or from nurses at the various plague hospitals that he supplied with patients. Some of them might be from the many witches whose deaths he'd caused over the years.

There were other possibilities, too, and I wouldn't put any of the ones that sprang to mind past him. Like I said earlier, crime detection was a much more primitive endeavor then than it is now. There was no way for police to lift fingerprints, test DNA or even organize a cohesive search across London's loosely connected boroughs. Unless a criminal was caught in the act - or was followed by an unshakeable cloud of rumors - his crimes, no matter what they might be, were likely to go unpunished.

Malm Westminster was a respectable man, a man above suspicion. If he took advantage of his patients or staff, who was to know, or indeed believe his victims? I'd known Westminster to be a despicable character, but I'd never suspected, well, whatever this was. What was this?

I decided that I couldn't stand around here brooding any longer, and as I crept deeper into the house again, the air seemed to thicken with my growing sense of righteous anger.

Thoughts of Westminster's taunting demeanor and his insinuations, the way he'd belittled and essentially bullied my entire family for years, echoed in my mind, fueling the resentment and disgust I felt for him. The urge to shock him, to punish him somehow, had only grown with the discovery of his little jar collection.

Returning to the living room, my eyes sought out a gilded vase displayed on a marble pedestal, its delicate beauty a manifestation of the wealth and privilege that Westminster had shrouded himself in like a protective shield. Without a second thought, I pushed the vase onto the floor. Now, I'd never promote the destruction of beautiful artifacts, but sometimes, just sometimes, it's all right to make an exception. The vase shattered into countless pieces that flew across the room. The noise echoed off the walls and ceilings. I looked down at the scattered pieces.

It had felt good to release some of the anger from my body - so good, in fact, that I reached for another vase. There were plenty to pick from; Westminster's sense of decor could be described as a form of overblown, indiscriminate maximalism, a magpie's nest. There were plenty of shelves filled with fine china, statues, vases.

Over the course of the next five or ten or fifteen minutes - I lost track of time, admittedly - it all went onto the floor. Everything that wasn't small or valuable enough to carry. When I'd had enough and was overcome with exhaustion, I left by the front door, closing it neatly behind me.

Only as I made my way back down the garden path to the gate did it occur to me that all of the sound I had been making could have awakened and even summoned the neighbors. Indeed, someone could have seen me as I waltzed out the front door with my characteristic mane of pale golden hair gleaming in the moonlight.

I can only put it down to my vampiric arrogance, a thing not so easily shaken. I was still so used to being able to move about effortlessly and soundlessly that I constantly had to remind myself of the potential consequences of attracting attention.

With my makeshift bags filled with the spoils of my audacious breakin, I made my way back through the narrow streets from Westminster's Temple Place residence to the Graves home in Bride Lane. The night had been a triumph, a bold move that I very much hoped would send shockwaves through Westminster's world. He would have to be exceptionally dimwitted to not get the memo - the message that no one is untouchable.

This, I admonished myself, included me. Had breaking into the home of someone I knew - and was known to resent - perhaps been foolhardy? I wasn't sure, and it was too late now, at any rate.

In my mind's eye, I saw Westminster return to his home after a long night of threatening and torturing the neighborhood's population of the sick and dying. Stepping through his front door, it wouldn't take him long to sense that he had had a visitor.

As it turned out, my smugness was exceptionally short-lived.

I WAS NAVIGATING through Thornhill Mansion's second floor corridor once again, this time moving in the opposite direction.

What, really, was I doing here? What kept drawing me back to this place? Wouldn't it make more sense if I were to haunt my own grand villa in Queen's Wood when I went on my out-of-body excursions?

Yet here I was, and when I reached the end of the corridor, I pushed the door inward. I stepped through the door into a bedroom which was furnished with a closet easily large enough to hold a king's wardrobe, and an imposing four-poster bed and a lacquered desk under a garden-facing window, all carved of the same gleaming, lacquered mahogany. The room was shrouded in darkness, all but the desk, which was bathed in the light of a purple and red stained-glass Tiffany lamp.

Bending over the desk was Venedict, with a fountain

pen in his hand and a notebook full of scribbles in front of him. He was as beautiful as ever, youthfully androgynous, with his large amber eyes, button nose and cruel mouth. He turned halfway around at the sound of the door as it swung open.

I stood completely frozen. How to even begin to explain my appearance here, in ghost-form, wearing a white flannel nightshirt?

Venedict's large amber eyes fixated on the dark corridor behind me. "Who's there?" he demanded. So he couldn't see me. But how come Octavia could?

"Make yourself known!" Venedict pushed back his chair, slammed his notebook shut with what seemed like excessive force, and stood up. "Whoever you are, step forward."

"Venendict," I said, somewhat hesitant, "Can't you see me? Can you at least hear me?"

Despite the bad blood that had come between us, Venedict might be willing to help me out of my predicament - he might at least offer some insights, or consult some of the occult books in his well stocked library on my behalf. He might even contact Csilla on my behalf.

But that he could neither see nor hear me became abundantly clear when he stepped forward, and through me, and out into the corridor.

He shivered, as if he'd stepped into a freezer. "Damned ghosts," he declared, having surveyed the corridor. Then, as the room faded from my view, he returned to his desk and popped his notebook back open.

THE DREAM EVAPORATED like dew in the sun the moment I opened my eyes. Forgetting, for the umpteenth time, the low and slanted ceiling above my bed, I banged my forehead against it as I sat up.

Cursing under my breath, I slipped out from under the covers and stepped out into the middle of the room. Here I stood very still and alert, trying to discern the nature of the disturbance that had interrupted my sleep. Ah, there there it was, a faint whiff of burning leather.

All had been peaceful when I'd returned home after my little visit to Westminster's abode in the wee hours of the morning. Now, something was off.

Still wearing my white flannel nightshirt and breeches, I thundered down the rickety wooden staircase, my heart beating in my throat and threatening to leap out of my mouth. Something was burning - hopefully not Graves & Sons. The Great Fire of London wasn't due until next year, at least there was that.

I reached the ground floor and was quickly led by the smell of dark smoke coming from the workshop. A cacophony of thoughts were already tumbling through my mind. Had Westminster seen me leave his home after all? Was he already exacting his revenge?

I choked as I tore open the door to the workshop and a cloud of dark, acrid smoke billowed outward.

It took a few seconds to clear, and when it did I was able to make out the outline of Elizabeth's lithe body illuminated by the crackling fire which was rising from the floor.

She raised her gaze to meet mine. She seemed both anxious and proud to have been caught red-handed. Sparks crackled around us as she looked at me defiantly.

Then my heart dropped as I noticed my plague doctor's

garb gathered in a miserable little heap on the floor with white hot flames rising from it.

I lunged towards the tiny fire. In a state of panic, I reached into the licking and dancing flames, trying to save whatever I could. The flames burned with a vengeance as I tried to grab the leather pieces before they were completely charred. But it was already too late. The mask, the apron and the coat all were already completely blackened and sticking together. And moments later, all that was left were some smoldering ashes. I'd only just about managed to save the heavy leather gloves, and what good were they on their own?

"What have you done?" I whipped around to look at Elizabeth with more vitriol than she'd ever sensed from me before. "Why would you burn my things? Do you have any idea how valuable they are, what you're putting at risk by doing this?"

"I don't care! I worry about what will happen if you continue down this dark path that you're on." Elizabeth was trying to sound defiant, but the hardness in her voice was already melting in the heat of my anger. "I fear what will happen if you're discovered."

I shook my head, fighting to get a grip on my emotions.

"Elizabeth," I said in a much quieter tone of voice. "I know that you only wanted to protect me, I understand that, but really you've no idea what you've done."

"And you, Gabriel, have no idea how blinded you've become by something like greed. You're simply not seeing the danger! You're not yourself! You're different."

"Gabriel, Elizabeth! What on earth is going on here?"

We both froze as our mother's voice cut through the thick smoke that still filled the workshop, despite the now open door to the shop.

Slowly, I turned my head enough to allow myself a glance over my shoulder. The smoke in the room was quickly thinning, and there she stood in the doorway, arms folded across her chest. Confusion and disappointment were both clearly visible in her pale blue eyes as she shifted her gaze between her two children. "I implore you to explain yourselves. But keep your voices down, by all means, unless you're hell-bent on rousing the entire neighborhood."

I answered her, my voice trembling with frustration, "Elizabeth accidentally knocked over a flammable liquid that I've been experimenting with as a means of stopping the plague from transferring from corpses."

Glancing at Elizabeth out of the corner of my eye, I was silently imploring her to take my lead.

Slowly, Elizabeth nodded.

Silence hung heavily in the room while our mother weighed my words, apparently debating whether or no to press for a deeper truth. Meanwhile the remnants of my burned disguise were blowing across the floor in the form of soft gray ashes. The smell of charred fabric hung in the air, clinging to the walls and our clothes and hair.

Marie Graves' eyes scanned my face and then the room with obvious disappointment. But then she sighed and said, in a voice that brooked no argument. "I want you both to clean up this mess. And then we will never speak of this again. Now I will go back to bed, and when I come back down here in a few hours it will be as if this incident never took place. Is that understood?"

Elizabeth and I both bowed our heads and silently nodded.

The crackling of the fire had subsided and was soon replaced by the soft rustle of movement as we set to work.

FIFTEEN

T he floorboards creaked beneath my weight as I stepped into the workshop. The hidden secret I had buried beneath them was now calling for my attention.

I knelt down, the coolness of the wooden floor sending a shiver up my spine. My hands brushed against the rough surface, as I carefully pried open the floorboards, revealing the hidden burial place of plague doctor Ellery.

He had been there for weeks now, and it was only really my frequent fumigations of the space with sprigs of lavender and cedar wood that kept it from stinking to high heavens. Still, with the floorboards out of the way, the pungent smell of the corpse rose into my nostrils, making me gag.

If only I was a vampire now, the sights and smells of death wouldn't have bothered me. I remembered reading in some scientific journal about how humans have an instinctive revulsion for disease as a way to keep themselves safe from getting sick. As a vampire, I had been above and beyond all that, so disease had seemed neither threatening or disgusting to me. I'd almost forgotten that it had ever been any different. Of course my time spent here had thoroughly reminded me.

Now I reached down and grasped the plague doctor's lifeless form and hoisted him up and onto the floor. Loath to touch the rotting corpse with my bare hands, I'd put on Ellery's own thick leather gloves. They were all I had left after Elizabeth's rebellious attack on my plans earlier today and they still had blackened fingertips and reeked of smoke.

Ellery was heavier than expected, his body bloated with the gasses of decay. There was a big open wound in the crown of his skull to remind me of the violent end he had met at my hands.

I wrestled the corpse onto the floorboards and proceeded to wrap it in a sheet and, after assuring myself as best I could that no neighbors were watching, I dragged it across the dark courtyard and into the stable. It was late evening now and the best chance I was going to get at carrying out these clandestine deeds undisturbed.

Once inside the stable, I placed Ellery's sheet-wrapped corpse alongside the similarly shrouded figures of my father and Dwight which I had already unearthed from their shallow graves in the dirt floor. It was time to get rid of every trace of evidence that Westminster or one of his ilk might sniff out and pin me to.

I first burned my father's and Dwight's corpses, dousing them in oil before standing back to watch their funeral pyre. I'd carefully splashed some water on the ground around them - it wasn't yet time to let the entire shed go up in flame.

A somber silence enveloped the space as I watched the flames dance and consume their bodies. It took a while, but when it was done I carefully gathered their ashes. Then, I set the remains of plague doctor Ellery aflame and left the shed, allowing it to burn to the ground in its entirety.

Ellery's ashes I didn't collect but simply washed away by throwing several bucketfuls of water onto the smoldering remains of the burnt-down shed.

At one point my mother opened a window in the building behind me, but she didn't call out to ask what the hell I thought I was doing, burning down her shed. Marie Graves was an intelligent woman and she probably assumed that whatever I was getting rid of was something connected to the plague doctor's garb that Elizabeth and I had been fighting over earlier. And so, once she had assured herself that nothing had caught fire accidentally, she closed the window again.

Once I had obliterated both the three corpses and the shed - which didn't take long, thanks to the oil I'd splashed liberally over the thin boards it was made of - I carefully gathered my stash of stolen wealth from the various hiding places where I'd been keeping it. I retrieved gold coins and precious stones from underneath loose floorboards, pearl earrings from a box tucked away in the loft, gold and silver rings from a hollowed out crossbeam in the attic, the two stuffed pillowcases I'd taken with me from Westminster's home and hidden in a cupboard.

I sealed all of these things inside an unremarkable pinewood casket, ensuring its contents were secure and hidden from prying eyes.

Before I'd begun my corpse-burning spree, I had headed over to Isadore and Isadora's villa, where I had asked to borrow their magnificent black coach, accompanied by their trusted driver, whose name I had finally learnt was Nicholas Lacey. Glancing out the window of Graves & Sons,

I could see that the coach was already waiting for me outside in Bride Lane.

I wasn't wearing any disguise - it wasn't necessary. After all, the sight of a coffin builder carrying a pinewood coffin into the street during the worst outbreak of plague that London had ever seen was nothing unusual.

The casket was heavy with treasure when I carried it out to the waiting vehicle. I struggled to carry it on my own, but I managed to load it into the coach. I also brought with me a shovel and a small round ceramic vase containing a blend of Dwight's and my father's ashes. The carriage rolled through the winding streets, its wheels echoing the beat of my restless heart.

When we reached our destination, Cemetery Bottom Wood (which, much to my annoyance, had later been renamed Queen's Wood), I asked Lacey, the driver, to wait for me at the forest edge. Used to complying with his employers' unusual schedules and requests, the man didn't even lift an eyebrow.

I unloaded the heavy casket and half carried, half dragged it along the damp ground, deeper into the woods. I wanted precisely no one to see where I intended to bury my treasure. Moonlight filtered through the canopy of leaves overhead and cast a mesmerizing glow over the timeless and familiar forest floor.

How I loved this place! This was my true home. I was overcome by a sense of nostalgia for the future. When I'd first arrived here, I'd been so thrilled that traveling back in time had proven possible that I'd immediately started toying with the idea of making several more trips back to my former life, but after eight weeks or so of actually having lived it, I'd had more than enough. The dusty, cramped and dirty London of 1665 just wasn't for me.

Finding the exact clearing in the woods I knew would be mine, I began to dig a grave. The soil was rich and fragrant, an earthy embrace that would soon welcome the secrets I entrusted to its depths. As I shoveled the dirt, I imagined my majestic Villa Graves with its beautiful gardens and the artificial lake that would one day inhabit this spot.

It took me a while to get there, working on my own as I was, but once I was satisfied that the hole was deep enough, I pushed the heavy casket into the earth and covered it up again. Then I sat down in the spot, taking my time to memorize every detail about it with crystal clarity. After all, what good was risking your life for riches if you were to lose track of where you'd buried it?

When I was sure I had remembered the spot clearly, that I'd managed to sear it into my brain, I sprang to my feet and wiped away any dirt that clung to me. It was now time for the second part of my reason for being here.

I retrieved the small vase containing my beloved relatives' ashes from my jacket. I wore the black suit I'd arrived in from the future; it was suitable funeral attire.

With the vase cradled in one arm as carefully as if it were an infant, I tipped it over and spilled out its contents into the sky with a puff of breath. I imagined that it carried the spirits of Dwight and my father away on invisible clouds, and that they would always roam these woods and be part of this land.

～

My mission had taken several hours more than I'd anticipated, and so again it was early morning by the time I returned to Graves & Sons. I thanked Lacey as I stepped from the coach seat and onto the cobblestones of Bride Lane which were glistening after a brief shower of rain. Again he didn't deign to answer but simply rode off in the direction of Knightsbridge.

Exhausted from the night's events and covered in dirt, I decided to first have a wash and then to make straight for my bed.

I was still in the bathroom, letting the warm water wash away the grime of my endeavors, when suddenly I heard brusque voices rising from the shop premises downstairs. What the blazes?

Alarmed, I quickly got dressed and rushed down the creaky staircase to find out what was going on. There had been quite enough drama around me these past few days and nights, thanks.

Just as I stepped down onto the shop floor of Graves & Sons, the door swung open with a forceful shove or perhaps a kick, aimed at it from whoever was standing outside in the courtyard.

Probably unsurprisingly, it was Malm Westminster who came barging in, flanked by two searchers, one of whom I recognized as Widow Nesbit's eldest son, Blaine. I'd played with him often as a child and had, ever since my earliest recollections, considered him a wimpy and spineless weasel. The fact that he had grown into a broad-shouldered, barrel-chested adult hadn't changed my perception one iota.

Blaine Nesbit had nothing but his hulking build going for him. Somehow he possessed the unfortunate combination of his mother's hawkish facial features and his deceased father's ginger hair. Now as he stepped into Graves & Sons, he wore the sort of shit-eating grin that wouldn't have looked out of place on the face of a 21st century corporate worker bee who will do anything to please and impress his boss.

The other searcher, a much shorter and younger man with sandy brown hair, was someone I didn't recognize.

My heart raced as I watched them stride towards me, their boots clacking against the wooden floor. Malm's face was twisted in a snarl, and I could see the veins bulging in his powerful neck. It was clear that he was both furious and looking for someone to aim it at.

"Westminster," I said. I was trying to remain calm despite his clearly combative attitude, "To what do I owe the pleasure?"

"What do you think I'm doing here, Graves?" Westminster practically spat the words out, stopping just inches away from me. We were of even height, but bis bulky, thickly muscled figure combined with his anger made it seem like he was towering over me, filling up the room. "I am finally putting an end to your occult activities! The parish has received no end of complaints, but, in case you want to know, I have been holding a magnanimous and protective hand over your family, admittedly for Elizabeth's sake. But this has been going on for long enough. I am no longer able to turn a blind eye!"

Oh, really? I strongly doubted any of what he was saying. Sure, Widow Nesbit had probably made her accusations against me and my family known to Westminster - but then again, was there a family in the neighborhood that had not been on the sharp end of her suspicions?

What seemed much more likely to me was that Westminster, rightfully of course, suspected me of breaking into his house and discovering his private collections. I'd taken the lock of Elizabeth's hair with me when I left - a move I now regretted.

Looking into Westminster's flinty, gleaming eyes, I knew that he wanted to punish me for my audacity. I had no doubt that if he found anything he could pin me to, he would.

My heart pounded in my chest as Westminster and his men began to search every corner of the Graves property, starting with the premises of Graves & Sons. Elizabeth was away on one of her shifts, but my mother, alarmed, came down to see what was going on.

"What is happening here, Malm?" she demanded. She was equally anxious and angry, and I for one could practically sense the electricity radiating from her aura. It would have repelled a less intimidating man than Malm Westminster.

At the sound of my mother's voice, he spun around to face her, his eyes flashing. "I hate to be the bearer of bad news, Marie, but I'm afraid I am here on an official errand. Gabriel is suspected of conspiring with dark forces. It is quite likely that he has been responsible for several of the unfortunate events that have been occurring in this parish - and neighboring parishes - of late. We are here to put an end to it."

My mother's face was pale with fear, but admirably, she still fired back at the imposing figure standing in front of her. "Oh, don't be so silly, Malm! You've known this family for twenty odd years. You know that no son of ours would ever, as you put it, conspire with dark forces. In fact, what are you implying, exactly?"

Westminster scoffed. He took a sweeping step closer to my mother, who stood her ground, refusing to let him intimidate her. "I assure you, if we find as much as a shred of evidence that Gabriel, or indeed anyone in this house, has been communing with spirits or otherwise dabbled in the dark arts, he will be held accountable. And there will be nothing I can do to delay the consequences."

Westminster's suspicious eyes fixed on me again, while his men scoured every nook and cranny, turning things over without regard for what they might scuff or shatter. They meticulously combed through the shop, and then the work-shop, and then the courtyard where a dark spot was the only lingering sign of the shed that had stood here until last night.

I tried to steady my breathing as I followed the search party outside.

"Wasn't there a shed that used to be here?" Westminster demanded, walking over to where the dark ashes lay in a heap.

Eager to show his commitment to the cause, Blaine Nesbit crouched down and scooped up a handful of ashes in his gloved hand. "These ashes smell fresh, sir," he said, helpfully. He held the ashes up towards Westminster, who didn't even glance at them.

"That is true," I conceded. "But I decided to get rid of it. How else would I make space for a herb garden?"

Westminster's eyes flickered with annoyance. "A herb garden? And why, pray tell, would a coffin builder start a herb garden?"

I kept my voice steady as I gave him my best white lie. "We use the herbs for the posies and plague cures we sell here at Graves & Sons. With the Black Death showing no real signs of relenting, I thought we'd better start growing our own. It's just so much more convenient."

"Really, is that so?" Westminster spat on the ground to show his dissatisfaction with the explanation I'd given him. But he couldn't argue with it.

The search continued upstairs. Westminster was

getting more and more red-faced and frantic as his men ran out of rooms to ransack and duck feather pillows to tear open.

At long last they were forced to give up, and to my relief, they'd found precisely nothing they could use against me. The evidence of my illicit activities had either been washed away or were buried in a secret place in the woods. But it had been a close call, a damned close call.

"Should we search again, sir?" asked Blaine, his eyes shifting nervously to Westminster, cleaving to his authority like a child clinging tight to his father's hand.

"No need," Westminster snapped at his subordinate, his cheeks flushing a deep beetroot red. "We've wasted enough time here."

"Before you go, I have something I'd quite like to share with you."

I was about to make a daring move, but I couldn't stop myself. I had found Westminster's buttons and now I wanted to push them as hard as I could. I had the upper hand and I wasn't going to simply let him walk away without a thoroughly bruised ego.

"Hmm?" Westminster grunted, irritably. Now that his triumphant hunt had proved futile, his entire demeanor indicated that he couldn't wait to be out of here.

"I have purchased a plot of land in Cemetery Bottom Wood. My father and nephew are there, overseeing the construction of a villa."

I hadn't purchased my piece of Cemetery Bottom Wood just yet, but Westminster and his cronies didn't know that. "In fact," I added, "I have you in part to thank for my family's good fortune, and I would like you to know that."

Westminster's expression shifted from annoyance to

uncertainty. Still, he couldn't help but ask, "And how is that?"

"Surely you remember coming here on the night before the Bakers' funeral? You challenged me to think bigger - to see the Black Death not merely as a tragedy engulfing the city, but also as an opportunity. A blessing, even. At first I have to say I simply could not wrap my head around the scope and magnitude of your vision. Why, I even thought some of your words were rather glib and cruel." Here, I paused to tilt back my head and laugh, as if I couldn't believe how hopelessly naive I'd been. "But that only goes to show how small my own thinking was, at the time. As the plague gathered momentum, the scales finally fell from my eyes and I began to see that you were right. The plague has been a smorgasbord of opportunity, and I've learned, in my own way, to make the most of it."

Westminster looked utterly bewildered, and for once he had nothing to say.

"We should go, Westminster," Blaine Nesbit piped up. "We have more homes to visit."

Westminster nodded briskly, but his usual sense of bombastic self-confidence had taken a hit. "Very well. But Graves, mark my words. This isn't over - you and I aren't done. Whatever you might be up to, I will find out, and I will not let you get away with anything!" The words squeezed out between his clenched teeth and up this close, his eyes looked bulging and bloodshot.

"I appreciate that, thank you, Westminster. You're always so generous with your time and attention."

He drew in a sharp intake of breath, opened his mouth as if he was about to say something, but then he closed it again.

Without bidding me or my mother farewell, he turned

on his heel and practically stormed out of Graves & Sons. Through the window we watched them disappear around the corner, Westminster stomping angrily ahead while his two searchers trailed behind.

I must say, I felt not only relieved but also rather triumphant. Not only had Westminster had to leave empty-handed, I'd also managed to humiliate him and make him falter in front of his lap dogs. Had he shown up a few hours earlier, he would have found Ellery's corpse, as well as the remains of my father and Dwight. Not to mention all of the stolen wealth, a not insignificant portion of which had come from his own opulent abode.

"Gabriel."

I turned around, mildly startled by the sound of my name. I'd halfway forgotten that my mother was still here, standing in the midst of the chaos that our visitors had left behind. The look of concern I saw in her eyes put an immediate dampener on my gleeful high spirits.

"Gabriel. Promise me you're done playing with fire." She meant it both literally and metaphorically, of course.

I nodded. "I am done, I promise you."

I knew that she was right. I'd already stirred up enough of a storm; there was no need for me to add any more fuel to the fire of the hatred that Westminster clearly held for me.

Besides, I had more than enough wealth now to purchase half of Cemetery Bottom Wood as well as to secure the new premises for Deep Graves on the Old London Bridge. I could schedule the opening night for the upcoming full moon, only a week away. All the puzzle pieces were going to come together then.

CHAPTER

SIXTEEN

"Have you seen Elizabeth?" There was a slight tremor in my mother's voice as she stepped into the Graves & Sons workshop.

I stopped my work with the hammer and chisel and looked up from the workbench. I had started preparing a new pinewood casket - a child's. It was September now, and although no one else had sensed the tide turning, I knew that the Great Plague had slowly started to simmer down. Soon, life in the city would go on, and with it, its regular share of mortality. I saw no reason not to be prepared.

I shook my head, my tools frozen in mid-air. Elizabeth's shift at Clayfield was over for the day. I had greeted her when she returned home just a few hours earlier, and I had not seen or heard her leave again.

I lowered my tools, a worm of worry already nibbling at the edges of my consciousness. "I haven't, no. I thought she was upstairs."

"She went back for something she forgot at Clayfield." My mother's voice quivered despite her best efforts at remaining calm. "It shouldn't take her this long to make it there and back, should it? I don't want to alarm you, but I am starting to worry."

"She will be making her way back right now. I'll head out and meet her halfway." I hoped I sounded sure of myself as I quickly wiped and put the tools away. I very much wasn't, but I couldn't let my mother see or sense that I shared her rapidly growing unease.

My mind was racing with possibilities, none of them pleasant. Something told me that no matter what might have befallen Elizabeth, Westminster had something to do with it.

My mother looked at me and I knew that she was thinking the same thing. After a brief silence while I cleaned my hands and removed my apron, she said what neither of us really wanted to acknowledge; "I fear that this has something to do with what took place here earlier. Westminster was enraged when he left - dangerously enraged."

A shiver ran down my spine; my mother and I both knew that I'd provoked him.

"It could be just a coincidence. But stay here, and don't answer the door for anyone until I return. Until *we* return," I quickly corrected myself.

Then I reached out and placed both hands on my mother's slightly shaking shoulders. "I am certain it will not take me long to find her. I'll be back with her in no time."

My mother nodded slowly. I could tell that she very badly wanted to believe in what I was saying. That made two of us.

~

ACTING ON PURE INTUITION, I waited in the shadows outside Malm Westminster's home on Temple Place. I had no guarantee that this is where he would be and so I was betting on a hunch. All the windows facing the street were dark, just like they had been last night.

After about twenty minutes, my determination to wait for him here began to waver. What if I was wasting my time here while he was somewhere else?

Wait. Just as I was contemplating heading to Clayfield, Westminster emerged from the shadows that swathed the front door. He was wearing his full plague doctor regalia, and he put on the mask while standing on the porch. Something about his stance and the outline of his beak-masked face against the dimly lit building reminded me of a bird of prey preparing for its nightly hunt.

The night sky was so dark that I was able to follow him through the narrow, cobble-stoned streets without there being much risk of him noticing me. It also helped that he seemed to be in a hurry, moving with quick and agile steps through the darkened streets without turning around or casting a glance over his shoulder even once. Still, I kept as much distance between us as I dared to, without risking losing sight of him.

I followed his shadow as he made his way through narrow alleyways and stepped over a decaying body left in a gutter, left there to be picked up later by the next plague doctor passing by on his round.

My intuition was that Westminster was going to lead me to Elizabeth. I was sick with worry over what he either planned to do or had already done to her. If his collection of hair was anything to go by, he had some rather unusual appetites, and there was no telling how far they went.

Once lively and full of people, the windy streets were

now mostly empty thanks to the plague's stranglehold on St Bride's and its surrounds. Despite the light breeze, a smell of decay hung in the air like a billowing curtain, draped heavily over the usual smells of animals, feces and other forms of waste. All was quiet, except for the occasional, mournful tolling of a bell from one of the city's many churches.

We'd made it as far as Covent Garden when, suddenly, Westminster changed directions. He disappeared into a dark alley that turned out to lead us back towards the river. We were looping back on ourselves, Westminster's footsteps quickening as we continued east.

We walked on for perhaps half an hour, both of us ducking in and out of pools of shadow. When we reached the docks, the scent of brine wafted up from the river. The dark waters of the Thames shimmered under the light of the stars. The usually bustling harbor was blanketed by stillness and a light fog.

Westminster's footsteps sped up as he approached a warehouse. Suddenly, the air around him seemed to crackle with an electric charge of terrible excitement.

Hiding behind some oil barrels, I watched him reach into an inner pocket of his coat and withdraw a heavy set of keys. He unlocked the multiple padlocks that protected the warehouse, looking left and right before disappearing inside and closing the door firmly but quietly behind him. He'd clearly done this many times before.

And now what?

I circled the perimeter until I found a small window at the back of the building. I made my way over to it, noting to my relief that the tiny square of the grimy, glass-paned window stood ajar. It was only a small square, about chest height, but I figured I'd be able to squeeze through.

I took a deep breath and pushed the window fully open, trying not to make any noise. I then squeezed my blessedly slim frame through the opening, scraping my elbows and the sides of my arms on the wood in the process, but barely noticing.

Soundlessly, I lowered myself to the floor. My eyes, having already adjusted to the moonless night outside, didn't take long to adjust to the dimness inside.

There was only the sound of my own heartbeat beating against my eardrums. The air I was breathing was heavy with dampness mixed in with the pungent scent of burning oil. A flickering light danced across the room, illuminating the wooden walls and the simple wooden shelves that lined them.

My heart skipped a beat - the shelves were filled with jars that contained an assortment of teeth and what could only have been bones in different sizes. The jars and their contents gleamed under the flickering light of many oil lamps. Nails protruded from the opposite wall, and from them hung locks of hair in a wide variety of colors and textures. Clearly an extended version of the collection I'd found in Westminster's home.

I blinked, trying to stop myself from imagining the moments when those locks of hair had been severed from their owners. None of these tokens had been given freely. They seemed more like trophies of the kind that a serial killer might collect from his victims.

We tend to think of serial killers as modern monsters, don't we? The uncomfortable truth is that the mortal serial killer might be a much older monster than the vampire.

I let my gaze continue gliding along the wall, taking in the vast collection of trophy jars. They were horrifying, but it was the sight that awaited me in the corner of the warehouse that sucked the air out of my lungs. Elizabeth, chained to the wall by heavy rusty chains. Her eyes were cast down to the dirt floor. I could see, even from a distance, that she was badly bruised.

Westminster was nowhere to be seen. But he was somewhere, all right. He wouldn't have left again so soon.

It was highly likely that he had only vanished into the shadows momentarily to retrieve a weapon or a tool with which he intended to extract some of Elizabeth's teeth or cut her long blond hair from her scalp.

Or worse. In other words, risky as it was, with Westminster looming nearby, now was the time to act.

I moved into the open warehouse space and approached Elizabeth as quickly and silently as I could. I wanted to clasp a hand over her mouth to prevent her from screaming, but her eyes fluttered up from the floor and locked with mine before I was close enough. She startled, her chains rattling and giving off a series of muted metallic clinks. But seeing that it was me, she managed to stifle her scream. Her pale green eyes shone with fear.

"Gabriel!"

I both felt and heard a sudden rush of air behind me before a powerful force hit me between the shoulder blades. The force of whatever had hit me would have knocked me to the ground if Elizabeth's warning hadn't allowed me to take half a step forward before Westminster's fist, or whatever he'd used, had made contact with my upper spine. Now, instead of falling I merely stumbled forward, staggering to regain my footing.

I spun around, my gaze immediately landing on Westminster. His plague doctor's mask had been discarded, but his face, contorted with anger, was much more disturbing. His heavy jaw was set in a tense, maniacal smile and the light from the flickering oil lamps in the space around us danced in his eyes.

"I see you've discovered my little secret." His heavy eyebrows rose high onto his forehead. "Well," he breathed out, as if with relief, "I'm afraid I am going to have to insist that you take it with you to your grave."

"I'd rather not."

I reached out behind me, my fingers reaching for something, anything, that could be used as a weapon, but there was nothing but air. Looking around, there was also nothing useful within easy reach. Except, perhaps, that oil lamp over there, sitting on an upturned wooden crate.

Westminster took a step closer, his sinister smile widening as he reached out to grab me. I drew back, and grabbed the handle of the oil lamp I'd been eyeing up.

"I warn you! Stand back, Malm. Stand back or you'll regret it. Come to think of it, I think you'll regret it either way."

"*You* should not be doling out warnings to *me*!" Westminster was indignant. "You're more a worm than a man, I know that, and I doubt you are a fighter."

I swung the lamp at Westminster's head, but he was surprisingly quick to dodge. The glass shattered against the wall, and the oil spilled on the floor, spreading an acrid scent. Westminster's face twisted in anger.

"Careful!" he warned. "These things that you see here mean more to me than a simple gravedigger like you could possibly imagine, let alone begin to understand. If you break anything-"

"I am an undertaker, thank you very much," I corrected him, grateful for his folly in pointing out to me a weakness I could exploit against him. I lunged for the shelves nearest to where I stood. My arm crashed into it and I grabbed it, rattling it until most of its contents fell to the floor. Glass jars shattered, teeth and femurs flew everywhere across the ground.

"No, stop!"

Encouraged by the effect my move had had on him, I reached for the next shelf. This one, too, tipped over as I pulled it. Everything it held spilled to the floor in a cacophony of sound as wood splintered and glass shattered.

Westminster groaned, as if I'd wounded him. Or perhaps he was just outraged by my bad manners.

I reached for a drawer next, and as it slid open, several woven bags tumbled to the floor, some of them falling open in the process. I registered dully that they held severed fingers and complete hands in various stages of decay.

Westminster's face had gone a deep shade of red, and there was a vein pulsating in his forehead. "Don't make matters worse for yourself and Elizabeth than they already are," he warned me through gritted teeth. His eyes shone with unhinged intensity. "You are making me very angry, Gabriel. So very angry!"

I stared back at him. "You're an absolute monster, Malm." It was the simple truth, at least as I saw it.

"How dare you!" He reached for an oil lamp of his own to swing at me. I ducked away and the lamp shattered against the wall, this time uncomfortably close to Elizabeth, who winced as the splinters flew.

"You're the one who should be fearful now," I told him. "You, Westminster, have made *me* very angry. You've threatened my sister, threatened my plans!"

"Stay back now!" Westminster barked.

"Why do you only attack women, Malm? Are you afraid you can't win a fair fight?"

Malm grinned, his eyes glittering like dark beads. "I have nothing to prove to you, of all people," he insisted, spitting on the floor to show his contempt. "But if it's a fair fight you want-" I saw him reaching for something secreted in a hidden pocket or the folds of his heavy leather coat. He wanted me to believe that he was armed, but he was not. He simply lunged at me, either trying to land a punch or to grab me. I jumped to the side and out of his reach. Realizing he'd missed, he quickly retreated several steps, probably only so he could take better aim.

But I caught the slight flicker of doubt in his eyes. He was not used to being challenged, and he didn't like it one bit. The way he liked to inflict harm, whether on supposed witches, plague victims or the unfortunate women who happened to attract his attention, was from a vantage point of power and control. My accusation was true; he didn't like to fight fair.

"Give me the key to unlock Elizabeth's chains," I demanded. "Give them to me now and I might decide to let you live."

"Never, never." Westminster was still backing away from me, the heavy flesh of his neck shaking with anger and resentment as he shook his head. "Ah, Gabriel, I've always despised you! You've always had an air of unearned entitlement about you. Who do you think you are exactly? Let me tell you right now who you are, you're nothing and no one, and you never will be! No matter the feeble attempts I've seen you make, no matter your affectations, you and yours will always be down in the dirt, digging graves and building coffins for those slightly better off. You're just too self-important to see it, and because of your arrogance, you've clipped your sister's wings, crippled her chance at soaring to a higher station in life. Who knows, I might in all seriousness and earnestness have taken her hand in marriage. Denied that opportunity, I will simply take her life. And take her any other way I can."

"You disgusting old vulture! I'd rather die by your hand than spend a moment at your side!" Elizabeth shouted and I could tell from the rattling of her chains that she was kicking and thrashing in them. Her defiant anger made me proud. Westminster ignored her completely. "By the end of tonight," he sneered, stepping closer now again, "both of you will be dead! Neither of you will leave here. What will your poor mother think?"

With a flourish, he threw down an oil lamp and stepped away as a wall of flame leapt up between us. Then he spun around and sprinted for the rickety stairs that curved their way up into the warehouse rafters.

The anger that had been boiling inside me like an awakening beast was now fully alert. With my arms up to protect my face, I leapt through the flames and went after him.

CHAPTER
SEVENTEEN

I climbed the stairs as Westminster beat a hasty retreat into the overhead maze of rafters. He moved with a sort of animal agility that I wouldn't have thought his thickset body capable of. But Westminster was a man full of surprises.

Crates and boxes crashed around me as Westminster pushed them over in his wake. I dodged them as best I could, but one struck me hard on my arm and nearly took me with it as it tumbled towards the ground, now ten feet or so below us.

"Damn you," Westminster sneered up ahead. "I'll make you regret coming here!"

The metallic scent of rust and the musty odor of aged wood were in my nostrils as I kept climbing. The flickering light from the oil lamps and flames below cast dancing shadows on the rough wooden walls while also having the effect of making everything look slightly distorted.

I'd only blinked, but when I opened my eyes again, Westminster had ducked out of sight. Crates were stacked along thick wooden beams up here - there were plenty of places to hide. I glanced up at the heavy wooden beams above me, trying to detect any flicker of movement. At any moment he might emerge to attack me from an unseen corner. And as I knew all too well, a desperate man will do desperate things.

A sharp clang reverberated under the warehouse roof, and instinctively, I ducked. And just in time - a heavy, rust-stained meat hook whizzed past my head, narrowly missing its mark.

I jumped to the side, barely avoiding another swing of the hook on its chain. My heart raced. If that hook connected with my skull, it'd all be over. If I went down, Westminster would never let me get back up again. Not to mention that I would probably break my spine if I fell from this height.

Westminster had confidently declared that I was no fighter, but what did he know? All those untold hours building coffins weren't the same as being a practiced fighter, but it counted for something. I was nimble and strong, and I was about two decades younger than him. And if I could find just a sliver of an edge, I would use it for all it was worth. All in all, I felt relatively confident about my odds.

Now, if only I had a weapon of my own.

My centuries as a vampire had skewed my thinking - I'd broken into Westminster's home, I'd humiliated him in front of his men, and tonight I'd followed him through the streets of London without even thinking of bringing a knife or a gun. What had I expected - that I could easily over-power him with my bare hands or command him with my voice?

If the situation hadn't been so dire, I would have laughed out loud at my own careless stupidity.

Instead, I kept scanning the planks and beams around us until my attention caught on a piece of broken metal pipe. Whatever powers reign in the universe, they had heard and answered my unuttered prayer.

As Westminster's hook whispered past my head yet again, I ducked down and grabbed the rusty piece of metal, noting to my satisfaction that its end was sharp and jagged where it must have broken off from somewhere. Westminster didn't seem to notice it when I slipped my hand holding the pipe behind my back.

I took a step towards him and he retreated a step. I was trying to close the distance between us, Westminster to maintain it - he needed it if he wanted to keep taking swings at me. I could use this to my advantage, and I did, by forcing him backwards onto one of the cross beams under the roof.

There was a deep drop below us now.

He didn't like it and was baring his teeth at me like a rabid dog. But he was determined to get at me with the meat hook and so he kept stepping backward.

He was preparing to take another swing at me, the chain whispering as he spun it round and round in his hand. I wasn't going to let him, though. I pitched myself forward, letting my own surprise weapon appear from behind my back.

He didn't even see the pipe before it had made contact with his shoulder, tearing right through the heavy dark leather of his coat. He staggered and let out a grunt which was half surprise, half pain. But he didn't drop the chains to clutch his injury as I'd hoped.

"Too far!" He bellowed, "Now you've really gone too far."

I certainly had - there was no going back now.

Westminster's dark, beady eyes gleamed with resentment. He couldn't wait to make me bleed for my misdeeds.

My only response was to accost him with the broken pipe again, this time going for his neck. Side-stepping it as best he could, he let out a furious growl. His heavy leather boots shuffled to remain firmly planted on the cross beam and he only just managed it. He made a small, heavy jump backwards that made the beam shiver under us.

He started spinning the chain in his hand again. He was trying to get enough traction on his swing to knock me down, but he didn't have the space for it. Grunting with exasperation and fury, he pulled in the chain so that he could hold its tail in one hand and the rusty hook in the other. Now he could both swing and claw at me. Seeing that I knew what his intention was, he grinned at me.

But before he could swing the chain or jab the hook, I attacked him again with the broken pipe. Metal clashed against metal as he parried me by raising his meat hook, only just in time.

He jabbed it at me and also swung the tail end of the chain again and again, almost blindly.

My approach, we both soon discovered, was much more measured, my strikes as unpredictable as those of a snake. Westminster couldn't know when the next one would come, so he was caught off guard over and over again. Several times I managed to tear through his plague doctor's coat and even to draw blood from the pale, hairy flesh underneath.

I was certain I had him, but then he moved out of my reach quickly by jumping to another beam. He landed heavily, laughing, making the entire structure shake.

I'd thrown myself at him with such force and speed that for a dizzying second, all of my energy went to steadying myself so I wouldn't fall. The dirt floor was perhaps 20 feet below, impossibly distant. I'd rather not find out what would happen to my mortal body if I fell from this height.

Then, in a split second, the hook on Westminster's chain found its mark. I gasped in indignant fury when I looked down and saw it snagging around my ankle.

Before I could react, my entire body was wrenched suddenly sideways, the force pulling me off balance and sending me hurtling towards the edge of the beam. I fell on my side, my body slamming against the wood. Shooting pains cascaded through me and colorful lights danced in the darkness of my skull - beautiful aurora borealis.

Octavia, I said silently, if you're going to appear at all before the end of this adventure, better make it now.

Of course, when I opened my eyes, she wasn't there. She hadn't answered my prayer, or whatever we might call it.

Instead I found myself locking eyes with Westminster, who had stepped back onto my crossbeam and was closing in on me. The doubt I'd seen in his eyes was gone, replaced with glee now that he had the upper hand.

His features were twisting into a sadistic, leering smile as his shadow loomed over me. He looked at me with a predator's gaze, watching my attempts to raise myself on my elbows and sit up without any attempt to disguise his amusement. As soon as I was nearly there, he planted a heavy boot in the middle of my chest and forced me back down. If he wanted to, he could probably crush my rib cage under his weight.

"Don't push your luck, Gabriel. You've already run out. You're completely, but completely at my mercy now. How do you like it?"

"To be perfectly honest, this isn't really doing it for me."

"You disgust me."

He kicked me in the ribs, then, like the vulture he was, Westminster bent over me and rummaged through my pockets, his knee now firmly holding me down in lieu of his boot. I wiggled and tried to throw him off, but I wasn't able to get enough momentum and force behind my throws and thrusts.

I knew what he was going to find before his fingers closed around the vials of ectoplasm. He held them up to the flickering light, his eyes illuminated by their radiant glow. The sinister grin that tugged at the corners of his lips looked distorted and practically demonic thanks to the shadows the dancing flames cast on the wall behind him.

"Ah, but Gabriel, what do we have here?" His voice dripped with excitement. "Are these perhaps the results of your necromantic witchcraft? Do not try to lie to me now, Gabriel! I knew the dear Widow Nesbit was onto something when she voiced her suspicions about you."

My blood froze in my veins as a dreadful thought occurred to me: What if Westminster decided to drink my precious ectoplasm? I couldn't decide what was worse - the prospect of him gulping down my return ticket to the future or killing me with his bare hands.

"Are these perhaps the *true* plague cures?" Westminster wondered out loud. "Are these what have kept you and your family shielded and safe from the reaper's scythe?"

"No, no, these are nothing," I said, keeping my tone as casual as I could make it under the circumstances. It was a tall order, and I must confess, I don't think I pulled it off very well. "They're just herbal tinctures - my mother prepares them and we sell them in the shop. They're placebo more than anything."

"I warned you not to lie." Westminster's voice was now low and menacing as he regarded me. "These are not nothing. You wouldn't be carrying them around with you like this, wrapped in fine silk, if they weren't powerful potions, magical talismans of some description." His eyes were narrow, glittering beads. "Do not make the mistake - again - of insulting my intelligence. Tell me what these really are. Tell me."

He pressed down hard on my chest with the sole of his boot as he hoisted himself back up to a standing position, forcing the air from my lungs until I sputtered and heaved. This seemed to amuse him, so he did it again while letting out a cackle. My head was spinning and for a moment I couldn't tell what was up and what was down.

"All right, well," I gasped, struggling for breath, "They aren't nothing, and they aren't plague cures. They contain poison."

I spoke the words as they occurred to me, and now a sense of calm determination settled over me. If I could make Westminster eat the lie I'd just given him, he wasn't going to drink my ectoplasm. And even if I couldn't convince him that the vials contained poison, planting a seed of doubt that they might could be enough. He wasn't going to risk his life in order to find out, was he?

"You lie again, Gabriel!" Westminster swept down and smacked me hard in the jaw with his fist. My head snapped to the side and I spat out a jet of blood. It described a perfect, crimson arc through the air.

"You may be a coward, but you are no poisoner, no killer. Trust me, I would know. It takes one to know one, as they say."

I lifted my hand to feel my jaw. I noted with relief that nothing seemed to be broken - I did not intend to re-enter immortality without my teeth.

"I am, and I've poisoned both my father and my

brother, and even my innocent nephew. What I told you earlier about them overseeing the building of a villa a plot of land in the woods was a lie, meant to throw you off."

I relished the doubt that my words caused to flicker deep in the plague doctor's eyes.

"Surely not. Why would you do such a thing?"

"So I could take the business, of course! Isn't it obvious?" Taking shots at his intelligence was either sure to work, or to fan the fires of his murderous rage. Given my current situation, it was a risk worth taking. "With my father, Thomas and Dwight out of the way, I now own and control it all."

Bewildered, Westminster looked at the two small vials in the palm of his hand and at the swirling silvery liquid they contained, as if he could ask them that way to reveal their true nature and purpose. After a moment of deliberation, he straightened back up, squared his shoulders and looked straight at me like a hawk.

"Drink them and you will die, I promise you." I watched him, my heart pounding in my chest.

"You wouldn't harm your own family, Gabriel. You share those all too common weaknesses called loyalty and compassion, at least when it comes to your own." He spoke the words with disdain, as though they were distasteful to him. "I, on the other hand, am blessedly free from the qualms that make other men weak. No, these are plague cures, true plague cures, and you are lying to me, hoping to keep them to yourself."

Apparently, he had made up his mind not to believe me.

I couldn't let him imbibe the contents of those vials. I slowly propped myself up on my elbows, carefully gauging the moment to strike.

"Imagine," Westminster invited me, his voice becoming

animated, "imagine the possibilities when I become immune to the specter of plague! Even the Black Death will bow and tremble before me, naturally. No longer would I be regarded as a mere plague doctor, no, no, I would be feared and admired like never before. Revered. You, Gabriel, were never worthy of what this potion can do."

While Westminster continued his monologue I laced my fingers together underneath the crossbeam. Then, while his eyes and attention were both held rapt by the two little skull-topped vials which he lifted again to admire in the flickering light of the rising flames, I kicked his legs out from under him by swinging up my right leg, hooking it behind his knee and pulling sideways with as much force as I could.

The element of surprise caught him off guard as much as the impact itself. Stunned, he staggered, teetering on tip toes on the edge of the beam. His eyes were wide with disbelief - he simply couldn't accept this turn of events.

Time slowed as I watched him, teetering and swaying like a leaf in a gale.

"Help me!" he said in a small, frightened voice.

Then, as if he had expended his last energy uttering those two meaningless words, he lost his balance. With a half-choked gasp he plummeted, hurtling towards the dirt floor below.

The air was sucked out from the place where he had just been standing. And in that vacuum, the vials of ectoplasm hung suspended in mid-air.

Breathless, I threw out my hands to catch them while holding onto the beam by squeezing my knees around it. I already knew that it was too late. After all, time doesn't stand still for mortals.

But then I felt a hand, unnaturally cool and smooth,

grip mine. I opened my eyes, and there was Octavia, hovering in the air. Opening her delicate ghostly palm, she revealed the two vials, whole and unscathed. She'd caught them. And now she released them into the palm of my hand.

I held the vials, both in one hand. The delicate glass was blessedly cool against my palm as I closed it around them. Then I pocketed them, my entire body shaking with spent adrenaline.

"Octavia," I managed.

"Don't thank me. I'm doing this for me, remember?" she said in her small, petulant voice. But she gave me a genuine smile. "Please figure all the rest out soon and return to the present. The more time you spend stuck here in this cesspit, the more nerve wracking it gets for me. As this situation has just proven, there are so many things that could happen to you, that could snuff you out. It was fun in the beginning, watching you struggle uphill, but at this point it's just giving me anxiety."

"All right, well, I'm doing the best I can. You could have asked Venedict for some assistance, you could have asked Csilla."

"I wanted to do this myself."

"Do what?"

"Help you of course!" Despite her semi-transparent state, I could very well see her rolling her eyes at me.

"Well, I could have used some extra reinforcements, but at this point, I believe I've got my return to immortality both figured out and within reach. Isadore and Isadora are going to turn me on the full moon in just over a week."

"They seem reluctant to give it up, their blood. Pressure them or they might just keep dragging their feet until you're an old man."

"I should hope not. Like I said, I've got this in hand. I agree with you, the idea of waiting much longer is deeply unsettling. But first things first. Right now, I need to get myself and Elizabeth out of here."

"Indeed. If you burn to a crisp we'll both be sorry."

Octavia was gone.

My legs shook under me - so much so that I could barely get up, stand up and walk downstairs where the body of the plague doctor, and, of course, my dear Elizabeth, were waiting for me.

Elizabeth, still chained to the wall, sat nearby, while Westminster's lifeless body lay crumpled on the floor. His neck was twisted at an unnatural angle, a reassuring sight.

What was less reassuring was the fire that Westminster had started. The flames he had caused to leap from the spilt oil on the floor earlier had traveled to the walls and were rapidly climbing. Already, the smoke was stinging my throat and making my eyes water.

"Gabriel, in his pocket somewhere," Elizabeth attempted to direct me. Smoke was billowing up around her to the point that I could barely make her out.

Kneeling beside the dead man, I quickly rolled him over. He'd been heavy in life, but he was even heavier in death. Now it was my turn to search through his pockets, and it didn't take me long to find a bundle of keys. I held it up for Elizabeth to see.

"It's one of the smaller ones! Gabriel, hurry!"

Keys in hand, I hurried to the wall and began where I crouched down in front of her and started trying the smaller ones in Elizabeth's handcuffs. The encroaching flames were already reaching their tendrils towards her, inching closer. If I didn't find the correct key soon, I would have to attempt to break the metal rings that secured the chains to the wall in order to free her.

After trying about half of them, I finally found the one that made the lock click and the handcuffs spring open. I draped my arm around Elizabeth's shoulders, half-lifting, half-dragging her towards the door. It was unlocked, and as soon as we were outside in the cool, fresh air.

As soon as we had reached a safe distance from the warehouse, which was now consumed by flames and smoke, I turned towards it again. I'd been seized by an idea.

"Wait here."

"Where are you going?" Elizabeth reached out for me, to stop me from heading back towards the burning building.

"I will not be a moment," I assured her as I slipped out of her grip, "Wait for me here."

Moving through the thick smoke, I returned to the building, back to where Westminster lay on the floor. With Elizabeth safely outside, I swiftly stripped Westminster of his plague doctor's outfit. Frantically, I searched for the mask, and there it was, lying nearby. Though slightly torn, it was all still usable.

My wealth-gathering spree had been cut short, but I wasn't quite done with it yet. There would be one last raid, and then I would hang up the beaked mask for good.

Standing in the billowing smoke I pulled on the attire. Once this was done, I pulled a few burning pieces of wood over Westminster's lifeless body, deciding it would be best if it was consumed by the flames and never found. It was only a shame that the evidence of his crimes would be going up in smoke with him.

I made my way back outside to where Elizabeth was waiting. She startled when she saw me and murmured,

"Unbelievable." But she left it at that - too exhausted, probably, to argue.

"Let us go," I said, taking her hand and pulling her along with me.

"Shouldn't we alert more people so that the fire can be extinguished? It could easily spread."

"Don't worry too much about that. The Great Fire of London is next year's catastrophe."

She looked at me, not understanding. She opened her mouth, then she closed it again, letting it go.

We would make our way back through the darkened streets, back to Bride Lane and our home.

And tired though I was, I would then head back out again, still wearing Westminster's own beaked ensemble. By the time the first rays of sunlight burst through the horizon, I would have emptied Malm Westminster's villa of every last thing of value it contained. I would have loaded it all into the Elysion twins coach and be well on my way to Cemetery Bottom Wood. Here, I would bury Westminster's treasure next to my existing loot, and in that tranquil place, I would also bury the plague doctor's garb. And that would be the end of my criminal career.

Well, more or less. You really can't walk the world as an immortal without ever setting a foot wrong. But that's a philosophical musing for another time.

EIGHTEEN

I walked along London Bridge. The cool breeze brushing against my face brought with it a refreshing change from the heat of the plague-stricken summer. The city was slowly emerging from the depths of despair, as London always does in the wake of disaster.

The long shadow of Malm Westminster already felt like a distant nightmare, no more ominous or threatening than a scarecrow in bright daylight. He did not seem to be missed by anyone. As far as I was aware, his sudden disappearance didn't inspire any kind of investigation.

Without having had to discuss it with a single word, Elizabeth and I had agreed that our mother was to know nothing of what had transpired that night in the warehouse on the harbor. Only the two of us knew what fate had befallen Malm Westminster. Apart from his victims, only we knew what a monster he'd really been. And only I knew how perilously close he had come to thwarting my plans, which were finally nearing their crescendo.

Octavia's feelings on the matter mirrored my own; dilly-dallying around here until I was old wasn't an appealing prospect. It was about time that I wrapped up the loose ends.

Stopping momentarily to lean against the stone railing, I gazed out at the tranquil waters of the Thames which shimmered and rippled under the gentle rays of the sun. The sun! For the first time since I'd become mortal again, I was reminded of how much I was going to miss it when vampirism descended on me once more. Not long now.

I kept on walking until I reached the southernmost end of the old London Bridge. Here, I stopped in front of the tall, elegant timber frame building that had housed the first incarnation of Deep Graves.

Similar to the building on Bride Street that housed Graves & Sons, it had a shop on the ground floor and living quarters above. A crucial difference was that this building had three instead of two floors of living quarters and that they were ample.

And don't even get me started on the view. The windows upstairs faced both the narrow bridge street and the flowing waters of the Thames. I'd fallen in love with this building from the moment I first laid eyes on it as a child, accompanying my mother on one of her shopping trips. Even at that young age I'd dreamt of one day owning a coffin shop right here on the Bridge, in the heart of the city's most prestigious shopping district. It was a dream I'd fulfilled, and was about to fulfill again with the opening of Deep Graves tomorrow night.

With all of the riches I'd stolen from Westminster's villa and other places I could have bought this place many times over, but there was no need. For sentimental reasons, I wanted the same property again.

Securing it had been easy. I'd been able to offer the old clockmaker, a Mr. Elden, a kingly sum for his shop. The poor old man had lost most of his family to the plague and without sons to take over after him, he was more than happy with the chest full of gold that I had Nicholas Lacey assist me in carrying in and placing in front of him - irrefutable proof of my sincerity. Needless to say, he'd accepted right away.

Elizabeth had been thrilled at the news of our immediate move, but our mother had proven difficult to convince. Again and again she'd suggested that she should stay behind in the Bride Lane property, just in case Thomas returned from his adventures at sea.

But it was a done deal. I'd already found tenants for the narrow apartments above Graves & Sons. Their tenancy would be up on August 31st 1666, two days before the Great Fire of London. Up until that date, I would keep the shop and workshop as a storage facility and workroom for the fine coffins and caskets I would be selling at Deep Graves.

On the day of our move, several neighbors came out of the woodwork to wish us good luck. Others, including the omnipresent Ethel Nesbit, seemed to prefer watching from behind curtains or through doors that had been cracked ajar. But whisper as they might, they couldn't stop us.

Nothing could stop my plans now. As I gazed up at the newly installed brass letters and coffin-shaped sign above the door, spelling out Deep Graves, I knew this as surely as I knew anything in this universe.

I HAVE a memory of walking upstairs in the building on the old London Bridge.

It had been November of 1665, and the last visitors had just left after the grand opening of Deep Graves.

Everything had gone perfectly. I had known in my heart that I had set myself and my family up for a prosperous future, and that the sweep of the Black Death was now certainly retreating.

I had reached the first landing and then the first floor where Elizabeth and our parents had their bedrooms; my dwelling had been on the top floor, true to tradition. Thomas had his own floor waiting for him, should he ever decide to lay claim to it.

Our parents' bedroom door had been closed; they must have already been asleep after a long evening and several glasses of sweet wine.

As I had walked past Elizabeth's room, its door had stood ajar. She had hung a mirror on the wall, a half-length mirror, and she had been getting dressed for bed. As I had walked past, her back and shoulders had been reflected in the mirror, completely covered in red roses, the signs of the plague.

I had frozen on the stairs, struck by lightning. In that moment, Elizabeth had looked up, our eyes meeting in the mirror. Something unspoken had passed between us. We both had known that I had discovered something she had been hiding - the fact that she had fallen prey to the plague and must have been in its grip for quite some time.

Quickly, Elizabeth had pulled up the sleeves to cover her shoulders. "Gabriel, I wasn't- You weren't meant to see! Don't tell Mother and Father!"

As I had stepped forward, I had reached out towards her, but then I had stopped myself. If the signs of the plague had already been so visible on her skin, the plague had a true stranglehold on her.

"Why," I had said in a voice that was as terrified as it was angry, "Why have you been hiding this?"

She had started crying, blinking back the tears. "I was scared! I hoped I was mistaken when I first found them. I have been hoping, stupidly, that they would go away! I have been trying to treat myself with some of the remedies I learned at Clayfield. I thought I could cure myself and that I would never have to tell anyone!"

"You should have told me, Elizabeth. I could have done something sooner!"

But what, exactly?

The doorknob leading into our parents' bedroom had twisted, and our mother had opened it from within, standing in the doorway. She had already been crying, having heard our voices and deduced the general drift of our exchange. She had let out the deepest sigh, so deep it seemed as if her spirit had left her body.

Later that night I had turned up at the Elysion residence in Knightsbridge. Of course it had been in the middle of a thunder and rain storm, and I had been completely soaked.

I had only had one thing in mind: finding my patrons and demanding that they grant me whatever powers they had. At this point, I had still not know exactly what Isadore and Isadora were, only that they were somehow immune to diseases, immune to ageing; immortal, or something very much like it.

I had beaten on their door and called out for them until they emerged, both of them bewildered to see me there. Without waiting for an invitation to come inside, I had pushed past them while explaining in a big rapid rush of words my predicament. Isadore and Isadora had both followed me through the hallway as I spoke, and by the time we had reached the living room I had demanded that they lend their assistance. I had told them that if they had any special powers, now was the time to make use of them.

I had never demanded anything of them, but I demanded that they share their powers with me.

They had obliged, turning me into a vampire, something they had apparently already been discussing, and my showing up on their doorstep, essentially demanding a miracle, had cemented their decision.

They could have done nothing more.

But even so, by the time I had made it back to the house on London Bridge, reeling from all of the new power coursing through me and determined to share it with Elizabeth, it had already been too late.

I had found Elizabeth tucked into her bed, stone cold dead, our parents and Dwight all gathered around her, dissolved into desperate tears. It was as if the insidious disease had exploded through her the second she was no longer able to keep it secret.

Despite the marvel of my new vampiric powers, everything in that moment had seemed utterly meaningless.

Burying my sixteen-year-old sister a few nights hence had been the worst night of my life, and of my afterlife.

And the fundamental failure of it had haunted me, like a ghost in the firmament, ever since.

THAT WAS how it had happened in 1665. But this time, things would turn out very differently.

Of course the plague wasn't over yet, but the opening night of Deep Graves was tomorrow night, under the light of the full moon on September 24, 1665.

Everything was ready - the new shop was decorated and decked out with caskets, many of them filled with flowers. These had been collected, picked, and arranged by my mother and Elizabeth. And I had an array of new coffins and caskets on display that I had been working on since my raids as a plague doctor had come to an end.

Most things in my little apartment upstairs were still in their bundles and crates, and for the time being I had more important matters to attend to than unpacking.

I stood in front of my beaten copper mirror, admiring the fine suit that I'd had made specifically for this occasion. It was deep emerald green with embroidery and plenty of detailing. This was the suit I was going to wear tomorrow night when I became immortal, as well as tonight, when I made my case for immortality.

Slipping out of the shop downstairs where my mother, Elizabeth, and a few assistants were preoccupied with preparations for the opening, I walked across the bridge, through my old neighborhood and into Knightsbridge.

Darkness was falling softly around me, and although it wasn't chilling, the mist hanging in the air enhanced the sense of excitement that filled my heart and quickened my steps.

Reaching the Elysion residence, I stopped on the doorstep and steadied my heartbeats and my breathing before I rapped on the door. It was early in the night, but the vampires would no doubt already be awake.

A maid came to the door and opened it. I recognized her as Kavya, the shy young woman who had served me tea and biscuits on my last visits to the Elysion home.

"Mr. Graves," she said, surprised to see me. "Come on in." She called out to her master and mistress as she led me through the foyer and into a lavishly decorated living room furnished with several pieces of ornate furniture, including several sofas and armchairs. Thick and heavy velvet curtains hung in front of the windows, sweeping the floors.

Between them, I was able to glimpse a sliver of the beautiful and tranquil garden beyond.

"Wait here, please, Mr. Graves," said Kavya before turning on her heel and leaving the room, presumably to alert Isadore and Isadora to my unexpected presence.

I stood in the middle of the room, looking around, taking it all in. Then a door opened into what appeared to be another adjacent living room, a smaller one.

Isadora appeared in the doorway. Behind her I could see several easels and canvases, all of them covered with white sheets. Paintbrushes and tubes of paints and pigments took up various table surfaces. If I was not mistaken, Isadore had picked up his painting practice again. Perhaps both of them had. I sincerely hoped so.

My hope quickened and I smiled to myself.

"Gabriel!" She greeted me warmly. Stepping into the room, she reached out her arms and gave me a hug. I didn't recall her ever doing that before. "It is good to see you."

"Where is Isadore?" I asked. I wanted them both here for this. I wanted them both to get onboard with me.

"Oh, he's upstairs. I'm sure he'll be down in a moment. If only he can tear himself away from his brooding. There's something on his mind, you see." She smiled, but the smile was brittle.

I nodded. I thought I understood what she meant. For so long, he had shut himself off from the possibility of creating, of enjoying art as he had in his mortal life. My words the last time I was here had stirred something in him, made him question his resolve. Perhaps he was going through some kind of internal battle that hadn't yet been won one way or the other. As you've probably already guessed, that was why I was here - to make sure the battle was won, one way rather than the other.

"Well, you look resplendent," Isadora said, eyeing my fine tailor-made outfit. I bowed my head slightly, accepting the compliment. "This is what I intend to wear tomorrow night for the opening of my shop, Deep Graves. This reminds me-" I withdrew from my inner pocket, where it had been lying next to my heart, a cream-colored envelope on thick parchment. The words were all handwritten in my looping, forward-leaning, dramatic hand. I handed it to her. It was an invitation to the opening, which I had set for the evening, specifically to ensure that my patrons would be able to appear.

Isadora immediately opened the envelope and read the invitation, her eyes flowing rapidly over the words. Almost at once, she said, "Thank you, Gabriel. We will definitely be there. I am very proud of you, you know. I've seen you develop as an artist through the years, and this is a new pinnacle. No doubt your family is also very proud." She folded the invitation and placed it on the table.

"And Isadore?"

She sighed. "I'm sure he would be delighted to come, too. Now, if the opening is tomorrow night, no doubt you're very busy. Why are you here, inviting me personally? You could have sent a courier." She searched my face with her glimmering eyes, as if her question was a test. It was definitely a test.

"That is true," I conceded, "but no courier could convey or speak the words that need to come from me. No courier could express the request that I'm about to make, as adequately as I hope to be able to."

Isadora's shoulders stiffened slightly, but then she inclined her head to indicate that she was listening. There had been no noise of footsteps approaching in the hallway outside, but suddenly, Isadore appeared in the doorway.

"Isadore," I lit up at the sight of him.

He had arrived at just the right time. I'd rather not have to explain my errand twice. It would be better if they both heard me say it once and both were able to take in the entire narrative, the entire plea that I intended to lay out for them.

"Gabriel," he said, giving me a sort of hesitant smile. He was looking a little disheveled, unlike his usual elegant and impeccably groomed self. His hair, gathered in a short ponytail, looked somewhat frazzled. And the buttons of his shirt had been put together unevenly. I noticed paint splatters on his elegant hands and even a few on his marble white chest, forming a vivid trail disappearing behind the thin fabric of his voluminous shirt.

He noticed me looking at the paint spatter and nodded. "Yes, indeed, after your last visit, I have started painting again. And I must say that it has returned to me much quicker than I would have ever expected."

"He feels conflicted at the moment, I think it's fair to say." Isadora explained.

"Well?" I prompted

"Well, what if I don't deserve the enjoyment that this gives me?" Isadore folded his arms in front of him, a defensive stance.

"Maybe it's not about what you deserve," I said. "Maybe it's about what the world deserves. Don't you think the world is a better place for all the beauty in it? Isn't beauty in art and literature and music what people have always used to comfort themselves and to create a bulwark against the meaninglessness of it all? Isn't art of redemptive quality in and of itself, something that doesn't really belong to its creator but to those who enjoy it?"

I might have been pushing my luck at this point - I

mean, I could plainly see the emotions warring on his face, but I still pressed on. I had to. As Octavia had said, if I merely waited, I could grow old. And I really did not want that to happen to me.

"Perhaps you could put your art out into the world, even if you had to do it under some kind of alias, to disguise your true identity. You would not be harvesting any accolades, of course, but you would still have the knowledge that you are participating in the creation of more beauty and meaning in the world. And that would have an impact on some. It would move those who observe it. You have the means," I looked around to indicate their beautiful and richly appointed home. "You have the means to create. You have the skill and you have the time. Doesn't it look to you like you've been blessed? And that you owe it to the world to share those blessings rather than keep them locked up inside you just because you feel, well, what exactly? Guilty?"

Isadore frowned. I'd offended him, but he didn't try to rebuff my words. He bit his lip, one of his tiny fangs nearly punching a hole, and absentmindedly, he licked the drop of blood from his lip where he had punctured it.

"Now listen to me," I said. "I haven't come here on a casual visit, and this is not just me showing up personally to extend an invitation to my most important patrons and supporters. I've come here tonight because I have a very important request to make - a big request. You already know what it is," I pointed out. "I have made this request before, but never have I made it so firmly and heartfelt as I am now. Because you see, this is it. With the opening of Deep Graves, I've reached the pinnacle of my mortal potential. Definitively. Tomorrow night marks the completion of my mortal life. I feel this very strongly. The rest of my potential, the potential that my spirit contains, can only be expressed through a supernaturally extended lifespan. I know that I can keep developing and growing as an artist, as a craftsperson, as a businessman. And I would like the opportunity to do so. I know that the two of you-" I looked from one to the other of the twins, "can give me that gift, that opportunity. No one else. And I would like to humbly request that you bequeath it to me, tomorrow night or never."

Isadora was nodding thoughtfully, and there was something sparking in her eyes. I could see that I had won her over. But Isadore still seemed undecided, uncertain of which foot to stand on.

Just then Isadora took a step towards me. In a firm, clear voice she said, "I will help you, Gabriel. Your mind is made up, that much is clear. What's more," she looked to her brother, as though encouraging him to see what she was seeing, "as an immortal you'll be able to keep serving humanity for generations to come, perhaps for millennia."

"I'm not sure I agree with this," Isadore said, his arms still folded in front of him. "I'm still fundamentally opposed to creating any more like us. I'm not sure I could bear it on my conscience if I am responsible for bringing Gabriel from the world of mortals into ours, into our dark realm."

"Oh, Isadore," Isadora said, "please lighten up a little for once in your afterlife! Don't you see? You're not taking it upon your conscience. Gabriel is taking it upon his own."

"I am indeed, and enthusiastically." I wanted to leave Isadore with no wiggle room for objections.

"Unlike what Minuetta did to you," Isadora said, now turning completely to face Isadore as she implored and persuaded him on my behalf, "we are not forcing anything on Gabriel. We are merely complying with his own wishes. I for one think we actually owe it to him. He has always meant much to us, always served us, always impressed us. He is even trying to give you back the gift of art. Isn't all of that worth a bit of blood?"

Isadore didn't respond right away, but took a step back from his sister. "Don't put me on the spot like this," he said in a quiet but somewhat menacing voice. "I will not succumb to pleas and pressure. And as you well know, there are never enough hours before sunrise - so I'll have to get back to my painting."

In an instant, he was gone, the doorway where he had stood as empty as before.

Isadora's shoulders sank, but she turned to me and spoke the words I had been longing to hear. "So, Gabriel," she looked me in the eyes, "I'm going to help you, regardless of Isadore's decision. I'll be there tomorrow night, and after all have left, I will share my blood with you to fulfill your wish."

CHAPTER

NINETEEN

The grand opening of Deep Graves proved to be a resounding success, surpassing its initial interaction, surpassing even my own expectations. The turnout was even greater than I had dared to hope. Shopkeepers from all across the old London Bridge flocked to witness this new addition to their ranks. Relatives and friends from the St Bride's and St Paul's neighborhoods also made their way to our doors.

Among them I spotted Blaine Nesbit, who had likely been sent by his nosy mother to spy on us. But as I greeted my guests, whom we had to let in one or two at a time in the hopes of minimizing the risks of contagion, I felt fully in control of the unfolding evening. After all, I had my eyes on the prize that I knew awaited me at the end of it.

Now that my time as a mortal was nearly at an end all over again, I could allow myself to actually enjoy the last few hours of the ordeal.

Candles flickered softly, casting a warm glow throughout the shop, illuminating the beautiful (If I must say so myself) displays of coffins, caskets and fragrant flower arrangements.

I had hired a talented musician to sit and play his lyre in the corner of the room and fill it with sweet, melancholy melodies. A journalist from the local newspaper that circulated on London Bridge appeared, scribbling in a small leather-bound notebook.

A celebratory mood hung over the evening, and barely an hour into it the crowd had swelled to the point that it was clogging up the bridge outside. The commotion itself attracted even more visitors.

I made a point of interacting with all who came to visit Deep Graves, but the lion's share of my attention was constantly drawn to Isadora. She was by far my most important guest this evening, and I couldn't help myself but keep tabs on where she was at all times. With my goal so near at hand, I suppose I on some level feared that she might change her mind or otherwise slip through my fingers.

As the evening wound down I paid the musician and the wine servers handsomely, and was relieved when the final guests trickled out and tottered off into the evening mist that had draped itself over the bridge.

I helped my mother into the horse-drawn carriage that Isadora had arrived in earlier. Nicholas Lacey was tasked with returning her to Bride Lane where she would spend one final night. I preferred to spare her from witnessing what was about to transpire. No doubt, if my mother knew what was about to happen to me and to Elizabeth, she would not only be deeply disturbed but also attempt to prevent it.

I bade her goodnight tenderly but without lingering, not wanting to give her the slightest reason to sense anything amiss. Even so, a sense of unease shimmered in her sky blue eyes as she held my hand and said, "Gabriel? Promise me that all is well."

"All is exceptionally well, Moeder. I will see you tomorrow."

In some parallel timeline, this was probably true. I stepped back from the carriage and turned around before my mother caught any glimpse of treacherous tears in my eyes.

With the shop emptied, I went back inside and locked the door, practically shivering with anticipation. The moment of my turning was at hand. Only Isadora, Elizabeth, and I remained in the building. A few remaining candles flickered, casting a dim glow in the room.

"Are you ready?" Isadora asked, searching my eyes, perhaps for any sign of doubt. But there was none.

"I feel as though I have been ready for hundreds of years," I said, offering a reassuring smile.

"Now, I had hoped," she said as she went around, drawing the curtains, "that Isadore would also be here to participate in this. With our combined blood, you will undoubtedly become an exceptionally powerful immortal. Still, I believe my blood will guide you well on your journey. And perhaps Isadore will be more inclined to share his blood with you once you are already turned. Maybe then, he won't feel like he is transgressing, bending nature, or whatever he likes to call his reasons."

While Isadora finished drawing the curtains, I made sure the door was securely locked so that no intruders could stumble upon the unholy scene that was about to unfold.

"Give me just one moment."

Before proceeding, I quietly ascended the stairs and

peeked into Elizabeth's room. She was already in bed in her new bedroom overlooking the Thames, immersed in her reading. Through the half-open door I whispered a soft "Goodnight."

I didn't tell her that, within the hour, I would awaken her, wrenching her from her human existence and immersing her into an immortal one beyond her current comprehension.

Yes, it would have been nicer of me to have asked her whether she wanted this gift of immortality - but truth be told, I didn't want to give her the opportunity to refute it.

Walking back downstairs, a sense of déjà vu washed over.

"Would you like me to explain how the transformation is done?"

"No," I shook my head, "Just do it."

I walked right into Isadora's arms and she immediately sank her sharp fangs into my neck, tearing through my artery. Every mortal instinct within me screamed to fight back, to resist, to pry this wild creature's jaws away from my neck. But I managed to find calmness and surrender, allowing it to happen.

To facilitate the process, I had positioned a casket in the center of the room and emptied it of flowers, which now littered the floor in a disorganized manner.

I settled myself inside the casket, my body slumping against Isadora as my strength ebbed away from me. She kept drawing my blood with deep, purposeful pulls that felt like they were tugging and pulling at my very veins. The exchange was powerful, and the sensation consumed me. The rush of blood in my ears merged with the pounding of my own heartbeat, or perhaps it was Isadora's, drowning out all other sounds.

My senses were overwhelmed by the fragrance of lilies that hung in the air, pleasant moments earlier, but now suddenly cloying. Then there was a feeling of being carried away on a dark current, of drifting towards eternity like a small boat on a great and uncontrollable sea.

The room spun and swam around me, reminding me of the sensation I experienced when physically dissolving during my time travel. Dully, I realized that this sensation meant I was dying. I was beginning to disappear. Then, all was perfectly dark and perfectly still.

But after a while, I heard Isadora's voice calling out to me, urging me to drink. She pressed her wrist against my parted lips, and I eagerly latched onto it. This was it!

With all the strength I could muster, weakened as I was from the blood loss, I clamped down, drinking hungrily from her wrist. I relished every drop, savoring the taste of her blood as it revitalized me, giving me a new lease on immortality. Let me tell you, there is no taste in the universe that can compete with that! Some of her black vampire blood had spilled onto her arm, and I licked it up, ensuring not a single precious drop went to waste.

"Keep going," she encouraged, her voice shaking faintly with approval at the urgency and greed with which I was embracing vampirism. "Take as much as you can. I want you to be as strong as you can be, as strong as you desire. So don't hold back."

I was all too happy to comply. And pulled deeply, latched onto her arm until finally, I was full. I fell back against the soft satin lining of the casket as Isadora withdrew, collapsing to the floor in a heap of satin and pale, trembling limbs.

Reignited by the blood I had consumed, my senses

gradually returned. The vampiric essence was spreading through my veins like pure, delicious liquid power.

I opened my eyes, gazing at the ceiling. It seemed to ripple and come alive above me, despite being made of solid wood. It seemed to emit a hum, to resonate with an electric charge so subtle, no human senses could ever have picked it up. As a vampire I had come to be used to this, but now, it was magical, even miraculous, all over again.

Slowly, I sat up, amazed that I felt light, strong, and fully alive. I chuckled to myself, levitating effortlessly out of the casket. Standing upright with remarkable ease, I could have wept. Okay, I did weep a little.

There really is no comparison between being a mere mortal and being a vampire. Of course mortals are able to experience intensity and beauty, but it just pales in comparison to the heightened senses and perceptions that come with vampirism. I simply don't know what else to tell you.

As I stood in the middle of Deep Graves, my entire world seemed to fall back into place. "Oh, it feels awfully good to be back!" I exclaimed, to no one in particular.

Isadora looked dazed as I reached down and offered her my hand. She took it and I pulled her up from the floor and into a tight hug. Isadora was now my only maker, and I would be forever grateful to her. If she ever needed me, if she ever required help with anything at all, if she was ever threatened, she would be able to count on me without question and without fail.

"Now," I said, tearing my attention away from the mesmerizing beauty of the room and of Isadora so that I could focus on the task at hand. "The first thing I must do now, above all else, is to share this magnificent gift with Elizabeth."

"Let me help you do it," Isadora offered without skipping a beat. "She will become a stronger vampire if we combine our efforts."

"If you feel strong enough right now," I replied, mindful of the fact that every last drop of blood singing through my veins at this very moment had come from her.

Isadora nodded earnestly. "I'm sure she will benefit from my strength. Just help me afterwards into one of the caskets and make sure Elizabeth and you are in one as well before dawn. You must never forget to always hide from the rays of the sun during the day."

"Of course," I assured her.

I went to fetch Elizabeth, climbing the creaking stairs alone. I couldn't fathom how to begin explaining to my sister what was about to happen to her, but I was determined to offer her some form of rationale, a bit of a heads up that Isadora was waiting downstairs in the shop, and that she came bearing an unfathomable gift.

I hesitated in the hallway outside Elizabeth's bedroom. Then, slowly, I pushed the door open. It creaked as it swung inwards, but she didn't even stir.

Kneeling beside her bedside, I very gently shook her shoulder until her pale green eyes sprang open with a startled expression.

"What is it, Gabriel? Is something wrong?"

"There's nothing to worry about anymore, Elizabeth. All is well. Now please don't be afraid." I'd taken an oil lamp with me upstairs and now I lifted it to illuminate my vampiric features.

Elizabeth scrambled and sat up in bed, her eyes widening as she took in my changed appearance.

"Gabriel, you're, you look..." she searched for the right word. When she didn't find it, her voice died in her throat.

"Different," I finished the sentence for her. "Yes, sister. I've just been given a great gift. And, if you please..." I extended my hand to her. "It is a gift that will also be offered to you. Come with me now."

She looked at my hand, frowning softly. My hand was perfectly pale, and my fingernails had transformed into gleaming, tapered shards of glass. She hesitated. But then she took my hand, choosing to trust me.

She was still half asleep as I guided her down the staircase in her nightgown. "The transformation you are about to undergo may not be pleasant," I explained. "In fact, it might be quite frightening. But I ask you to trust me. Do not resist it, do not fight it. Embrace it. Your life will be forever transformed. Your physical body will be immune to sickness, like the plague and its ilk. You will be impervious to old age. You will die momentarily, but then you will live forever."

"Gabriel." The last traces of sleepiness had left her voice and instead made way for fear. "You're frightening me. I'm not sure what you're really saying, and I'm not sure I want to find out." Her eyes searched my face as we descended into the shop, and then her gaze fell upon Isadora, who was sitting in a corner of the room, in a big, high back chair, surrounded by coffins and caskets and clocks, all of it illuminated by a multitude of candles.

No doubt Elizabeth was noticing, finally truly noticing, the pale luster of Isadora's skin, and the crystalline glow of her eyes that was too vivid to be human. Her entire body stiffened. "Something is wrong."

Elizabeth let go of my hand and backed up against the staircase until she bumped into the bottom step. "Why is she here?"

It was only now I registered that, unfortunately, there

was quite a bit of blood spillage on the front of Isadora's ivory colored blouse. Not to mention that the entire shop floor looked like a tornado had gone through it, knocking over flower arrangements and even a few caskets in its wake.

I looked at Elizabeth, trying to find the right words to calm her fears - but what really could I say? Nothing reassuring.

Isadora stood up, her skirts rustling, and approached my sister, extending her lace-gloved hands. But Elizabeth did not take them. Instead, she crossed her arms in front of her chest.

"Gabriel, why is she here?" she repeated, her eyes somehow both blazing with anger and pleading for an explanation.

Isadora reached for a lace handkerchief and delicately wiped away a few drops of blood that had gathered at the corner of her ruby-red mouth. "Oh, I do apologize for this," she said softly. "How careless of me. But Elizbeth, you mustn't be frightened."

"Elizabeth, I don't mean to shock you, but the sight of blood is something you will have to get used to," I explained. "As a nurse, you have already witnessed plenty of it, always in connection with suffering. However, blood is also a symbol of life, vitality, strength, and beauty. These are things you will come to understand."

Elizabeth looked at me, incredulous.

"Trust your brother," Isadora interjected. "And trust me." Then, looking over at me, "This process will be easier if Elizabeth willingly embraces it. If she accepts the gift being offered to her, even if she doesn't understand all of its implications."

"What gift?" Elizabeth demanded, placing emphasis on

the word gift in such a way that it made it sound like an insult. "And what implications is it you're referring to? How can I know if I will accept it if I don't even know what it is? I feel as though this is all rather unfair."

"You're right," I admitted. "This must all seem rather mad to you. But that's because I haven't found the right way to explain everything to you. There is another, deeper component to my plan for tonight that I haven't shared out of fear that you would misunderstand or reject it."

Elizabeth motioned for me to continue, and I took a deep breath. "You know that Isadore and Isadora have been coming to our shop for a very long time. You also know that their continued patronage has been crucial for our family's prosperity and survival over the years."

She nodded, still unsure of where this was all going.

"Well," I continued, gesturing towards Isadora, "you may have noticed that they have never aged. It's because of what they are, the type of beings they are."

"And what are they?" Elizabeth's eyes were fixed on Isadora. Isadora gave her a small smile, an almost apologetic one. "We are what are most often called night demons. The Slavs call us ubirs and the Turks, ubiors."

Elizabeth's shoulder stiffened.

"Here in England and in many other parts of the world," I interjected my own insights, "we will come to be known as vampires. We're blood drinkers. Immortals."

"Blood drinkers?"

Elizabeth began to shiver, and panic started to take hold of her. She looked at Isadora, disbelief and fear evident in her eyes. "So you're a blood drinker, a demon, here to offer us immortality? At what cost? What have you done to Gabriel?"

I opened my mouth to further explain the intricacies of

the situation to Elizabeth, but she vehemently shook her head in protest. "No," she said firmly," stepping away from me in a rush of cool air. "I want no part in this whatsoever."

Suddenly, she bolted towards the door, and when she reached it, rattled the handle. Having locked the door myself, I knew that it wasn't going to budge.

"Elizabeth, please calm down." Closing the distance between us in just a couple of gliding steps, I gently took hold of her shoulders. Her resistance melted away and she let me guide her back to the chair where Isadora had been sitting. Here she sank down, trembling all over and repeating the word "no" over and over again.

TWENTY

lizabeth was still protesting as Isadora and I moved in from either side, both of us clamping down on her neck and piercing her skin. My fangs had only just appeared, brand new and sharp as razors. I used these to render and tear her skin until the blood from an artery spurted into my mouth. Momentarily, all resistance seemed to have left her, but suddenly she frantically tried to fight us off.

Of course, her strength was no match against that of two two powerful immortals, and we had no trouble whatsoever holding her still in the chair until, finally, she stopped fighting, weakened from the blood loss.

"Don't fear what is to come, Elizabeth," I said, pulling back, whilst Isadora was still drinking from Elizabeth's slender throat where she was tethered by the mouth like a ravenous animal. Isadora's jaw had come unhinged, and even I have to admit that there was something quite disturbing about the contrast between that unnaturally unlocked jaw and her delicate features and well-tailored dress.

"Elizabeth," I took her hand in mine, feeling her fingers clench and unclench against my palm like a trapped bird struggling to get free, "there's nothing to fear. Immortality has found you whether you want it or not. Receive this gift as best you can. And I will be here to guide you through it, every step of the way. That I promise you." They were probably no comfort to her right now, but I felt they were words that had to be said.

Finally, Isadora pulled free from Elizabeth's throat and stood back, swaying as if intoxicated by the blood. But then she leaned back in, offering her own neck to Elizabeth.

"Now, drink, drink."

Elizabeth at first refused by turning her face away. But the intoxicating scent of the black vampire blood must have called out to her, weakening her resolve. Hesitantly, she bit down on the tender flesh Isadora offered to her. Soon she was drinking from Isadora's immortal flesh, hesitantly at first, but then with the urgency of someone who is drowning and trying to keep her head above the water. She was no longer able to fight what she was becoming as she pulled on Isadora's blood with all her might. Isadora looked up at me with an exhausted but proud expression on her face, as if to say, Look at our creation.

When Elizabeth had drunk deep enough from Isadora's fountain of immortality, she tore her mouth away from her maker's throat, rose to her feet and staggered backward. I grabbed her and steadied her, lest she fall on the floor. It was now my turn to offer some of my blood to my sister, and I did, offering her my wrist. Now Elizabeth did not even hesitate for a split second but sank her teeth into my skin, her jaw clamping onto my wrist with tremendous force.

"Yes, drink Elizabeth, drink," I encouraged her, "As much as you can." Elizabeth, who had been fighting so bravely and forcefully earlier, now seemed to have completely surrendered to the change which was coming over her. A powerful ripple went through her. I was beginning to feel myself weaken, and I knew I would have to stop her sooner rather than later.

My heart sang as I watched her change. As the vampiric blood coursed through her veins, her skin turned marble white, her hair to spun moonlight and her eyes to glowing citrines. The miracle had been granted! I was proud, delighted, and frankly, extremely relieved.

Then something interrupted this perfect moment.

The doorknob of the door leading to the street and the bridge outside started rattling and twisting. Someone was clearly trying to gain entry. The rattling was followed by a fist against the door, knocking loudly.

My gaze met Isadora's. Who would show up at this time? Had anyone suspected what we were up to?

"Gabriel," a voice called through the door. I recognized it instantly as Isadore's. Had he changed his mind after all? Did he want to participate in the transformation of me and Elizabeth, had he come to offer his own immortal essence - or to try to stop us? Well, he'd missed the boat if that was his intention.

I got up from the floor where I had sunken down on the floor, weakened from blood loss, and opened the door. And sure enough, there stood Isadore on the doorstep, his cape drawn tightly around his shoulders, a closed-off, impenetrable expression on his face. He didn't wait for me to invite him in. Being a vampire really isn't like the fairytales. No one ever waits for an invitation.

Isadora straightened up and dabbed at the blood on her chin, as if she was feeling self conscious and wanted to make herself presentable now that her brother was here.

"I see I have come too late," Isadore observed, striding into the room. He looked around at overturned furniture and blood spilled on lace.

"You have not come too late, Isadore," I said, "you have come just in time. As you can see, my own turning is complete and that of my sister is on the way." I gestured towards Elizabeth. She had only just opened her luminous, newborn vampire eyes and was taking in her surroundings in stunned silence. I knew what she was seeing, sensing, and experiencing - a powerful cacophony of sensual impressions unlike anything she had ever experienced before. It was little wonder she was overcome.

"I've been pacing all night," Isadore confessed, shaking his head forcefully, "wondering what to do. I was power-less, unable to make a decision, but finally, I determined that I would stop you," he turned accusingly towards his sister, "from making any more night demons, from spreading this horrible curse that we are afflicted with, least of all to our dear friend Gabriel, who we always agreed we would protect."

"But this is protection," I stepped forward to allow Isadore to direct his frustrations at me, rather than Isadora. "This is the ultimate protection you could offer me, the ulti-mate gift. As you know, I asked for this myself. I have desired all my life to become what you are."

"You do not understand the darkness that has now come into your life through this curse of blood," Isadore said, his tone dripping with melancholy.

"Do not be so harsh on yourself," Isadora said, trying to calm her brother down. She stepped towards him and reached out for him, but he twisted away from her. "Our blood is not only a curse, it is also a blessing and Gabriel very much sees it that way. He has just told you so himself.

In fact, he has on multiple occasions. Why will you not believe him? Allow him to carve his own path through this universe. We do not all feel as you do, Isadore."

"I couldn't agree more," I said. "This is the path that I've chosen for myself. And, well, also for Elizabeth."

"Oh, but this innocent soul hasn't asked for this," Isadore protested, kneeling in front of Elizabeth, placing his hands tenderly on her shoulders. She looked at him apprehensively. "It's me, Isadore," he told her gently. "Surely you remember me? You have seen me many times in your father's shop. And I can only tell you that I am sorry, so deeply sorry for what my sister has done to you, for the damage she has done. It hurts me. It hurts my soul, I assure you. If only there was some way I could undo what she has done, what she has perpetrated against you and against all creation."

"By god, do you hear yourself? Try not to be so dramatic, Isadore." Isadora was growing exasperated with her brother. "You are being quite histrionic. You're tarnishing everything with a brush of how you choose to see things. You always assume that your view is correct."

Isadore froze, and I could see his shoulders visibly tensing up at Isadora's words "You went against my wishes," he said quietly, his voice cold and tart. "The dark blood" he said slowly, as if picking his way forward through the conversation very carefully, "is not a condition that a doctor might be able to cure. Rather, it is a curse of the most Satanic and twisted kind. Gabriel," Suddenly he stood up again and with one fluid movement spun halfway around to face me, "you have tempted me to pursue art, beauty, and meaning again, to believe that I could once more have access to these things. You made me contemplate the possibility that I could participate in the world once more."

"I should think that I've given you a great gift," I said. "Besides, I only tempted you with the truth."

He was pacing the floor, clearly agitated.

"Let's just agree to disagree," I suggested, but Isadore was having none of it.

"No," he frowned as he halted his pacing mid-step. "This is no simple disagreement. I'm afraid this is something more serious than that."

"I don't want you to blame your sister for what has happened here, for granting my wish. If anything, I convinced her. You were there when I did. So if you must be mad, be mad at me."

Isadore shook his head with increasing conviction, not taking in my words, "I should have stopped her. I should have stopped you!"

He was practically stomping around the room, emitted magnetic radiant tense energy from his very pores. The heat of his anger seemed to spark from the core of his being.

"Isadore, please calm down," Isadora pleaded. She took a step towards her brother again, but again he flinched. "There's no need to turn this into some kind of disaster. It isn't according to anyone here, except you."

"So, my point of view isn't valid, is it?"

Now, Isadore was offended as well as angry.

As if sensing the impeccable timing of the moment, Elizabeth suddenly looked at her own hands and started screaming. For a moment, she completely lost it. Yelling again and again, "What have you done? What have you done, Gabriel? What have you done?"

She seemed horrified by the marble white smoothness of her skin as she reached up to touch her face, feeling the cool, smooth texture. Decidedly inhuman.

"Isadore," she called out, "you're right. I did not want to

become this! I did not ask for this. And if I had been given the choice, I would have said no. In fact, I tried to say no. I tried to refuse this curse, and I was given no choice!"

Isadora looked down, her hands clasped behind her back. "This is technically true," she admitted, deeply uncomfortable and perhaps a little embarrassed as Isadore glared at her.

"But it is for your own good," I interjected, addressing Elizabeth alone. "You cannot see it now. But you will come to understand that this has been my only way of saving you. I have had visions," I reached for her, crouching down and taking both of her hands in mine. "I've seen visions of your death, your horribly untimely death. It may seem as though the plague is over, as though it has already rolled by like an ominous cloud. But I assure you, it still lingers in the streets, it still stalks the city. It is very much still a looming danger. And in my vision, you caught it, Elizabeth. And you died because of it. That is the reason why I have done this, why I have invited what you have just described as this curse into our lives. But it is not a curse; it is a blessing. At worst, it is a double-edged sword, a blessing and a curse in one. But you have me," I said this with the utmost sincerity. "You have me to guide you when you're frightened. And I will illuminate your path through this darkness because I have walked it before. All this is something that I may explain to you in time, but not tonight."

Elizabeth shook her head, a gesture that seemed to imply both rejection of my words and disbelief. "This is all wrong," she insisted. "Everything looks beautiful and vivid to me now, but it feels wrong. It feels as though I've crossed a threshold that should have never been crossed."

"Indeed, indeed," Isadore chimed in. I had to quell my urge to hiss at him to shut up, to stay out of it. He went on,

"That is how it is. And now, if only I could find a way to undo it." Suddenly, he lunged forward and grabbed me by the lapels of my jacket, tearing the fabric. "You have made a tremendous mistake tonight, Gabriel. You have made an enemy of me."

"There's no need for such statements, for such black and white thinking," Isadora grasped her brother's arm, trying to wrench him away from me. But Isadore was adamant and stood his ground. He was staring directly into my eyes, his hazel ones radiating disdain. "You have seduced my sister to cloak you in eternal darkness. Not to mention how you have transgressed against your own sister. Forcing this cursed existence upon her when she is so innocent, so pure and so completely undeserving of your thoughtless cruelty. Don't you see? You've condemned her to become a monster, a murderess."

I could feel my own anger now boiling and rising to the surface, but I did not want to act on it. Isadore and I were evenly matched in size and strength, and it was anyone's guess who would be stronger in a fight. He had at least a century of vampiric age on me, but I wasn't as much of a fledgling vampire as he thought I was. And I might have the element of surprise on my side. Still, I did not really want to test this theory.

But Isadore didn't appear to be thinking rationally. Suddenly he shoved me against the wall, against the grandfather clock standing there. It gave a loud melancholy chime as my back crashed into it. Several pieces of wood broke on impact and he let go of me as I fell and slid to the floor. Elizabeth, panicked and angry though she may be with me, immediately ran to my side and started brushing away broken pieces of wood and little metal screws that had rained down on me, along with shattered glass.

"Are you hurt?" she asked in a soft, frightened voice. She didn't even look over her shoulder to see whether Isadore was contemplating another attack.

Isadore's eyes, ignited with fury, were locked on me. Isadora came up behind him, wrapping her arms around him and trying to pull him backward, but he didn't let her. He clearly wasn't prepared to let this go.

"Isadore, please," I said, rising to my feet, only slightly aided by Elizabeth. "I suggest that you and Isadora go home now and that we leave each other alone. No good can come of this."

"It is already too late," Isadore rejected my proposal outright. "Didn't I tell you, you have transgressed upon something that was sacred, namely human life?" He shook his head. "I'm afraid there's no going back now."

"What do you intend to do?" I challenged him. "Would you erase our years of friendship, simply because I now have different blood in my veins? Would you have me killed for simply becoming what I am now? No, Isadore," I shook my head, hoping to convince him, "you're smarter than this. Don't let this momentary anger get the better of you."

He hesitated. Clearly he hadn't decided what he intended to do. He was merely angry, and I was trying to think of something that would bring him back down to earth, steady his nerves and cool his temper, at least for long enough for Elizabeth and I to get out of here.

I knew that the coach would have returned to the bridge after delivering my mother safely to the house in Bride Lane. It would be waiting out there right now, as I had ordered. Unless, of course, Isadore had seen the coach on his way here and had told Lacey to return to Knights-bridge, in which case, my plan would be harder to execute.

Either way, I needed to get myself and Elizabeth to

Highgate where, with a little help from the ectoplasm, I would bring my little mission to a close.

But right now Isadore was in the way. I had not counted on making an enemy of him. But there you go. Sometimes things don't go according to plan, and you have to improvise with what you're given.

Isadore had fallen silent, his eyes alighting on something that was lying on the floor. I followed his gaze.

To my great horror, I saw the vials of ectoplasm lying on the carpeted floor. They must have fallen out of my pocket when Isadore had torn my jacket. Now, he was looking at them with great interest, forgetting his anger.

"Oh, but what are these?" He asked with curiosity. Before I could answer, he knelt down and picked up one of the vials. He held it up to the light, studying it much like Westminster had only a few nights earlier.

My mind raced for a plausible explanation. I couldn't very well call them poison in front of him. He would easily be able to tell if I was lying.

"They're talismans," I said, improvising. My voice sounded calm, but inwardly, I was shaking. If I could sweat as a vampire, I would be now.

"Well, they look like paint to me," declared Isadore. "What an interesting substance." He shook the small vial in his hand, watching the silvery, swirling fluid move around.

I had to dissuade Isadore's interest away from the vials. I feared this interest of his more than his anger. I would have to tread carefully.

"Isadore," I said, reaching out my hand towards him, indicating that he should give the vials back to me. He hesitated, now holding both vials protectively.

"Please, Isadore," I said, "they have tremendous sentimental value to me. Each of these vials contain something of my mother and my father. They represent a way of always carrying them with me, so that even when I have lost them both, I'll still have them nearby."

I hoped this would work. If I understood the fibre of Isadore's character correctly, it was bound to.

TWENTY-ONE

"No," Isidore shook his head slowly, as if he hated having to deliver bad news, "Gabriel, you no longer have the right to such sentiments. Such tender feelings belong to the world of mortals, and we should have no part in them." As he spoke, he closed his fingers around the vials.

"It's too late for me to stop what you've become," he continued after a deep breath, "But the very least you could do in return is to let me have these. I will use them for paint; no doubt they will shed a little bit of humanity on my inhuman arts." With these words, he slipped the vials into his own pocket while looking me dead in the eye, as though daring me to try to defy him.

Which of course I would have to, one way or the other. A noble confession this might not be, but these vials meant more to me than if they had contained a strand of hair from each of my parents. I knew that I could always communicate with my parents in my own way, and I didn't need any physical tokens to feel connected to them. But without the ectoplasm, my hopes of making my triumphant return to the future with Elizabeth would be extinguished.

Silently, I contemplated my next move. I could fight Isidore here and now or I could let him walk away and attempt to retrieve the vials later. The question was, how much later? And would I be able to ever find them again once I let them out of my sight?

No, I couldn't risk it. I couldn't risk showing up on Isadore's doorstep tomorrow night, only to find that he had already cracked the vials open and poured their irreplaceable contents onto his canvases.

"Isadore," I said, deciding to give him one last warning, "give these back to me this very moment, or I guarantee you, you will regret it with every fibre of your being. I have always been grateful to you and Isadora for your patronage, support and encouragement, everything you've done for me. But if you steal these vials from me, I will never forgive you and I will never let you live it down."

Isadore seemed, if anything, satisfied that he had found a sore spot, and he stubbornly shook his head. "No, I can't give them to you. Surely you will manage just fine without them."

His words spurred me into a rage and in a flurry of movement, I crossed the space between us. With the palms of my hands placed upon his shoulders I ran forward until Isadore's back slammed against the wall at the opposite end of the room.

I pushed him with such force that he left an imprint on the mahogany wood panelling and shattered a display case as he reached blindly for something that would allow him to pull himself to his feet. Damn it, it felt marvellous being this strong again.

The floor was now entirely covered in shattered glass, splintered wood and shredded flowers. Isadora had grabbed Elizabeth's arm and was guiding her toward the corner of the room, protecting her from her brother's rage as well as mine.

Isadore staggered as he rose to his feet, but he soon refound his balance. He let out one long, ragged breath and looked up at me through a lock of hair that had tumbled over his eye. "Gabriel," he said in a low voice, "have you gone mad? The dark flame has already made you feel invincible, but I promise you, you're not. And you do not want to fight me. Certainly not in front of your sister. You've already frightened her half to death."

Instead of dwelling on his words, my eyes scanned the room in front of me, looking for something I could use to threaten or hurt him. I didn't like having to even think along these lines, but Isadore wasn't giving me any other options. Believe me, I would have taken them.

My eyes fell on the pendulum from the broken grandfather clock lying on the floor somewhere to my right. I contemplated taking it and stabbing Isadore in the chest or in the throat with it. Yes, this was my best option.

And so, I reached for the pendulum and approached him again. His eyes widened as I advanced. He narrowly flung himself to the side and avoided me, and we circled each other in the middle of the room. Isadora screamed.

"Gabriel," Isadore's voice was somewhere between frightened and bemused. "What the devil has gotten into you?"

"What has gotten into me is that this is your last chance, your very last one. Don't make me do something I would rather not do. You know I care about you, but you're backing me into a corner. I'm determined to get those vials back. And I hope that it won't be at great cost to you."

"Gabriel, Isadore, please," Isadora cut in, her voice tense with worry. "Stop this fighting! This isn't worth it. It is utterly senseless. Isadore, just give him back the vials. We can easily find other rare paints for you to use."

"But I want these ones," Isadore said out of the corner of his mouth. His eyes and attention were fully on me. He launched at me, grabbing for me. But he didn't expect me to have adapted so quickly to my new vampiric abilities. He had no idea that I knew exactly how to navigate and move to make the most of my supernatural strength.

I let him lash out first.

I dodged, and then when he was tipped forward, his entire weight on the tip of his toes, I drove the pendulum from the grandfather clock through his neck.

It went in one side and out the other. Isadore blinked and immediately made a rasping sound as blood splashed on the wall and on the broken glass on the floor.

He half-turned towards me and I let go of the weighted part of the pendulum which I had used as a handle. While the rest of us stood frozen in a semi-circle around him, Isaodre fell to his knees, clutching at his throat, unable to utter any words although he was clearly trying.

Isadora also fell on her knees, right at his side while Elizabeth pressed her body against the wall, terrified of what she was witnessing. Her mouth was moving but she wasn't forming any words either.

Kneeling next to her brother, Isadora tried to pull the sharp end of the pendulum from his neck. But he was trying to push her away. With these two suitably distracted, I leapt into action.

I lunged forward, dipping my hand into the breast

pocket of Isadore's coat where I'd seen him put the vials. I felt them at my fingertips and I grabbed them, swiftly withdrawing my hand. My eyes flashed only momentarily over Isidore and Isadora, who were desperately struggling on the floor. What a mess, what a tragedy! Should keep them busy for a while.

I had to step around the twins to get to Elizabeth. She was stiff with fear and didn't react or respond to me in any way when I gently took her by the wrist.

"Elizabeth," I said, "we must go now."

She shook her head, stammering, "We should help him... We should help them. Isadore is badly hurt, Gabriel. You might have killed him."

She tried to pry my fingers away from her wrist, but I wouldn't let go. "He's an immortal," I said, "I doubt I've killed him, but I do hope I've slowed him down. Now, come on, my dear. Chop chop!"

Isadore and Isadora seemed not to hear or care about anything that was going on around them. Isadore had fallen onto his back, still gasping and choking. Isadora was bent over him, attempting to remove the pendulum which Isadore, for some inexplicable reason, was holding onto on the other side of his throat, preventing her from pulling it out of his airway and arteries.

I put my arm around Elizabeth and pulled her with me, guiding her towards the door, away from the pitiful, terrifying sight of the struggling twins. We didn't have time to dwell on it. It was time for Elizabeth and I to make our escape to Highgate. We had only a small window of opportunity and we had to use it.

Outside on the streets, in the rain a few meters away, I was relieved to see the dark silhouette of the horse-driven coach. Lacey sat patiently in the rain, the water dripping from the brim of his hat. Thank god for this man!

I pulled Elizabeth with me over the cobblestones to the carriage. "Lacey," I said, startling him. He had seemingly been sleeping or at least waiting in some sort of meditative state.

Immediately, he straightened his shoulders and turned his attention to me. "To Highgate," I instructed him, "via Swain's Lane."

"Understood, sir." As he prepared to descend from his perch to open the doors for us, I quickly held up my hand to stop him. "We'll get in ourselves. We're in a tremendous hurry. Ride like you've never ridden before!"

"Yes, sir," he said again, and I opened the carriage door, ensuring that Elizabeth entered before me. She was looking over her shoulder back towards Deep Graves as if expecting the Elysion twins to pursue us, or perhaps expecting some kind of specter of my sins to follow us like a shadow.

But no one was following us, at least not yet. The shop door was half open and a small square of light spilled onto the gray and rainy street.

As soon as Elizabeth and I were both safely inside the opulently upholstered carriage, we immediately set in motion. Moments later, we had cleared the bridge and were winding our way through the streets of central London.

My heart was still racing at an uncomfortable speed, tension still coursing through my body and rippling through my energy field. But as we drove past St. Paul's Cathedral, I allowed myself to relax a little.

"Gabriel," Elizabeth said in a hushed voice, as if Lacey could hear us from his perch on the coach box, "What have you done? What were those vials? What are they really?"

"They contain something very precious and rare," I

replied in an equally low and quiet voice. "And soon you will know what it's for."

"I don't want any more secrets. And certainly no more surprises," Elizabeth's voice was pleading. "I've seen too much in the last two hours. I've experienced things I never wanted to experience - I've had enough." She slumped back in her seat, folding her arms across her chest. "I really don't know what to think of all this," she continued. "I'm furious with you. And worse, I'm disappointed. I don't know how I'm going to forgive you."

"You will," I promised her, placing a hand on her arm. But she pulled her arm away.

"Do not try to console me right now," she sneered, and her sheer defiance made me smile, because she was clearly recovering from her state of shock.

"Very well, then," I said. "If you'd rather be in silence, that's fine by me."

Looking out the window at the rainy night time streets whizzing past, it struck me how exceptionally narrow they were, with the 1600s buildings leaning in over the road and nearly touching each other in places. At least there wasn't much traffic. Despite the plague having somewhat retreated, fear still loomed over the city and everything moved at a slower pace. Most people kept to themselves, hoping to avoid breathing in any deadly miasma, which left the streets mostly empty. Through the window, I caught glimpses of a woman drawing water from a well, a few figures standing in doorways conversing, and even a plague doctor next to a cart loaded with just a few corpses - a modest harvest, compared to what it would have been only a few weeks earlier.

"Elizabeth," I turned from the window to look at her,

"Isn't it true that I've always done what was best for our family?"

"You've always done what you thought was best." She didn't look at me. She was looking straight ahead with an unreadable expression, probably trying to process everything that had happened tonight.

"I hope Isadore is going to be alright," she said finally. "We should have stayed to help him. You haven't even told me why we're going to Highgate - why are we going to Highgate?"

"You'll see," I replied. "We're going on a journey."

I was in a great mood, but suddenly, a sharp piercing pain shot through my innards like a bolt of lightning. I stiffened in my seat, emitting a pained groan before I could stop myself.

"Gabriel, what's going on? Did Isadore hurt you? Did he wound you in any way?" Elizabeth looked alarmed, her pale green eyes wide with fear.

I shook my head. "No," I managed to say. I'd almost forgotten this part of the vampiric transformation. How could I have been so forgetful?

At first, when the dark blood courses through your veins, you're filled with renewed vitality and energy. It's a pleasurable experience as you feel the immortal powers taking over. However, soon afterwards, your body begins to eject all of its human tissue. Your inner organs liquefy and come out as a gush of oozing liquid. This was beginning to happen to me now, and the pain was indescribable.

Groaning, I fell forward in my seat. "Tell the driver," I managed in a hoarse voice, "tell him to keep driving no matter what. To get us to the fields of Highgate, to the bottom of Swain's Lane. Now, Elizabeth, I'll explain everything later."

I could barely get the words out. My jaw was clenching involuntarily as the black liquid started rising in my throat, then spilling out over my lips and onto the carriage floor. Its movement was sickening, much like the movement of a ship.

I was caught in a tide of intense pain that rolled over me in waves, almost blinding me. I was barely able to make out Elizabeth as she pushed aside the small window panel to speak to Lacey. She was saying something, but the rushing in my ears and the pain were too intense and I couldn't follow it. I allowed myself to slump to the narrow floor of the carriage. I knew I had to lie still and let it pass.

Hopefully, it would be over by the time we arrived in Highgate. I wasn't sure how long our journey would take, but I estimated about an hour, perhaps a little longer. In the depths of my pain, a thought occurred to me in a searing flash. Why hadn't Isadore and Isadora infused the horses with the vampiric blood? If they had, we would have traveled much faster. Of course they didn't want to arouse suspicion by traveling at anything other than a normal speed wherever they went. This was understandable, but not practical at all in our current predicament.

I must have passed out for a moment, because suddenly, the carriage floor came into view again. Elizabeth was lying next to me, slumped over. It looked like she had fallen from her seat. Her dress was bunched up and ballooning around her. Her mouth was open, and black liquid was seeping out of it. She was convulsing violently, and her eyes were open but entirely vacant.

"Elizabeth," I reached out to touch her cheek, then stroke her forehead. "Fear not, this will be over soon. This is the last pain you will feel as part of your turning. I'm sorry I didn't warn you about it. But in truth, I'd actually forgotten." I wondered if I had truly forgotten or if I had just blanked out how unpleasant this part of the process was.

I was still in pain, but I was able to move. I managed to get myself up onto my hands, knees and elbows, and then back up into a seated position. As I was about to sink back into my seat, something heavy was thrown against the side of the carriage, making the entire cabin shake.

I pulled aside the purple velvet curtain and looked out. We had left London behind us, and we were nearing High-gate, via the streets of Kentish Town.

My heart quickened with shock.

A figure was moving next to the carriage. It was Isadora outside in the rain, running alongside the carriage. She was soaked to the bone, her face was contorted with fury.

At least Isadore was nowhere to be seen. Had I actually managed to hurt him badly? Wounded him fatally? Isadora certainly seemed maddened and furious as she threw herself against the carriage again.

Now it was my turn to pull aside the little window to speak to Lacey. I did this in the most forthright way possible, grabbing the back of his neck. "No matter what you see or hear, you keep driving until I tell you to stop. Do you understand?" I heard him audibly swallow and he nodded.

I did not enjoy threatening this man who had done nothing to deserve it. But right now, I wasn't prepared to take any chances.

The window on my side of the carriage shattered in that instant.

Isadora's arm reached in, flailing wildly as her hand reached for either me or the handel on the inside of the door. I quickly ensured that the doors on both sides were locked from the inside. Of course, with her strength, Isadora might be able to rip the doors from the wagon itself. She might be able to do this and then drag us out into the rain. This was something I couldn't control.

I cast a quick glance at Elizabeth, who was still on the floor, oblivious to her surroundings.

I wasn't sure exactly what I intended to do, but I opened the carriage door on my side and climbed out onto the roof of the moving carriage.

"Isadora," I called out into the rain, "I do not want to fight you, but I will if I have to. And here I am! You choose."

CHAPTER
TWENTY-TWO

I sadora was catching up to the carriage again. As she got close to it, she jumped, grabbing onto the edges of the lacquered roof with her long, tapered fingernails. That was her mistake. I stomped on her fingers, forcing her to let go.

She landed on her feet and stood panting in the middle of the street behind us, fast disappearing as the coach driver swung his whip above the panting horses. Their backs were glistening with exertion, or it could have been the rain. What Lacey might have been thinking of all of this I had no idea, but to his credit he kept on driving just as I'd instructed him to do.

The road forked. As we took a left turn up Highgate Road, really not much more than a muddy trail at this point in time, Isadora disappeared from sight.

I was about to climb back into the carriage when she started catching up again. She shouted after me, "Gabriel, I never wanted this violence."

"Neither did I," I called back to her. "So why don't you

stop pursuing us? We need not create any more enmity between us."

"This is all your doing!" Isadora was relentless, and the rain was coming down hard and heavy from the heavens above.

Her hair was wet and plastered to her face, hanging in streaming strings, black with rain.

"Isadore never meant anything by what he said," Isadora pleaded, swerving and swooping in from this side of the road and then the other, "He wasn't really threatening you or intending to take your precious vials."

Oh, really? It had certainly seemed otherwise to me.

I was determined to prevent her from gaining entry into the carriage where she could harm Elizabeth, and to not let her get onto the roof either. I was also conscious of having to protect the driver. As a mortal man, he was vulnerable to her potential attack. The fact that he had served his mistress well for years did not necessarily mean that she wasn't willing to sacrifice him in order to stop me.

Highgate wasn't far away now. We would be there within five to ten minutes. "Isadora, just give up," I implored her. "Stop following us, you will not be able to stop us. And you will only end up forcing me to do you harm as well. And I really do not want to do that. Do not back me into a corner the way Isadore did. Learn from his mistake. Turn around, Isadora. Your brother needs you - go tend to him."

"You have to answer for what you have done!"

Isadora was crying. And in truth, I felt terrible for her. Worse than that, I felt guilty for having hurt Isadore. I still didn't know how badly, but I didn't have time to stop. I could not afford to waver. The second I let my guard down she might seize her chance to throw me to the ground. She might attempt to take the vials, she might crush them.

It seemed that the fulfillment of my plan was hanging by a thread. Not to mention, I had created a spectacular mess in my wake by making powerful enemies of the Elysions. This was something I hadn't anticipated, foreseen, or wanted.

But here we were, and Isadora was only making it worse by continuously hurling the full weight and strength of her body against the side of the carriage, making it rattle and crushing more of the glass inside the window. At one point she managed to rip one of the handles off the door. But fortunately, the door itself held; it was strongly built, and she knew this, having commissioned it herself.

"Isadora," I called out through the rain, "I will break your neck if I have to."

Once again, she was out of view, nowhere to be seen, but I wasn't ready to believe that she had given up the chase.

Did I really have to prepare for her attacks all the way to Highgate? How was I going to deal with her once the carriage stopped at my destination? I had to think this through and quickly.

I didn't get the chance.

Suddenly both of the horses whinnied and stood up on their hind legs, kicking with their front hooves. The reason was Isadora, standing right in the middle of the street, looking up at the horses, the carriage, and me with a steely expression on her face. She was willing to risk anything to stop me, it would seem.

While the horse stopped abruptly in the rainy streets, the carriage swerved and then fell on its side with a thunderous crash. Lacey and I were both thrown off the carriage roof - him from his seat in the front, I from the roof behind him.

I saw all of this happen almost in slow motion. I was able to land on my feet, about ten feet or so from the carriage, which was now lying on its side, two of its wheels spinning listlessly in the air.

Isadora was still standing in the middle of the road. Behind her was the field that would one day become High-gate Cemetery. We had nearly reached my destination. But Isadora had managed to cut our journey short.

I wasn't sure what she intended to do. Surely she must realize that Elizabeth and I would be able to overpower her together. She might be a stronger vampire than both of us, having lived longer, and had more time to get used to her strength and immortal body. But there were two of us.

"Isadora," I snarled, my voice a low growl, "do not come any closer. I don't know how much clearer I could possibly be."

I was keeping an eye on her while also trying to keep an eye on the carriage. Thankfully, I saw the door handle move and then the door swung open. Elizabeth's pale blonde head emerged. A crash like this might have fatally injured a human body. But that's no longer what Elizabeth's was. She levitated up through the door that was still able to open and landed daintily on her feet in the street, an amazed expression on her face. Her first real taste of vampiric power! No doubt she was going to love being a vampire as much as I did, given time.

There were a few houses across the road. I saw a light flickering in one of the windows, but no one came running out to see what was happening. Either the occupants hadn't noticed us, or they didn't want to get in the middle of what seemed like a dangerous fight or maybe a holdup.

Lacey had been flung across the road and he was lying in an unnatural position with his head in a puddle. Too bad. Now I could never thank him for his assistance.

I made a mental note to reward his descendant, Hyacinth, all the more in the present in order to make up for it, or at least to appease my own conscience.

Seeing the driver's lifeless, crumpled form, Elizabeth ran to him, trying to pull him up and out of the water, turning him over. But his neck was clearly broken, twisted at an awkward angle.

"Elizabeth," I called out to her, "get the shovel from the carriage, we're going to need it."

Elizabeth's gaze slid from me to the carriage, then to the driver and back again. She seemed uncertain what to do for a moment. But then she went to the carriage to retrieve the shovel I had placed under the seat earlier this evening.

Isadora had other ideas.

"I'm not sure what you think you're doing, Elizabeth," she said in a warning tone, cutting off my sister's path.

"Isadora, let her through!" I demanded, "We will do you no harm unless you force us to. And right now, you are getting really close to that territory, don't you think?"

"What I think is that you must pay for what you've done to Isadore." Isadora's tone was almost reasonable.

In a swift leap, I put myself between Isadora and Elizabeth. I sensed Elizabeth moving behind me, no doubt retrieving the shovel from the carriage as I'd told her.

Isadora was half following her with her eyes, but she also tried to keep focused on me. There was barely a foot between us now. Both of us were standing like cats with bushy tails, regarding each other, ready and waiting for the other to strike.

"I've got it!" I heard Elizabeth call out from behind me.

"Hold onto it," I told her, "no matter what."

I was glad that Elizabeth's turning was complete. If I had had to carry and drag her while she was completely unconscious and still gushing the black liquid, the task in front of me would have been more of an uphill climb.

I reached for the vials of ectoplasm. The pocket where I'd been keeping them had of course been torn to shreds earlier, but I had transferred them to a trouser pocket, terrified all the while that I would somehow lose them, or that I would crush them. Neither of these things had happened.

"Elizabeth," I said again, my eyes still locked on Isadora's, "come and stand right behind me, as close as you can be, and listen to me. Be ready for anything."

I sensed Elizabeth moving up close behind me. She let me know that she was there by placing the palm of her hand against the small of my back.

Isadora snarled, not liking that Elizabeth and I were conspiring and that she didn't know what our endgame was. Elizabeth, of course, didn't know either. But I had a plan in mind. We would run for the fields.

Once we were there, in the right spot, I would keep Isadora at bay while Elizabeth dug a grave with the shovel. As soon as the grave was ready, we would consume the ectoplasm, leap in and disappear back to the future. At least, I hoped this is how it would go.

Reaching one hand behind my back, I grabbed Elizabeth's and squeezed tightly.

"Isadora," I addressed our unexpected opponent, "Elizabeth and I are going now into the fields and you will not follow us. Do you understand? I am more than willing to explain my actions tonight at some future time. But right now, Elizabeth and I have something we must do."

I was looking into Isadora's eyes, searching for the person I knew was in there, the person who had guided and protected me throughout my life in her own subtle way. I knew she was in there somewhere, no matter what I had done tonight.

Isadora's shoulders hunched forward, and she bent slightly as if in defeat.

"I hope you'll believe me when I say that I never meant either you nor Isadore any harm," I said, "I was simply defending myself, simply taking back what is rightfully mine. Do you see what I mean?"

Isadora shook her head slowly, but she seemed uncertain.

I spoke to her very gently, not wanting to upset her, not wanting to fan the fires of anger that I had seen burn so bright in her only moments earlier.

"Isadora," I said, "I'd much prefer to be your loyal friend and ally throughout the centuries that await us. And this is only possible if you let me go now. We can draw a line right here." Slowly, I held the hand that wasn't holding Elizabeth's out to Isadora.

"The animosity between us doesn't have to follow us into the future. It is entirely up to you."

Her eyes were half-closed while she regarded me. She let out a deep sigh, one that seemed to emanate from the depths of her soul.

"That is what I wanted all along," she finally said. "But I'm afraid you forfeited that opportunity when you stabbed my brother's neck without remorse. No, I'm afraid that our bonds of friendship and alliance cannot withstand such an attack."

"I know I've made mistakes tonight, terrible mistakes, but only in self-defense, only in desperation." My hand was still held out to her, my palm still open and presenting my invisible offering of friendship.

She lunged out suddenly, trying to get not to me but to Elizabeth. Reacting on instinct, I blocked her with my arm and threw her to the ground. For a moment, she lay reeling before raising up on her forearms and lifting her gaze to meet mine.

"Enough." I told her firmly.

But the fires of hatred that I'd seen in her eyes were back again.

"Elizabeth, run, now!" I pulled Elizabeth with me as I set into motion. The two of us ran as fast as we could into the muddy fields across the road.

The road had been steady enough, but the field, soaked with water, was muddy and slippery beyond belief.

Behind us, Isadora had regained her feet and started after us, but she was far behind us, running up Swain's Lane, and then cutting left into the field, sliding in her high-heeled boots.

"Gabriel, I curse you!" she shouted, her voice nearly drowned out by the thickening curtain of rain and by the sudden thunder that rolled over us. "I curse your name."

Ignoring her, I guided Elizabeth towards the spot where in the future, the Circle of Lebanon would stand. It didn't take me long to sense its exact location. As a mortal man, I would have felt rather lost. But in my immortal state, I was able to sense quite clearly where the ley lines were running like veins underneath the layers of rotting leaves, mud and earth.

The Circle of Lebanon was the intense heart of the entire circulatory system of ley lines that criss crossed this area like the veins in a metaphysical body. I stopped, marking the exact location with the shovel.

Elizabeth looked frightened, of course, but she immediately knelt down and started digging with her bare hands. I joined in with the shovel, which I would have let her use if it wasn't for the fact that I intended to use it to protect us against Isadora, should she attempt anything reckless.

She was fairly close now, circling us like a shark that had tasted blood.

"Gabriel, what do you think you're doing? What are you attempting?" She demanded to know. She sensed that some kind of ritual was going on, but she couldn't discern what it was, and this infuriated her.

I didn't respond, but focused instead on the task at hand: digging a grave, big and wide enough for both Elizabeth and I to lay down in. As soon as we were in it, we would swallow the contents of the vials of ectoplasm, and we would ride out on this thunderstorm, its metaphysical essence propelling us forward in time to the very moment, or as close to it as possible, where I had started this Promethean journey.

"Elizabeth, he intends to kill you and bury you alive here in this field." Isadora was now trying a different tactic.

"Do not listen to her, my dear," I told Elizabeth, who determinedly kept on digging.

"Hasn't your brother proven himself to be not who you thought he was?" Isadora challenged in a softly lilting voice, addressing only Elizabeth. "Hasn't he already lied to you several times tonight? How can you trust him now? He's already killed my brother, and now he wants to kill you. But Elizabeth, you do not have to follow him to the brink of madness and beyond. I can help you. I can offer you a safe haven and teach you the ways of your new existence."

Elizabeth didn't stop, but her movements seemed to slow slightly, and I thought perhaps she was listening to

Isadora's words, words that dripped like a sweet and seductive poison into her ears.

"Elizabeth, whatever you do, keep digging," I implored her. "We have eternity in front of us, but only if we act swiftly in this moment right now."

"Come to me," Isadora was keeping a safe distance, seeing the shovel clutched in my hands, but she was reaching out her own, palms up towards Elizabeth. "Gabriel can dig his own grave, but there's no need for you to join him. As Isadore said, and rightfully so, you are an innocent and pure soul. Do not let your brother's darkness taint your spirit. Let me help you, come to me."

"Gabriel, tell me she's lying," Elizabeth, still kneeling on the ground, turned her face to look up at me, doubt flickering across her features like a flame.

"She's lying," I said emphatically, although there was a grain of truth in Isadora's words. Even I had to acknowledge that I was not the pure and good soul that Elizabeth had always assumed. After all, hadn't I clandestinely brought her into an immortal existence she never asked for? Hadn't she seen me brutally attack Isadore, seemingly over the minor transgression of taking two small vials of paint from me? And wasn't it also true that she had seen me defeat Westminster without a shred of mercy? Hadn't she known for months that I had been stealing from the rich rather than trying to help London's poor and suffering? The list was admittedly growing rather long.

Reaching into my trouser pocket, I withdrew the two remaining vials of ectoplasm. The moment had arrived.

"I need you to trust me one last time," I said, my voice shaking slightly because I didn't feel certain whether she would. I looked into Elizabeth's eyes. "I need you to drink this. To the last drop."

"He's out to poison you!" Isadora shouted, her voice frantic. "But Elizabeth, do not let this happen. Do not trust him! Together, we can put an end to his evil. We can put an end to his rampage. Elizabeth, do not let him take the new life that has only just begun tonight."

"This is not poison, I assure you," I said, "but you must drink it. It will help us make the journey that lies ahead of us."

"A journey into the realm of death!" Isadora shouted, furious with me, her voice flashing like the roll of thunder overhead. The grave was finally wide and deep enough, and it was time.

Still holding both of the vials in one of my hands, I used my thumb to flick the little skull toppers open, making the vials' contents ready to be consumed. "Down the hatch, Elizabeth," I said. Elizabeth was hesitating, uncertain of how to move forward, clearly unsure of whom to believe or trust.

"Throw it to the ground, Elizabeth, throw it away," Isadora called out, trying with all her might to influence the outcome. "Drink it and you will die."

TWENTY-THREE

For a brief and terrible moment, I didn't know what Elizabeth's choice was going to be. She might smack the vials out of my hand, or she might accept the one that I was offering her.

With trembling fingers, she reached out and took one of the vials from my grasp. I let go of it, almost reluctantly, because I knew that if she were to throw it away now, I would have no spare.

"Elizabeth," I said, looking into her eyes, "You have known me my entire life, and you know that I would never hurt you. What I want for you is not death, but its opposite. And that is what this drink, this elixir is going to give you. I'm asking you now to trust me. I'm asking you to listen to what you know of my soul and my character. I'm not flaw-less. I'm not perfect. I'm not without sin. But you, I have always loved. So here's not to death," I held up my vial, clinking it slightly against hers, "but to eternal life."

Then, I knew I had to leave this final decision up to her. I could have probably forced the elixir down her throat. But I knew she would have to take this one step willingly, or the entire thing would have been solely my doing. I needed to leave her this little bit of agency in all of this. Otherwise, she might keep blaming me for the rest of eternity for having taken away her choices.

I tipped back my head and guzzled down the strange, thick liquid. It glided down my throat and left a trail of inexplicable warmth as it quickly spread to my limbs, making me feel light and warm and tingly all over.

Elizabeth's hesitation lasted only a moment longer. She tipped back her head and emptied her ectoplasm into her open mouth as well.

Now, if you really must know what I would have done if Elizabeth had thrown her vial on the ground, I'll tell you. I would have caught it before it could hit the ground and forced it down her throat. In a heartbeat. But I was glad that I did not have to, and that she would always remember having made her own choice.

"No," Isadora shouted, "No, you mustn't. Elizabeth, no!"

Too late. Elizabeth and I had both consumed our respective doses.

And the stuff was already doing its job. Our surroundings were already starting to blur and spin. I embraced this familiar feeling with open arms. I took Elizabeth's hand and pulled her into the open grave with me.

Inside it, a glowing mist had started to pool and rise, seemingly from somewhere deep inside the ground. "What magic is this?" Isadora hissed.

She was aghast and furious. Something was going on here that she did not understand and that she had been powerless to stop. She came at us now, but I was still clutching the shovel in one hand, signaling that I intended to use it as a weapon.

"Lie down, Elizabeth," I said, "I'll keep Isadora at a distance."

Elizabeth did as I asked, pressing herself into the muddy ground. The mist was already pooling over her and filling the grave with its ethereal glow. Isadora was still circling us, the rain was still pouring down.

"Stand back and do not interfere!" I warned in a sharp tone. Even if she were to fling herself into the grave with us, when the mist filled it completely, she wouldn't be able to travel with us through the rift in time. Not without ecto-plasm, and there was not a single drop left for her to get her hands on.

Still, as the grave was almost completely full of the swirling, glowing mist, and I felt the sensation of my body and consciousness dissolving, I sensed movement out of the corner of my eye. Isadora was throwing herself forward, pitting herself at us with all her might, whether to tear our throats or slash our arteries, or perhaps to yank us from the grave.

Then, as my consciousness finally evaporated, I saw the lightning emerging from the clouds far above. With a loud clap unlike any I had heard before, lightning struck and I heard Isadora scream.

As the electric charge shot through her body, all was quiet and still.

I was floating on a tranquil, glowing sea.

THE WORLD STARTED FADING BACK into view. I opened my eyes and found myself blinking up at the calm, cool stars and the pale full moon, half hidden behind a veil of clouds. There was no rain or thunder here, and I immediately took this as a good sign.

Slowly I sat up, expecting to ache, but I was light and comfortable in my body. There was no trace of pain, fatigue, or fear. Glancing to my left, I saw Elizabeth, her eyelids fluttering as she too regained consciousness.

I sat up in our makeshift grave, which didn't feel muddy or slippery at all. Beneath me, I glanced around and, lo and behold, the familiar and tranquil site of Highgate Cemetery West!

We were in the Circle of Lebanon, a thin and luminous mist that looked like a veil of moonlight cloaking the ground below us. It blew slightly and stirred, but apart from that, there was no other movement, no other sound at all, except for the almost undetectable swaying of branches and rustling of bushes and plants nearby.

"Elizabeth," I said, "it worked! We've arrived. We're home."

Elizabeth's eyes were open now and they were as clear and green as the first leaves in spring. "Gabriel, where are we?" she sat up, looking around, "This is a different place."

"It is not technically a different place but a different time. I have so much to explain to you and to show you." So much indeed.

I felt a sense of relief in my spirit as I stood up and held out my hand to Elizabeth, who took it. I pulled her to her feet effortlessly.

"This is a new time, a new chapter, a new life for you. And perhaps not tonight, but one night soon, I'll tell you the whole story of how this moment came to be. But you will have to suspend your sense of disbelief, because there's so much of this that defies rational explanation."

"Gabriel," she said with a hesitant smile, "I've experienced quite a lot of irrationality tonight. My sense of disbelief has long since left me, let me assure you of that."

For the moment we stood there and surveyed the cemetery that sprawled below us on all sides. I'd never been so pleased to see it. And in this moment, I felt that the Circle of Lebanon and indeed the cemetery itself had fulfilled its destiny. I had been instrumental in the construction of its original blueprint, inspiring and urging the architects and the landscapers to organize and design the layout in such a way that everything aligned perfectly with the ley lines. The ley lines, of course, were conduits of spiritual energy, and I had no doubt that they had strengthened and aided in catapulting me back in time.

Whether my plan would have worked without the cemetery, without this layout, I didn't know. All I knew, and all that mattered, was that I had completed my mission, however imperfectly and messily.

There were lots of potential implications I would have to consider. What was my standing now with the Elysion twins? And were either of them still alive? In the split second before we dissolved and went back to the future, we had witnessed Isadora get struck by lightning. And Isadore, well...

The answers to all of these questions would find me, I was sure, though probably not tonight.

I was about to leap into the air and levitate to the gravelly ground below the Circle when, suddenly, I caught sight of a dark figure moving in the cemetery. Someone was walking up the Egyptian Avenue, striding confidently towards us.

I was able to see perfectly well in the dark, and I recognised the figure almost instantly as Venedict Thornhill. My breath caught in my throat. I did not need to be dealing with any of the Thornhills tonight - especially not him.

Of course, the cemetery belonged to neither of us. It had been built on his family's lands, and his family tomb, in this very moment, was right beneath my feet. But my hand in the creation and design of the cemetery meant that I felt a sense of ownership over it, too.

Either way, here he was.

Elizabeth had seen him too, and she was squeezing my hand to gain my attention. I nodded.

"That," I said, "is Venedict Thornhill. He's closer to a foe than a friend. But I hope he is here with good intentions." I would have to explain the whole sordid history to Elizabeth at some point, but right now it would have to wait.

"Venedict," I called out when he was close enough to hear me.

His eyes were already locked on me. He was coming closer and closer, striding through the gravel which crunched under his boots.

Born during the Victorian era, he still dressed pretty much like a Victorian. Tonight he was wearing a loose white shirt with lace at the sleeves, a pair of tailored trousers, and knee-high boots. The last time I'd seen him, on the night he'd escaped his chain-wrapped casket (Made by yours truly, once upon a time), his hair had been its natural caramel brown. Now the ends were dyed a deep and vivid purple.

His hands were clasped behind his back, and he stopped now in front of the tomb on which Elizabeth and I stood.

"Gabriel," he said, his eyebrows raising slightly, "and could this be Elizabeth?" Venedict knew I had a sister who had died during the plague. I had described that to him.

And of course, Elizabeth resembled me a great deal with her pale blonde hair and pale green eyes. Venedict looked at her with great interest.

I doubted that he had quite forgiven me after my failed attempt at calling Elizabeth's spirit into Octavia's body. At least Octavia herself had forgiven me; that was a start.

Could this be why Venedict had decided to appear? Surely, there was no need for him to hold a grudge. Not with Elizabeth given immortal life in her own body and Octavia imbued with her own spirit, living with him again at Thornhill Mansion on top of the hill. Surely we could call it quits now.

"I am Elizabeth Graves, yes." Elizabeth was a little apprehensive about the newcomer, but she was being polite and friendly enough.

"A sight to behold," Venedict complimented her. "And of course you are. You're every bit Gabriel's sister. It couldn't be more clear. And I congratulate you," Venedict let his gaze glide from Elizabeth back to me, "for having apparently succeeded in somehow retrieving her from the mists of time. Octavia told me that this is what you were up to. A very impressive feat. Perhaps one night, you will share with me the secret of how you did it."

"Perhaps one night I will," I agreed. "But tell me, why are you here? Did you come here for small talk?"

"As a matter of fact, I sensed your presence. But you know me better than that. I did not come for small talk. I came to make you an ultimatum."

"Do enlighten me?" I was willing to listen, but my shoulders stiffened slightly at the sound of the word 'ultimatum'.

'Ultimatum' was a word I didn't mind using, but I did not like to have it directed at me.

"Now that you've found your sister and have succeeded in bringing her back," Venedict said, still looking up at us with his amber-coloured eyes. I'd always found them beautiful, and I still did, which of course annoyed me greatly. "I propose that you leave the cemetery to me. And certainly, that you leave the Circle of Lebanon and the Egyptian Avenue to me. Perhaps I will tolerate your presence in the rest of the cemetery since technically, I'll admit that I do not own Highgate exclusively. But this, the circular tomb, my family tomb, and its surroundings, surely you can leave that alone. I do not like you trespassing on the grounds where my ancestors are buried. Or digging into them, as I can see you have been doing. I'm sure you understand." He gave me a sardonic smile.

Venedict, of course, had no idea what Elizabeth and I had been through tonight. The last thing I wanted right now was any more drama. On the other hand, you could say I had been on a roll all night, not conceding anything to anyone, and I wasn't about to start now.

"For the most part, I do leave the Circle of Lebanon alone," I reminded him.

"Then why are you standing on top of my family tomb at this very moment?"

"I see no reason why I shouldn't tell you. It has served a crucial purpose in my journey from which I've just returned." I wiped some rain and mud from my chin, hating that he had the ability to make me feel self-conscious. Elizabeth and I were both soaked to the bone and splattered with mud.

In response, Venedict levitated and landed softly on the grass right in front of Elizabeth and me. He peered down into the grave. "What is this?" he asked, pointing to the swirling mist that still covered the inside of the grave. I wasn't sure how long it would take for it to disperse, but probably a few moments longer.

"If I am not mistaken," he said, "this looks like some kind of portal. I know how fond you are of secret passage-ways and the like. Is this how you traveled?"

"It is."

"This is an act of vandalism on my family tomb," Vene-dict declared, his tone shifting. "An act of vandalism on my property, and indeed a transgression against my ancestors."

Let me jump in here and add that Venedict had never been much of a fan of his own ancestors when they were still alive. But once they were dead, of course, he held them in high regard. This flippant attitude was very typical of him. He went on, "You have dug this grave, this portal, right into the earth, in which the bones of my family members are housed."

When he put it that way, it did sound rather bad, I'll admit that.

"In fact, I will not tolerate it," he added. "If I ever see you encroaching on this part of the cemetery again, I will have to take drastic measures."

"Oh, really?" I was not in the mood for this.

And Venedict was in no real position to threaten me. Vampiric blood had been flowing in my veins for nearly two centuries before he had even been born. He was smaller and lighter than me. If he were truly intent on fighting me, it would not go well for him.

The only advantage he had in this regard was my reluc-tance to hurt him. That said, I did have it in me to break his arm right now if I had to. That should make him think twice about approaching me with angry, entitled demands in the immediate aftermath of a hazardous journey.

I motioned for Elizabeth to stand back, and she did so

with a weary expression on her face. She, too, had had far too much conflict for one night.

"Gabriel, if you're going to use the land of my ancestors as a portal for your own deeds and travels," Venedict went on, working himself into a self-righteous frenzy, "you should pay me some price. Perhaps some more of your immortal blood will do. After all, after countless decades locked in my casket, I still feel rather depleted. There's so much I have missed out on, so much blood I could have drunk, so many adventures I could have had, so many experiences."

"And who do you have to thank for it?" I countered. "Only yourself. If you had not betrayed and pushed me away, you would not have spent the past century and a half locked away in that miserable crypt with your mansion falling to ruin around you. All that time, I suppose you expected me to come and rescue you, for old time's sake, despite everything. And I could have, but I simply did not feel inspired to. That is what you are truly angry about."

Venedict looked stunned, as if I'd slapped him. "I did not come here for you to insult me like this!"

He started circling me, and soon we were circling each other around the still open grave. Elizabeth had retreated enough to get well out of our way while imploring us to stop.

Venedict made a couple of false starts towards me, clearly to provoke me. I was getting quite exasperated with him.

"Venedict, back off. Not tonight of all nights. You haven't the faintest idea what a long and tiresome journey I have had, and how little in the mood I am for these antics."

He suddenly pounced, flinging himself at me with full

force, the weight of his body colliding with mine and his teeth sinking into my neck.

I began to protest as pain erupted and my blood spilled into his mouth as he eagerly clamped down.

I staggered backwards until we both lost our balance.

We tumbled together into the grave, where the tendrils of mist still swirled, suddenly drawing and pulling us in.

Venedict had already drunk a good deal of my blood. The warmth and light of the ectoplasm and the blood flowed between us. I opened my mouth and shouted in protest, but the two of us were already dissolving into the mist.

Also by Lucius Valiant

Dark Roots (The Thornhill Vampire Chronicles Book 1)

Deep Graves (The Thornhill Vampire Chronicles Book 2)

Foul Moon (The Thornhill Vampire Chronicles Book 3)

Grim Games (The Thornhill Vampire Chronicles Book 4)

About the Author

Lucius Valiant is a Danish-British author.

The first real book he recalls reading is Bram Stoker's "Dracula." And that, as the saying goes, was that. There would be no turning back.

Lucius's literary inspirations include classics of Gothic fiction, such as Mary Shelley's "Frankenstein" and Oscar Wilde's "The Picture of Dorian Gray," as well as horror, supernatural, and speculative fiction by writers such as Anne Rice, Poppy Z. Brite, and Stephen King. He also draws much influence from Britain's rich history, folklore, and legends.

All of these influences shine through like glittering, dark fairy dust in his writing, which readers have described as vivid, visceral, and cinematic, with a sprinkling of wry humor.

Visit his linktree to learn more, join the mailing list, and be kept in the loop about upcoming releases and secret subscriber treats: https://linktr.ee/luciusvaliant

AUTHOR NOTE

I've written a very strange book. This was the first - or at least the loudest - thought that went through my mind as I sat back and looked at the finally completed manuscript for "Deep Graves."

My second thought: I thought writing your second novel was supposed to be a lot easier than writing your first.

"Deep Graves" wasn't easier. I've made and discarded several different beginnings to the story before finding the one that worked. I've got attempts harking back to NaNoWriMo (National Novel Writing Month) in 2018, 2019 and 2020. But I just couldn't find the right inroad into the story and get past the first handful of chapters before I'd completed its predecessor, "Dark Roots". Once I'd managed that, "Deep Graves" flowed.

Telling Gabriel's story demanded a journey back in time. A journey much further back than I'd have preferred to go. Weirdly, perhaps, I feel quite comfortable navigating the Victorian era, in which a good chunk of "Dark Roots" takes place; I feel quite at home there. But going further back than that was daunting and made me feel out of my depth - like swimming into deep, dark waters where you cannot see the bottom and have no way of knowing what might lurk under the surface. It required a lot more research, and a lot more simply trusting the story.

Once you've finished reading "Deep Graves", please let me know whether you think I've pulled it off. If you loved the story, please leave a review. Reviews are the life blood of indie published novels - it's what allows other readers to find them and give them a chance.

And now, off to finish the next novel! In "Foul Moon" the third volume in the Thornhill Vampire Chronicles, we'll be returning to Harlan, to Thornhill Mansion and to the present day.

Lucius Valiant, December 2023